THE HOUSE THAT JACK BUILT

THE HOUSE THAT JACK BUILT

A Lars Winkler Novel

JAKOB MELANDER

Translated by Paul Russell Garrett

SPIDERLINE

First published in Denmark as Øjesten in 2013 by Rosinante & Co.
Published by agreement with Gyldendal Group Agency

This edition published in 2014 by
House of Anansi Press Inc.
110 Spadina Avenue, Suite 801
Toronto, ON, M5V 2K4
Tel. 416-363-4343
Fax 416-363-1017
www.houseofanansi.com

Distributed in Canada by
HarperCollins Canada Ltd.
1995 Markham Road
Scarborough, ON, M1B 5M8
Toll free tel. 1-800-387-0117

House of Anansi Press is committed to protecting our natural environment. As part of our efforts, the interior of this book is printed on paper that contains 100% post-consumer recycled fibres, is acid-free, and is processed chlorine-free.

18 17 16 15 14   1 2 3 4 5

Library and Archives Canada Cataloguing in Publication

Melander, Jakob, 1965–
[Øjesten. English]
The house that Jack built / Jakob Melander ; translated by
Paul Russell Garrett.

Translation of: Øjesten.
Issued in print and electronic formats.
ISBN 978-1-77089-439-6 (pbk.). — ISBN 978-1-77089-440-2 (html)

I. Title. II. Title: Øjesten. English.

PT8177.23.E53O5413 2014   839.81'38   C2013-907029-X
C2013-907030-3

Jacket design: UNO Advertising Agency, Munich
Text design and typesetting: Alysia Shewchuk

*We acknowledge for their financial support of our publishing program
the Canada Council for the Arts, the Ontario Arts Council, and the Government of Canada
through the Canada Book Fund.*

Printed and bound in Canada

MIX
Paper from
responsible sources
FSC® C004071

THE HOUSE THAT JACK BUILT

THE WIND TEARS through Øresund, whipping the waves into foam. The sun hangs low and red, with streaks of purple cloud on the horizon over the island of Amager. A flock of herring gulls squawks in the updraft. They circle above a carcass floating in the water, rising and falling in time with the sea. The first gull alights, tearing a chunk of white flesh from the body's swollen stomach; a second quickly follows suit.

On the chilly spring evening, a troop of Scouts scales the earthworks surrounding Charlottenlund Fort, marching single file up the grassy slopes. The young boys' knees are knocking, blue with cold. They walk bent forward, bracing themselves against the chill, and disappear behind the cannon batteries only to re-emerge farther ahead, halfway across the embankment, heading toward Strandvejen and the forest surrounding Charlottenlund Castle.

A tall, bony boy brings up the rear, scrambling after the others. He gasps for air in the strong wind. The distance between him and the other boys is growing.

They're singing up ahead. The wind breaks up the voices, throwing snatches back in his face.

Fatty and skinny went for a run
They'd only just begun when Fatty's zipper sprung
Skinny took a whirl — and kissed every girl
In the end he got so out of hand
He kissed Popeye the Sailor Man
Skinny, skinny, run for your life —
Here comes Fatty with a butcher's knife
Skinny, skinny, run for your life —
Here comes Fatty with a butcher's knife

The boys cross Strandvejen in a coiling line, then vanish between the trees on the other side. The lone straggler has to wait for a northbound convertible to pass. A blonde girl in the passenger seat smiles at him. Then she's gone and he can cross.

The echo of the boys' voices still resonates among the trees.

Skinny, Skinny, run for your life —

When he's in the forest, he starts walking faster, almost jogging. His rucksack bounces up and down, the cold metal frame banging into his kidneys. Soon, the only sounds are the wind singing in the treetops and his hoarse breathing. His heart pumps double beats. The trees spin before his eyes. A tree root stretches out, grabs his foot, and sends him plunging down to the forest floor. The gnarled branches reach out, catch him. His mouth is full of soil and rotting leaves; he cannot scream. Instead, he extends his arms in a silent cry for help.

Suddenly it's over. He's lying on the forest floor, gasping for air, moaning and spitting dirt and leaves. Alone in the twilight. Then the treetops begin to sing steadily louder. He sits up, wraps his hands around his legs, and buries his face in between his knees. His small shoulders tremble.

Then the voices reach him.

They ride the wind, howling with its every twist and turn, rising and falling in a slowly turning cadence as night overtakes the gentle twilight. He doesn't know how long it continues, the furious onslaught of voices. All he knows is that he has to succumb, allow the growing chorus to wash over him, and flounder in darkness and terror.

He's lying on his back, half-submerged in a pool of water, saliva around his mouth, his face completely covered in dirt. There is a wild look in his eyes when they find him, the men with their dogs and flashlights. They've been searching for him for hours. Didn't he hear them calling?

His grandfather takes him into his arms. Yes, he sobs into the neck of the large man with the familiar scent. The voices. He heard the voices.

One of the men walks around the clearing with his flashlight, roots around in the dirt with his foot. Say, he says, isn't this where the HIPOs caught that pilot—?

But Grandfather silences him with a gesture and a look. Grandfather's in charge, Grandfather always knows best.

And then they set off toward the house where Mother is waiting. His mother, who never speaks.

SATURDAY
JUNE 14

CHAPTER 1

"GUNNAR, COME HAVE A LOOK AT THIS."
There was excitement in Johannes's voice, and his small body trembled with anticipation. The boy was crouched down near the water, pointing at some dry residue hanging from a plant stem. It swayed in the gentle breeze.

The algae-filled water gurgled quietly at the edge of the sandy, overgrown bank. A light breeze sang through the tree-tops and branches overhanging the water. From the lake, a single gull followed the strange proceedings.

"Very good, Johannes. Come over here everyone, come see what Johannes has found." Gunnar smiled to himself. Getting the job as park ranger at Amager Fælled had been his dream ever since he'd come here as a boy scout. Of course, getting up ridiculously early in the morning and leaving his girlfriend home in bed wasn't much fun. But this—this made it all worthwhile. The kids were spread out behind him, squatting down, completely absorbed.

Gunnar waited until the children had all gathered around him before continuing. "This is a nymph skin from a large, brown dragonfly, one of our largest insects. A dragonfly's transformation is incomplete. Meaning, they don't have a cocoon stage." He looked around the circle to make sure everyone was following. The children were hanging on his every word. "They live as dragonfly nymphs in streams and ponds for up to three years. Then when they're old enough, starting here in May, June, and July, they crawl onto land and emerge from their nymph skins. Do you see those white fibres there? That's the nymph's respiratory system, which opens up in their final stage of development so that the dragonfly can emerge. They're called tracheoles—"

"But how do they move?" someone wanted to know.

"Well, they do have legs." Gunnar laughed. The next part was always a big hit. "But when they really need to get moving in the water, they let out a gigantic fart and then shoot off. Their intestinal system works exactly like a jet engine." He used his hand to show how quickly a dragonfly nymph could shoot across the water. The kids were about to fall over laughing. A couple of the girls pulled faces and whispered to each other.

Behind him, Ishmael pulled at his parka.

"Just a minute, Ishmael. I'm..."

The boy tugged at him again. "Gunnar, look. What is that?"

"Where?" He turned around.

"There." The boy pointed further down the bank. Partly hidden behind a couple of bushes, right at the water's edge, something large and yellow was half-submerged in the dark, still water.

It was getting hot. He should take his parka off.

8

"I don't know, Ishmael. Let's take a look."

With Gunnar in the lead, the children started walking down the bank. After a couple of steps, he stopped. Above them, a plane drew a white line across the blue sky.

"You'd better wait here, kids."

She was lying on her back, naked, halfway up the bank, the lower half of her parted legs in the water. Her skin was waxy, yellow. Dry and lifeless wisps of black hair covered her face.

He hesitated, then stepped closer. A fly flew out of the dark hollow below her eyebrows, buzzed across the still water.

Behind him, one of the children started to cry.

CHAPTER 2

JOHN PAUL JONES'S falling bass line provided a gloomy backdrop for Jimmy Page's spine-tingling guitar work. The Fender bass and Telecaster guitar resounded in his head in that indescribably fantastic way that made music better than drugs and almost as good as sex. Led Zeppelin's entire first album was stored on the internal hard drive of his mind; it was only a matter of switching it on and off whenever he saw fit. The lyrics to "Dazed and Confused" had never felt more true than today. The soul of one woman, at least, really was created below.

"Hey, are you listening?" On the other side of the large, dark desk, Ulrik Sommer, Chief Inspector of the Copenhagen Police's Violent Crime Unit, was silhouetted against the enormous panoramic window. His face was one black surface— apart from the eyes. They were gleaming.

"Yes." Detective Sergeant Lars Winkler rocked his almost

6'6", forty-four-year-old body back and forth on the balls of his feet, closed his eyes. The office smelled of linoleum, dust, and stale sweat.

Lars opened his eyes. Looking beyond the silhouette of his old friend, he gazed down Edvard Falcks Gade and over the treetops of Tivoli Gardens at the Star Flyer's towering spire and the Ferris wheel's gondolas. Beyond was the Radisson Blu Royal Hotel and to the right, the Ny Carlsberg Glyptoteket museum's small oasis of a garden. It had rained overnight, leaving the city fresh and clean.

Ulrik had had this view for many years, and there was no reason it shouldn't remain so. But inside, in the room, everything had changed. Somewhere along the line he and Ulrik had passed a turning point.

But Ulrik didn't seem to understand that.

"Hm." The chief inspector of Copenhagen's Violent Crime Unit rubbed his forehead, looked at his desk pad, and fiddled with the top button of his uniform. Then he cleared his throat. "Where did you go?"

Lars looked away, coughed. "I got on a plane to Athens, rented a car, and drove until I couldn't go any farther."

"I see. And where was that?"

"Does it really matter?"

"Well, as a matter of fact . . ." Ulrik sighed. "I am your friend."

"You wouldn't know it." Lars looked away. He had to get out. Now. "All right. Kato Vasiliki. A little seaside resort for Greeks. Nothing to do. A hole."

Ulrik appeared to be thinking. He was good at that. Appearing to be thinking. It was that ability more than anything else that had given him the extra star on his epaulettes. Then he smiled. It spread over his entire face.

"So everything's fine then." Ulrik folded his hands on top of the desk. "I'm glad you had a nice vacation. If anyone around here deserved one, it was you." He paused. "I'm prepared to let things continue as they were. I hope that..."

Ulrik didn't look him in the eye when he spoke. Lars wasn't listening. It was strange, really; he hadn't realized before how much Ulrik looked like a weasel. The animal's mouth opened and closed, but no sound emerged. Lars tried to feel something, tried to find his anger. But it was gone. There was only a vast, empty hole.

The weasel's mouth moved, formed sounds, words.

"...and to show you that I'm serious, I've kept this for you: lead inspector on a murder investigation. It was called in to HQ half an hour ago. Out on Amager Commons." The weasel passed a thin case file across the desk. Lars reached out to accept it. They brushed hands. Both looked away.

Ulrik got up, ran a hand down his uniform. "Welcome home. It's good to have you back." He hesitated. Then he held out his hand. Lars moved the case file to his other hand, then shook Ulrik's outstretched hand.

"Hold on," Ulrik said. "There's a girl from Kolding joining us. They say she's very bright. She's here to see how we do things in the big city. I thought you could keep an eye on her? You know, help her out a bit?" Ulrik looked at a piece of paper on his desk. "Bissen—Sanne Bissen."

Lars scrunched up his eyes and sighed. Just what he needed. "I'll go down and get a car."

Ulrik smiled. Probably out of relief.

Lars swung his jacket over his shoulder, opened the door, and turned around again. "The chief of homicide, is he in?"

Ulrik was just about to sit down again, but fell back into his chair, taken completely by surprise. "I think...isn't he off today?"

Lars left without answering, the door cutting off the rest of Ulrik's sentence.

He stood by the reception desk for a few seconds before

pulling the envelope out of his jacket's inside pocket. Then he nodded at Ulrik's secretary who was in the middle of a long phone call and went over to the row of mail slots and placed it in the chief of homicide's slot.

CHAPTER 3

DOWN ARTILLERIVEJ, MOST of the local businesses consisted of chop shops, which were interspersed with largely abandoned graffitied warehouses, bus hangars, and overgrown building sites. On the other side of the harbour, H. C. Ørsted Power Station stood out against the deep blue sky. Lars turned the car down Lossepladsvej, then down a dirt road toward the nature reserve at Amager Commons. He followed the track, listening to Detective Toke Hansen's crackling directions on his cell phone.

In the rearview mirror, he noticed the clouds of dust being kicked up by passing cars. Further ahead, he saw the black surface of the lake, the bushes and trees lining its far shore. Crime scene investigators in neon yellow vests stood along the edge of the water. He crossed the bridge and parked behind the Crime Scene Unit's van.

He picked up his radio. "Okay, Toke. I'm here now."

Lars set the handbrake and turned the key. The engine sputtered and died. He tapped his fingers on the steering wheel briefly, then climbed out of the car. In front of him, the road curved to the left. Behind the row of cars in the makeshift parking lot was a thicket of bushes and small trees. Toke's blonde spiky hair stood out among all the green.

Lars slammed the car door and headed toward Toke. "How's it looking?"

"You'd better come down and see for yourself." Toke lifted the tape for Lars, then guided him through the thick foliage toward the lake.

"Welcome back, by the way." Toke held a branch aside so Lars could pass. "Was it—did you have a nice vacation?" Lars didn't reply. Toke continued without missing a beat. "A park ranger found her. He was out here with a group of fourth graders from Peder Lykkes Elementary School, looking at water holes. He's waiting in one of the cars if you'd like to speak with him."

"On a Saturday?"

Toke shrugged. "It was the only day the park ranger was free."

Lars grunted, stepped over a mud puddle. "Has she been moved?"

"No. He says he didn't touch anything. Here we are."

The algae-filled water was completely still beneath the June sun. Above them, a lapwing shrieked. The activity along the bank was frenetic. Detective Allan Raben, who was always quick to perspire, was hunched over, examining something on the ground between the bushes and the water. A couple of uniformed officers stood a little ways back, sharing coffee from a Thermos. Three forensic investigators wearing white protective suits, face masks, and bags over their shoes, were busy scouring the area for clues. Bertil Frelsén, the chief forensic pathologist, was standing in the water, leaning over a yellowish-white body that was half-submerged in the water, half-lying on the bank. He was the only one wearing rubber boots. His gold-rimmed glasses rested halfway down the bridge of his nose; his hair stood straight up.

One of the crime scene investigators waved at Lars. His teeth gleamed against his dark face. Wallid Bint.

"Hey Lars." Frelsén's assistant shook Lars's hand. "It's nice to see you again. We're almost done here; then you can take over."

"Beautiful, Bint." Lars turned to Toke. "The park ranger can go home. Tell him we might contact him at a later stage. Where's this—Bissen?"

"Bissen?"

"Sanne Bissen. The detective sergeant from Kolding?"

"Right here." A hoarse female voice came from behind him. The Jutland accent wasn't as strong as he had expected.

He turned around and saw a pretty, blonde woman with an outstretched arm. A firm, dry handshake. She was tall, almost lanky. Her wispy hair covered her neck and ears but was pushed back from her animated grey eyes. There was a cluster of freckles drizzled across her nose and cheeks. She was wearing jeans and a pair of rubber boots that looked far too big for her thin frame.

"You must be Lars." She smiled. Lars tried returning the smile. It went surprisingly well.

"Welcome." He nodded at the body and then looked at her. "Can you give me a quick overview?"

Sanne looked at Toke, then at Frelsén as he waded through the shallow water. The forensic pathologist removed his latex gloves as he walked toward them.

"Well, you see—"

"Leave the poor girl alone." Frelsén stuffed the gloves into his back pocket. "Now this is interesting. The corpse has been preserved. The same procedure used on bodies that are donated to science."

Sanne's cheeks went red. "Are you saying someone abused the corpse?"

"A person who donates their body to science seldom leaves this mournful world with a bullet through the heart." Frelsén pushed his glasses further up the bridge of his nose. "Very tidy. Right above the left breast. Bint found a fine corona of gunshot residue around the entrance wound. Oh, and her eyes have been removed."

Everyone was quiet.

"Bint?" Sanne asked after a short while. Her voice only trembled a little.

"Wallid Bint," Lars explained. "We hardly ever use his first name." He turned to Frelsén. "So can you start from the beginning?"

"Come." Frelsén motioned for them to follow, walking through the water on the other side of the body. Lars, Sanne, and Toke lined up on the shore. Allan stood slightly apart from the rest.

A slight hospital smell mixed with the scent of algae lingered by the water's edge. Lars looked down.

She was lying on her back, naked, with her legs slightly apart. She had a root stuck in her back, so her chest was pushed up and out. The skin had an unnatural yellowish-white tone and rubbery appearance. The water covered her from the knees down; the rest of her body was on land. Either the dark pubic hairs were very sparse or they had just started growing back after a recent shaving. Rigor mortis had set her forearms at a ninety-degree angle, pointing to the sky. Her face was contorted in an expression of terror and disgust. The frayed entrance wound from a bullet was visible just above her left breast.

"Young woman," Frelsén started. "Presumably Eastern European, presumably a prostitute. Cause of death: a single gunshot to the heart. She's been here no more than eight hours, judging by the condition of the skin."

He lifted the body's lower leg, bringing the toes above the surface of the water. They all noticed the wrinkled skin, but the decomposition wasn't far advanced. Frelsén pulled a small Maglite flashlight out of his breast pocket, and directed the light at the mixture of sludge, seaweed, and sand below her left shoulder. Something was gleaming.

"Bint thinks it's glass," Frelsén said.

Lars looked across the small lake toward the suburban neighbourhood hidden behind the low vegetation.

"How long?"

Frelsén straightened up. "Since she died? That will require further examination. But I suspect her eyes were removed first—presumably under anaesthetic, considering the clean incisions. Then she was shot."

Sanne cleared her throat. "Was she…was she conscious… during?"

"When the eyes were removed? Unlikely. Afterwards? Judging by her facial expression, I'd say yes," Frelsén said.

"Jesus," Allan whispered behind them. Even the crime scene investigators stopped working.

Lars raised his voice. "How did she end up here?"

Allan looked down at his notepad. "Something heavy was dragged through the bushes. Bint found some fibres, possibly from a blanket. And there are footprints, size 11.5. There are also some tire tracks up by the dirt road." He pointed his thumb over his shoulder.

"Good," Lars said. "Let's get the dogs out here, see if they can find something."

"Welcome back, Lars." Frelsén rubbed his hands together. Then he shouted, "Come on, it's down here." A couple of paramedics were making their way down the overgrown slope, a stretcher balanced between them.

Lars closed his eyes. He wished he was back at Kato Vasiliki. Back at Nikki's beach restaurant with nothing to do but drink frappés and pints of Amstel and stare across the water toward Patras.

CHAPTER 4

IT WAS ALMOST 7:00 p.m. by the time Lars stood in front of his apartment entrance at number 2 Folmer Bendtsens Plads. Just as he placed the key in the lock, he saw an S-train rumble out of Nørrebro Station. The newspaper placards in front of the neighbouring corner store flapped as the train passed. A loose newspaper page blew out onto the road. Clinking bottles could be heard from inside the Ring Café. A drunk was being hushed by his buddies. Lars pushed open the door to the staircase and, with a weary movement, lifted the bag of Thai takeout, and tramped up the stairs. First day of work after two months of vacation. He could barely drag himself up to the second floor.

After the ambulance had driven away with the body, Lars sent Allan off to canvas the Amager hostel and the housing co-op. According to Frelsén, the body had been brought to the area shortly after midnight, so there was little likelihood anyone had seen anything. Still, questions had to be asked all the same. Sanne and Toke went to the red-light district in Vesterbro with a photo of the dead girl's face and instructions to ask the girls working the streets there if they knew the victim. Hopefully someone would recognize her. If not, identifying the body would take some time. When Lars got back to the station, he had started going through all the missing persons reports from the past three months. With no luck.

After too many cups of coffee and far too many reports, Lars was still alone at the station. Allan had not returned, nor had Sanne and Toke—Ulrik had been in to see him twice and they had exchanged a few monosyllabic words—so he'd gotten up to leave.

As he opened the door to his flat, he was greeted by a stuffy, slightly musty air. He hadn't been back at the apartment since he moved his stuff in the night before he flew to Athens, about two months ago.

The apartment consisted of a small hallway, two rooms facing the street, and a bedroom and kitchen that faced the rear courtyard. The tiny bathroom was located on the left, just past the front door. The urban regeneration company had finally fitted showers in the apartments here. The water sprayed over everything, but at least he had his own shower.

The first room contained the moving boxes with the stereo system, the LPs, a table, and a couple of chairs. He dropped the bag of food on the table, fell into a chair, and kicked off his sneakers. He threw his jacket in the corner behind him, then lit a King's and put his feet up.

Ah.

As the nicotine surged through his body and shot up into his brain, he looked around the apartment. Textured wallpaper, 1980s style. The walls and ceiling had probably been white once, but after almost thirty years and an untold number of cigarettes, they had turned an indeterminable yellowish hue. *Something should be done about that.* With the cigarette dangling in the corner of his mouth, he got up, put his hands in his pockets, and walked into the other room. More boxes, a threadbare couch, a TV. He opened the door to the balcony. The hinges squeaked. The cigarette smoke mingled with petrol fumes and the smell of hot asphalt. An eggplant-coloured Toyota on its last legs chugged out of the roundabout, clanking all the while. Roads, sidewalks, houses—everything was oozing with pent-up heat from the sun. He looked down Folmer Bendtsens Plads, below the elevated railway where Ørnevej met Bregnerødgade. On the far side of the roundabout was one of the ubiquitous green grocers as well as a store that, taking its sign at face value, sold "Muffler."

So this was home.

He flicked the cigarette butt over the balcony and went back inside, leaving the door open. He walked into the kitchen. It was a standard Copenhagen kitchen with two narrow windows facing a dark courtyard. He put away his groceries: milk in the fridge, coffee and oats in the greasy wall cupboard. Then he found the moving box with kitchen utensils, dug out a plate and a fork, and rinsed them under the tap.

He couldn't shake the image of the dead woman, naked and vulnerable at the edge of the water, the empty eye sockets staring out into nothing. Lars dried the fork, put it on the plate, and went into the living room. He was getting hungry, but first he had to hook up the stereo.

He managed to manoeuvre the amplifier, preamplifier, and speakers onto the low bookcase; he connected everything and plugged it in. Now all he needed was the turntable. The old Rega P1. He lifted it out of the moving box, placed it next to the amplifier, and plugged in the cables.

It took some time finding the box with the LPs but before

long he had eased the stylus onto *Get Yer Ya-Ya's Out* and dove into his cashew chicken with extra chilli.

A little while later, he plugged in the TV, adjusted it so he could see the screen from the other room, and turned the volume all the way down. A home-improvement program flashed across the screen. An actor was helping an accountant build a patio for his house. Lars lit a cigarette, laced his fingers behind his neck, and tilted his chair back.

Why had the murderer removed her eyes? Had she seen something she wasn't supposed to? Was there something she wasn't allowed to see?

He sent a billowy smoke ring drifting up toward the ceiling.

There was a violent crash from the apartment above followed by loud swearing.

Two more months in this vacuum, then he'd be gone.

MAY 1953

HE'S BEEN SITTING on the sofa since Grandfather and the men brought him back from the woods the previous night. In the morning, Grandfather takes one look at him, then grabs his doctor's bag to go on a house call. Mother is in her rocking chair, staring into space. As always.

Creak-creak, creak-creak, Mother rocks back and forth. He gets up and strokes her porcelain pale cheek. Her loose skin quivers, moves away under his fingers.

She needs a pick-me-up. He takes off his jacket, walks into the kitchen to make her some warm juice. He pours water into a pot and lights the old cast iron stove.

On his way down to the cellar for the cups with the English motif, the ones Grandfather forbids them to use, he checks in on Mother. She's sitting as he left her, stone-faced, her hands folded in her lap, in the rocking chair in the empty living room.

The sunlight enters through the window, casting squares and rectangles on the wide floorboards. Dust dances. He hurries down to the cellar, pushes past all the junk Grandfather keeps there to the wall-mounted vitrine with the china, then hurries upstairs to avoid the voices.

Back in the kitchen, the water is boiling. He fills the cup halfway with Ribena fruit concentrate, and tops it up with hot water. He crumbles a rusk into the thick juice mix and already has the teaspoon in his hand when he discovers a chip in the saucer. A piece has broken off the rim; the crack spreads all the way down the glaze. A sudden rage surges up in him. Everything has to be just right today. He tears the cup from the saucer. Juice and rusk crumbs spill out onto the kitchen table. The saucer flies into the sink, shatters. A shower of broken porcelain clatters against the drain.

He has to go down to the cellar again, force himself past all of Grandfather's things.

The door to the vitrine is open. Did he remember to close it earlier? The monotonous creaking of the rocking chair upstairs in the living room reaches all the way down here. He reaches for the last saucer at the very back of the shelf. As his fingers close around the porcelain, they brush the head of a nail sticking up in the corner. With a gentle click, the nail slides down and in: the vitrine swings open toward him. A black hole appears in the wall behind it. Musty air streams out, smelling of rot and chemicals.

He finds a candle stump on the bookcase below the cabinet and lights it. The darkness is so great it swallows the light from the flame. Tentatively, he places one foot on the bookcase, steps up. Through the opening in the wall, he sees a staircase leading down.

Fifteen steps he counts before reaching the foot of the stairs. He gropes his way forward, holding out the candle stump in front of him. Restless shapes dance at the edge of the circle the light casts. They spring to life with each flicker of the small flame. There are bookcases, boxes, and cases with hand-drawn labels along the wall: Cyclotol, Husqvarna, Composition B. Hirtenberger 5.6 x 50 Mag.

The bookcases tower above him. He raises the candle stump above his head. The light shines on a jar on the shelf. Two pale white, blurry spheres with grey pupils float in a cloudy liquid. Muscle tissue, frayed tendons form veil tails behind them. Remnants of Grandfather's medical practice? His heart falters, he gasps for air. He drops the candle stump on the floor; it sputters and rolls away. He drops to his knees, searches the floor with trembling hands.

Then they're on him, the voices from the woods. They fall into a slowly turning cadence.

When he emerges from the cellar, night has replaced day. Mother is still sitting in the living room, rocking her *creak-creak*. Grandfather has not returned.

He puts the jar down on the table in front of her. The pale white objects rock quietly in time with the movements of the liquid, and settle down shortly after. He's standing before her, a layer of dust clinging to his knees and forehead.

She doesn't look at the jar. Her lips curl into a strange smile; her pupils are pitch black. She looks up at him and speaks for the first time.

"Father took them. Father took everything."

SUNDAY
JUNE 15

CHAPTER 5

AN INSANE DRONING broke through his sleep, penetrating his ear canal. Lars sat up with a start, banging his forehead against the edge of the small bureau next to the bed.

"Ow, Jes—"

He doubled over, holding his hand to his head. The music started again. Blindly he fumbled for the infernal machine. He was on the verge of throwing it out the window when it occurred to him to switch off the phone.

Blessed peace.

Then an S-train thundered into the station across the street. The windows in the living room rattled. Welcome to Nørrebro.

He took a quick shower, ate some rolled oats, got dressed — loose-fitting dark blue shirt, jeans, and sneakers — had a cup of coffee and a morning smoke, then went out the door. They were meeting Frelsén at the Institute of Forensic Medicine at nine o'clock for the autopsy and post-mortem examination.

Twenty-eight minutes later, Lars was running across Blegdamsvej toward Frederik V's Vej. He ran along Fælledparken, Copenhagen's largest park, then looked up. Another one of those never-ending blue skies. A white Fiat 500 pulled up alongside him as he approached the entrance to the Institute of Forensic Medicine at number 11. Sanne rolled down the window.

"Good morning."

"Hey . . . I mean, good morning."

He stepped aside, allowing her to turn into an empty parking spot. He waited while she climbed out of the car.

"So we got lucky." Sanne looked up as she locked the doors. "It took a few hours but in the end we found two Slovakian girls. They didn't want to say anything at first, but I took them to a café and made sure Toke kept his distance . . . Oh, yeah, it took a few lattes as well."

"Good work. Tell me about it."

They walked up the stairs to the entrance. Lars stopped outside the door, moved aside to let a group of students past. Sanne continued.

"Her name was Mira, from Bratislava. The two girls shared a room with her on Mysundegade. We went there afterwards — to get her personal effects." Sanne swallowed. "It's all at the station."

"Who was her pimp?"

"They mentioned two Kosovo-Albanian brothers. Bukoshi, I think it was. Does that name mean anything to you?"

Lars nodded.

"The girls weren't very keen on saying much," she continued. "They say the brothers beat her in her room less than a

week before she disappeared. On..." Sanne pulled out a notebook, "...May 4."

"Denmark's Liberation Day?" Lars grabbed her sleeve and
pulled her toward the door. "Come on. They're waiting for
us—"

Just then the door opened and Ulrik walked out wearing a
freshly pressed uniform.

"Lars, Sanne." Ulrik nodded at them. "Glad I caught you
here." He hesitated, stuck his hands in his pockets. "I spoke
with the chief of homicide this morning, Lars." Ulrik looked
at him searchingly. Lars didn't say anything, waiting. Ulrik
sighed.

"You've asked to be transferred to the North Zealand
department in Helsingør—is that correct?" Ulrik was breathing a touch faster now.

Lars shrugged. "I need a change of scenery."

Sanne took an almost imperceptible step backwards and
looked from one man to the other.

"You might have considered letting me know first. As your
superior, as—your friend?"

"No, not really."

Ulrik caught his breath. "You can't be in charge of a murder
investigation if you're leaving the department. You're off the
case."

Lars pulled out a cigarette. At least this meant he could have
a smoke.

Ulrik continued. "You've got nothing to say?"

Lars shrugged again, then lit the cigarette.

Ulrik took off his peaked cap, wiped the sweat from his
forehead.

"I'm taking over the homicide investigation." He put the cap
back on. "A woman was admitted to the Juliane Marie Centre.
She was beaten and raped last night. You're taking that case.

You've got Kim A, Frank, Lisa Bak, and Toke. Sanne and Allan are with me." Ulrik's eyes flashed under his cap. "I understood you weren't thrilled about getting a new partner anyway?"

Dammit. Lars glanced at Sanne. And Kim A of all people. He filled his lungs with one final drag, then stubbed out the cigarette with a twist of his heel.

Sanne gave him a wounded look as she followed Ulrik into the Institute of Forensic Medicine.

CHAPTER 6

STAIRWELL 5, THIRD floor. The Juliane Marie Centre: Centre for Victims of Sexual Assault at Rigshospitalet. Lars stepped out of the elevator and scanned the signs hanging from the ceiling of the broad corridor. Department 5032 was to the right and down the corridor, parallel to Tagensvej. The idea behind the numbering system at Rigshospitalet was enticingly simple but in practice, it was more complicated to decipher than had been envisaged when the university hospital was built in the 1970s.

Lars walked the fifteen steps it took to reach the reception desk and showed the nurse his police badge.

"Lars Winkler, Violent Crime Unit. You received a rape victim here last night?"

The nurse studied his badge, nodded. "Early this morning. I'll get a doctor."

He couldn't hear what was being said on the phone but less than a minute later a doctor approached from the end of the hall. She was short, stocky, with mousy hair cut in a bob and piercing grey eyes behind red designer glasses.

"Christine Fogh," she said. "Follow me."

She led him into an office with a window facing the University of Copenhagen's faculty of medicine, the Panum Institute. The treetops of Amor Park softened the view of the building's massive grey concrete porticos.

The doctor sat down on the edge of her chair, folded her hands between her parted knees, and waited. She didn't offer him a seat.

The air was heavy in the small office. Lars looked around. The only other chair was by the wall opposite the window. He sat down, took a notepad and pen out of his inside pocket. Sweat was trickling from his neck and armpits.

"I was just assigned this case ten minutes ago. I don't even know the victim's name. Can you give me the details?"

"The details?" She turned her head and looked out the window.

"Who is she, where did it happen, when?" He attempted a smile. She removed her glasses, placed them down in front of her, the arms pointing at him.

"Do you know how many sexual assaults are reported in Denmark each year?" she asked.

"I don't have the precise figure in my head, but I believe it's around three hundred?"

"Five hundred. Almost two a day."

Lars didn't answer. Her face was aglow in the sunlight streaming through the window.

She turned to him. "And only one hundred result in a conviction."

He tried to rally behind an answer. That often it was one

person's word against another, that the figure also glossed over false reports, but she interrupted him just as he was about to speak.

"You also have to add to that the cases that are never reported. But this victim, Stine Bang…" She got up. "Follow me."

Lars followed Christine out of the small office and down the corridor.

"She was on her way home from Nørreport, heading toward Trondhjemsgade, at about 2:40 a.m.," the doctor continued. "She's riding her bike but gets a flat tire on Øster Voldgade, just past Nørreport. So she pushes her bike. Around Sølvgade, she senses someone following her. She starts walking faster." Christine's shoes clacked down the corridor as her account became more and more staccato. "Just past the National Gallery, a man grabs her, hits her over the head, forces her across the street and into Østre Anlæg." Christine stopped suddenly and lowered her voice. "He hauls her up the embankment, rains down punches and kicks on her. She's screaming but who's going to hear her? At the top of the bank, he continues the beating, tearing off her clothes and then pushing her forward. And there—in front of Danmarksmonumentet—he anally rapes her. She has a broken jaw and three broken ribs, internal bleeding, lesions and wounds covering her entire body, along with a severe concussion. We've started preventive HIV treatment." Christine moved toward the door on the side of the corridor opposite Tagensvej, grabbed the handle. Then she lowered her voice and stared into his eyes. "Oh, yes. And her sphincter was millimetres away from being torn apart. Were these the kind of details you had in mind?"

Lars swallowed and followed her into the room.

Stine Bang lay on the hospital bed. Her head was slightly elevated and almost completely covered with gauze; what remained visible was black and blue and swollen. The area around her closed eyes was distended, and her nose was crooked. She was missing two of her lower front teeth. The cardiograph beside the bed emitted steady, monotone beeps.

Lars stepped forward and was about to say something when Christine grabbed his arm.

"Shh, she's sleeping. You can't wake her up." She dragged him out of the room. "I just wanted you to see her. Come. We can talk in my office."

Back in her office, both Lars and Christine assumed their previous positions. The notepad remained in his pocket. Christine cleared her throat. She took off her glasses once more, and looked down.

"I'm sorry if I came across as aggressive before. But this kind—" She broke off.

Lars nodded. "I've got a sixteen-year-old daughter." He pictured his daughter, Maria, in a park, naked and beaten on the grass, unable to move or call for help. "If this is of any comfort, I don't think Stine will have any problems being taken seriously. Not by the police, the public prosecutor, or the court."

Christine observed him from behind her desk.

"When do you think she'll be able to speak with us?" he continued.

"It'll probably be a few days. Tuesday, maybe Wednesday."

"Did she give a description of her attacker? Who brought her in?"

"An old couple from Stockholmsgade were walking their dog around six thirty this morning. They found her half-conscious and ice cold at the foot of the monument."

"Meaning that she was lying there for—three to four hours?"

"Her body temperature was down to thirty-five degrees. She'll probably get pneumonia on top of everything else. As for

36

her attacker, she got nothing more than a glimpse of him. Black clothes, black balaclava. His Danish was flawless. Oh, wait a minute. Here." She passed a yellow Post-it note across the table. "That's her girlfriend's number."

Lars looked at the note: "Astrid" and a Nørrebro number. "Is she going to report it?"

Christine nodded. "Of course. Despite the statistics." Lars's cheeks were burning. Christine continued. "I'm well aware of the police's standard snapshot of a rapist: a social outcast with no friends. How, then, do you explain that two out of three victims know their attacker?" Lars cleared his throat. She'd hit a sore spot. Christine held a hand up to hold off his protests. "But I think you might be right in this instance. It's unlikely the attacker is someone she knows." She flipped through a pile of papers on her desk. "Here. We performed an evidence collection examination. We have sperm and saliva samples from the attacker. The lab has promised a DNA profile by the end of next week."

"No fingerprints?"

Christine shook her head.

He handed her his card. "The problem with cases like this . . . well, I'm sure you're aware."

"Yes, of course. Without prior contact between victim and assailant, the case is often solved by chance. Sometimes years later. If it's even solved at all."

Lars got up. Years later. If. Exactly. He cursed Ulrik in his head.

They shook hands. He didn't want to let go. She smiled. Then he nodded and left the office.

CHAPTER 7

AS LARS DISAPPEARED down the stairs, Ulrik guided Sanne through the corridors of the Institute of Forensic Medicine. "You'll have to forgive me," Ulrik said, still in shock. "You weren't meant to see that. I hadn't counted on it being so...hostile."

The fluorescent lights flickered. The long corridor was empty. Sanne nodded, went along with it. As always. On the farm, when the boys used to come by with their mopeds at night, revving their engines for the girls, had she ever done anything other than just go along with things?

Ulrik interrupted her thoughts. "I don't know how many autopsies you've witnessed in Kolding." His whisper echoed through the empty corridor. "But you've got nothing to prove. Just observe and listen to what's being said. Then we can discuss it afterwards."

Sanne tried to keep up with Ulrik, walking quickly through a door, down another short corridor. They were in a long room with several small bays on the right. The other side was clear, creating a long connecting passage between the bays. The large, grey tiles covering the floor and the white glazed tiles on the walls made the room resemble an old-fashioned operating room.

Ulrik led her to the far end of the room where three dark shadows were visible under the fluorescent lights. Allan turned around as they approached, waved them over.

"Where's Lars?"

Frelsén and Bint stood on either side of the examination table with Mira's body. A large, gaping incision revealing bluish flesh and yellow fat ran from a point between her breasts and her pubis. She was lying on a table with diagonal grooves that allowed blood to run off. Today, however, they weren't necessary.

Ulrik removed his cap.

"Lars has applied for a transfer to Nordsjælland's police. I've given him another assignment. Until further notice, I'll be leading this investigation." He looked around the room.

Frelsén snorted. "That is the stupidest thing I've heard in a long time," he mumbled to himself.

"Excuse me?" Ulrik took a step closer.

"Yeah, yeah. I won't be poking my nose into your affairs." Frelsén rested his hands on the table and leaned over the body, seemingly unaware of its presence. "But Lars is one of the best investigators I've worked with." He let his gaze drift from Ulrik to Sanne.

She was fourteen again. The mopeds barking on a hot summer evening. The engine vibrating between her thighs.

"I think we should get back to the autopsy." Ulrik was sweating.

"That's why we're here." Frelsén winked at her. "Bint?"

Bint eased his hands into the opening and reached inside the body. Sanne looked away. She had witnessed a couple of autopsies at Syddansk University Hospital, but the atmosphere had been very different in that bright room. There were no windows here. No one was getting out of this one unscathed.

"Liver, 1,456 grams." Bint turned to note down the weight. She focused on his hand, the felt pen dancing across the whiteboard. Heart, brain, and kidneys were already marked down. Her gaze followed Bint back to the table. Frelsén stood on the other side, studying the body's face.

"She's a strange mix. Eastern European—Czech or Slovak maybe. But there's something else too—Ukrainian or Georgian."

Sanne leaned toward Ulrik, whispered, "How on earth could he know that?"

"The face," Ulrik whispered back. "The bone structure, I suppose. I've never really figured it out. But he always hits the mark dead-on."

Sanne returned to her original position. Ulrik was still sweating. Bint struggled to keep the intestines from moving on the scale.

"There's no body odour, no gasses." Frelsén sniffed above the body. "In the old days we used to make a small incision by the belly button and hold a lit cheroot next to it—this was before the smoking ban. The flame could shoot up to three metres in the air." Sanne closed here eyes, happy she'd had a light breakfast. Frelsén continued, unmoved. "But this girl, she's pumped full of glutaraldehyde. It destroys all microbial bacteria."

"What?" Ulrik said.

"Glutaraldehyde. When I was at university, it was used to preserve the bodies for anatomy classes. They've switched to formaldehyde these days."

Ulrik's Adam's apple jumped. Allan took two steps back and sat down on the room's only empty chair.

"And how—?" Allan asked.

"The smell is unmistakable. There are needle marks on her inner right thigh. This guy knows how it's done—or rather how it was done."

"But why—" Allan tried to get up, but fell heavily back into the chair. "Why preserve her? You said she'd been beaten?"

Sanne stirred. Ulrik's gaze rested on her as she opened her mouth.

"She was beaten by her pimps less than a week before she disappeared. The bruises must originate from that."

"Highly probable." Frelsén pulled the electronic magnifier over her right breast. "Bruising on the chest and arms. From several days before she died. Take a look—the black is turning green."

"And when were you thinking of telling us that?" Ulrik had turned toward her.

"I didn't get a chance—before..." She repeated what she had told Lars about the Bukoshi brothers earlier, the words practically spilling out of her.

When she was finished, Ulrik nodded. He ran his thumb along the sweatband of his cap. "And her last customer?"

Sanne shook her head. "The last one she was seen with was driving a white Opel Kadett. But one of the girls ran into her an hour later—" She pulled out her notebook, flipped through it. "At approximately 9:45 p.m. on Halmtorvet, heading toward Skelbækgade. She'd scored drugs on—."

"Maria Kirkeplads." Ulrik nodded. "Have you been there?"

"I was thinking about going down there today."

"Take Allan with you. The drug addicts are peaceful enough, but the dealers can get aggressive when the police are in the vicinity. Where was Mira's usual corner?"

"Either Skelbækgade or Vesterbrogade, between" — Sanne checked her notes again — "Vesterbro Torv and Viktoriagade. I'll make sure I ask around there too."

"Try the corner stores." Ulrik put his cap back on, avoiding looking at Mira's body. "The owners always know what's going on. After you've been out to Maria Kirkeplads, bring the Bukoshi brothers in for questioning." He nodded at Frelsén and Bint. "I want the report on my desk as soon as the autopsy's been completed." He turned abruptly and walked toward the door.

Frelsén watched him leave, shaking his head. "I'm not finished."

Ulrik turned in the doorway. "Well?"

"The crushed glass we found beneath her shoulder."

Sanne shivered, remembering how Frelsén's Maglite had shone on something in the shallow water the previous day. Still, when Frelsén lifted the body's left shoulder from the table, she stepped closer. A dense pattern of major and minor wounds covered Mira's back.

"The waves pushed her back and forth, moving the body up and down on top of whatever it was, crushing the glass. We'll need the technician at the lab to put it back together, but I'd bet my right —" Frelsén stopped. He seemed to be considering something. A joke? His upper lip twitched, then he continued in a neutral tone. "It appears to be the remains of an ocular prosthesis. A glass eye."

CHAPTER 8

COPENHAGEN POLICE HEADQUARTERS. Broad, power-ful, impregnable.

Overhead, soft clouds drifted across the blue abyss. Lars nodded to the gatekeeper and entered the labyrinth of corridors and stairwells. As a young officer in the Emergency Response Squad, it had been his duty to check that the windows and doors in the entire building were shut before he left. He got lost on more than one occasion and had to look at the surrounding streets in order to regain his bearings. But at least now he knew every crevice in the entire building.

He poked his head into the claustrophobic office that Kim A shared with Frank.

"Can you guys come into my office? Grab Lisa too." He disappeared before they had a chance to answer. As always, Kim A looked right through him.

Toke was already sitting in his office when Lars stepped inside. He got up from the corner of Lars's desk a little too quickly, holding a copy of Stine Bang's chart.

"Well, it's about time," Toke said. "We've been waiting for you all morning."

Lars didn't answer. He hung his jacket over the back of the desk chair. He had been by Baresso Coffee at the corner of Skoubogade and Strøget, where Stine's friend Astrid worked. The previous evening, Stine, Astrid, and a third friend, Maya, had drinks at Stine's house. Later they cycled to Ristorante Italiano on Fiolstræde — near Jorcks Passage — and ended up at Penthouse nightclub on Nørregade.

Toke sat down, crossed his legs. "How's it going with the apartment?"

"Good, thanks." Lars sat down, rubbing his face with both hands. "I just have to get settled in. Say hi to your brother-in-law and thank—"

The door opened. Kim A and Frank walked in without knocking. The office suddenly seemed crowded.

"Lisa's on her way," Frank said, then sat down on the windowsill. Kim A positioned his more than 225-pound frame in the middle of the room. His fleshy cheeks quivered when he talked. Lars ignored him.

"I assume you've all been briefed on the case?" Lars pulled out a cigarette but he didn't light it. He just needed to have something in his hands. "I've been to see the victim, Stine Bang."

Toke raised his hand. Lars nodded and Toke slid a photo onto the table.

Everyone leaned over Lars's desk, studied the printout of the photo. Stine was lying on a stretcher in the corridor at Rigshospitalet, clearly unconscious. Christine Fogh was bent over her. Stine was naked, although someone had covered her groin

44

with a towel. Even in the grainy photo, the jumble of dark stains and wounds that covered her frail body was clearly visible. Her face was almost lost behind layers of congealed blood. Her nose was crooked, her eyes shut. Even if she'd wanted to, she wouldn't have been able to open them.

A quick knock and the door opened. Lisa Bak entered. She was small and nimble with big brown eyes and short, dark-blonde, spiky hair.

"What's up?" She smiled at Frank. Toke made room for her by the desk.

Lisa glanced at the picture; her smile disappeared. "What a fucking psychopath."

No one contradicted her.

"You haven't spoken with the victim?" Frank's freckled face was almost transparent in the backlighting.

Lars shook his head, told them about his meeting with Christine Fogh, and then recounted Astrid's statement. A guy had been all over Stine on the dance floor, then had followed her to the bathroom. He was about a head taller than Stine, and had light brown, curly hair. Astrid couldn't remember what colour his eyes were.

Lisa moved to the door and rested her back against it as he spoke. The others returned to their previous positions. Everyone avoided looking at the photograph.

Lars cleared his throat. "This guy that Astrid mentioned, we need to find him."

Everyone in the room nodded. Lars looked at each of them in turn. "It won't be long before the media gets hold of the story. This picture..." He pointed at the back of the printout. "It cannot end up in the tabloids or online. She's already been raped once."

Toke nodded, folded the picture, and returned it to his inside jacket pocket.

Lars leaned back in the chair. "Stine left Penthouse at 2:00 a.m. By bike, it isn't more than ten minutes to Øster Voldgade where she was attacked at 2:40 a.m. Stine was drunk, so let's say fifteen minutes. What happened during the intervening twenty-five minutes? Kim A, Lisa, you take Ristorante Italiano and Penthouse nightclub. Somebody had to have seen something. Frank and Toke, you speak to the cab drivers. There are a lot of cabs driving down Øster Voldgade at that time of night."

"Ristorante Italiano?" Kim A was already writing the name down on his pad.

The meeting wrapped up. After the detectives left his office, Lars leaned back in his chair with his hands behind his head. He needed a smoke.

He sat up with a start and reached for his cell phone.

"Christine Fogh? This is Lars Winkler, Homicide Department. We spoke earlier about Stine Bang?"

"I remember you, officer." Her voice was a touch deeper than it had been earlier that morning.

"Is there any change in Stine's condition?"

"No, we're keeping her asleep."

"One question. Can you tell me how tall Stine is?"

He heard paper rustling.

"I don't seem to have that information here. I'll call you right back."

Lars was walking in haphazard figure eights between the pillars of the colonnaded courtyard of the police station. Halfway through the cigarette, his phone rang.

"Elena." His ex-wife.

"Welcome back, Lars." She hesitated. "Did you have—did you enjoy your vacation?"

"Hmm." He took a long drag on the cigarette. The ember was now perilously close to his lips. The stench of burnt stubble stung his nose. He started coughing.

"Are you sick?"

"No, no," he assured her. "What did you want?"

"Have you sorted out the apartment?"

"Yes, I've just—"

"Listen, can you come by the boutique tomorrow? Let's say eleven o'clock?"

"That's not a good time. I'm in the middle of something."

"Lars, you know very well I can't leave the store." Honey and steel in her voice. "You've got Maria tomorrow, for the next two weeks. You haven't forgotten, have you?"

"Fine, fine, I'll try to be there. But—"

A bell chimed in the background.

"I have to run," she said. "Remember, tomorrow at eleven."

As usual, she got things her way. He put out his cigarette, and as he was making his way back through the building, Christine called.

"Five foot six."

"And her heels?"

"Two inches exactly."

"So he was about eight inches taller than her." Lars held the phone between his jaw and shoulder, noted down 5′8″ and 5′6″ + 2″ on his hand. "Thank you."

4 Folmer Bendtsens Plads, a corner store on the ground floor, or more accurately, a SUPER CORN RSTORE, if you believed the sign above the door. Lars was looking despondently at the red boards above the storefront, the dimly lit space behind

them, and the cases of factory flowers outside. Toilet paper and juice cartons were stacked in one window; the other had an ad for Jolly Cola and Jolly Lime. The place hadn't seen an interior decorator for years.

So this was where he'd be buying his King's from now on? The occasional newspaper?

A moped shot past. The slipstream made his jacket flutter. Someone shouted at the driver.

He stepped inside and looked behind the counter at the rows of magazines bathed in the merciless fluorescent light. The glossy covers shimmered in an extended palette of skin colours. From piggish pink to light mocha and chocolate brown.

He thought about Elena, about their phone conversation, and felt the beginnings of a bad mood. His gaze swept across the magazine covers again. He had accomplished so few of the things you were supposed to achieve in life.

"Ahem." Someone cleared their throat from behind the counter.

Lars looked up. A chubby kid with blond hair and watery eyes was standing behind the counter. He was wearing a T-shirt and jogging pants, and couldn't be more than seventeen.

"You've gotta be the only Danish guy working in a corner store for miles."

The boy laughed. "Most people are surprised. Still, not many have the guts to mention it. What can I get for you?" The guy turned sideways to reveal the magazine shelves behind him.

"Er, no thanks. I mean, not today ... I—" He went quiet. "Just give me two packs of King's Blue."

The guy placed the cigarettes on a pile of tabloids. The headline, "Political Hopeful's Secret Past as High-Class Prostitute," was in bold print, above a less-than-flattering picture of a female politician. Lars pulled out his wallet and ran his card through the machine.

"Well, I just work here," the guy said. "My friend's dad owns the store. He's from Iran. So you're not far off the mark."

Lars opened a pack and gave the young man an inquiring look. The boy nodded, still smiling broadly.

"Smoke away. Someone's always smoking in here." He gestured toward the storeroom. Languorous tones drifted out, a string instrument that Lars didn't recognize. The beaded curtains swayed gently back and forth.

He lit his King's, blew the smoke out through his nose.

"I've just moved in to number 2." He pointed a thumb over his shoulder. "How late do you stay open?"

"Well, we usually close around midnight, seven days a week. But I only really do a few shifts a week. I've got school as well."

Lars nodded. School was important. "Nice talking to you."

"Welcome to the neighbourhood."

Lars left the corner store just as an S-train thundered into the station. It was only when the whistling had died down and he was standing in front of number 2 with his keys in his hand that he registered the sound.

Maybe he was settling in here after all?

JULY 1944

SHE IS LYING in the darkness beneath the roof with her eyes open, waiting for that which comes crawling in the night. Up the stairs and into her bed. The rafters in the old timber frame give a little. A window rattles somewhere. The darkness presses on her. There is war in the summer night, and both inside and outside, blackout. Mother and Father are sleeping below on the second floor above the consulting room.

Nothing moves in the old house. Only the rising and falling of her chest, in time with her breathing. And deep down inside her, the little life stirs. She strokes the small bump under the rough blanket that scratches her skin through her nightgown. She wants to light the kerosene lamp, read a little. But there are no blackout curtains for the small window in the roof. The latest issue of *Family Journal* waits on the nightstand. She doesn't have time to read during the day. She has so much to do. School and Father's patients. And in the evening, cooking, washing dishes, packing Father's pipe. And now there is war.

The sky is torn apart by the terrifying roar of airplane engines. A monotone thrumming warns of incoming death. She attempts to count the planes, one, three, five... No, there are too many today. Having dropped their cargo of death and destruction on Berlin and Hamburg and Kiel, they're flying above Gentofte on their way home. Great cities in flames, with girls like her, and women and men and children. Over there, they are burning. Over there, the blackout is over.

She waits for the small *poofs* of the anti-aircraft guns. It won't be long now.

Someone turns in the bed below, a heavy body. She pulls the blanket up under her chin.

Poof, poof—poof, poof, poof. The sound is almost cute from down here. But there is also another sound. Something exploding, falling through the night sky. Screaming metal. She pulls the blanket all the way over her head, but no blanket will help tonight. The shrill screeching grows louder and louder. Then it's as though the house—no, the earth—is shaking. The crash is so tremendous, the world goes silent. Everything is completely still.

Then, little by little, the world begins to speak again.

The stairs creak, the rafters give. Somewhere outside, something is burning.

Downstairs, there's movement again. Someone is getting out of bed, getting dressed, walking down the stairs. Mother is shouting and whispering in the same breath.

"Be careful."

A little later, she doesn't know how long, the door opens with a crash. He shouts at her to bring water and cloths. She stumbles out of bed, puts her thin coat over her nightgown, and tiptoes down the stairs in bare feet. Her mother is standing in the hallway of the second floor, her nightgown clinging to her thin frame. Further down, on the ground floor, a kerosene lamp is lit. The flickering light casts dancing shadows over the walls and doors. There are bloodstains on the floor, just inside the front entrance. She hears clattering feet, men huffing. She hurries into the kitchen, fills the large pot with water, and lights the stove. Then she runs into the consulting room, finds the drawer with the folded cloths, and pulls out a large stack. Mother is on the landing, looking down at the ground floor. Then she turns on her heel and goes back to bed.

The blood trail leads to the cellar door. She follows carefully, so as not to fall down the steep staircase. She walks through the first cellar and over to the secret door.

Now she hears them. The flickering gleam from the kerosene lamp lights the spaces between the boxes. Her father is hunched over a man in uniform. It's difficult to see in the dark, but she can see the blood covering his face, and his neck is badly burnt. One arm hangs, strangely limp.

"An English pilot," Father says. "He's got several broken ribs. His arm might be broken too. Talk to him, Laura."

She walks over to her father, folds her hands, and swallows. Then she produces her schoolgirl English.

"Sir?"

With her translating, Father is able to make a diagnosis. She runs upstairs to get the water that's almost boiling. As she tries to balance the large pot down the steep stairs, water splashes onto her hands. Between them, she and Father manage to pull off the man's uniform jacket and shirt. She cleans his wounds. He's beautiful, she thinks. Black hair. Grey eyes, full lips. He's in a lot of pain. But he'll pull through, Father says. They must be sure not to say anything to Mother. She shakes her head. She is good at separating things. That which Mother can know and that which Mother cannot.

She grabs some gauze and morphine and some drinking water. She makes a splint for the pilot's arm from the barrel of a gun, binds it. He groans every time the barrel bangs against his broken ribs. Then she hurries upstairs and washes the blood from the carpet and stairs. She goes outside and walks along the garden path, searching in the darkness for any traces of him. She manages to wipe away the few stains. It's starting to rain. That should get rid of whatever's left. In the thicket by the swamp, out by the lake, the airplane is smouldering. A car horn cuts through the night. The Germans are coming.

"You have to stay down here and watch over him," Father says when she returns. He washes his hands in the spare water. All that blood on Father's hands. "I'm going up to the bedroom with your mother. I'll worry about the Germans when they get here."

She nods, darts up to the attic to find her *Family Journal*. So she'll get to read after all. She smiles when she returns to the cellar and sees Father walking up the stairs. He closes the secret door behind him.

Later, she hears knocking upstairs. Heavy blows that make the house groan. She's absorbed in her magazine; she doesn't react. Not even to the angry voices that follow shortly after.

Next to her, the pilot's wheezing measures the hours until morning.

MONDAY
JUNE 16

CHAPTER 9

THE ENTIRE TEAM gathered in Lars's office for the daily briefing. By mutual, unspoken agreement, everyone assumed the same positions as they did the previous day.

"Well," Lars said. "Let's hear it. Frank, Toke? How did it go with the cab drivers?"

Frank furrowed his blond brows, shook his head.

"Someone must have seen something? Toke?"

"Unfortunately not," Toke said.

A subdued atmosphere spread through the office. Lisa cleared her throat.

"We were at the Italian restaurant and spoke with the waiter who served the girls. They were in high spirits and got quite drunk that night. The staff at Penthouse were stocking the bar. They didn't notice anything either."

Lisa smiled. She was holding something back. "But then one

of the girls had a bright idea. Apparently, people upload images of themselves and their friends onto club and bar web sites. The young women reveal quite a bit, let me tell you."

Kim A straightened up. "That's not a bad idea. Take a closer look at her sexual history?"

Toke reached inside his jacket, pulled out Stine's picture, unfolded it, and placed it on the desk for everyone to see.

Lars counted to ten. "Neither Stine nor anyone else deserves — let alone is asking for — this." He jabbed his finger at the picture of Stine, naked, beaten, and bruised.

"Yes, but any defence lawyer in the country would bring up the victim's sexual history in court. We might as well be prepared for it," Kim A said.

"In front of a jury, with that image burned into their retinas?" Toke mumbled.

"I don't see it either," Lars said. "Carry on, Lisa."

"Do you mind if...?" Lisa reached across Lars, opened a browser on the computer, and typed in an address.

The page loaded. The air above Lars's desk was so heavy he almost couldn't breathe.

The image of a young blond girl appeared on the screen. She was in a short strapless dress, pouting and pushing up her breasts with both hands. Her cleavage almost reached her chin. A friend was pulling a face behind her. The flash made their pupils red. On the left, half-empty bottles and glasses filled a table.

"It doesn't look like six foot three and curly hair is going to be enough here," Frank snickered.

Lisa pointed her index finger at the top right corner of the screen. Just above her chewed nails, Stine Bang was dancing, smiling with her eyes shut, her arms raised high above her head. A tall guy was reaching around her from behind, his palms facing inwards. His curly, medium-length hair hid his face.

"Pig," Lisa mumbled.

"Aw, relax. They're just dancing," Frank said.

"Does anybody at the club know who this guy is?" Lars asked.

"One of the bouncers thinks a friend knows him." Lisa got up. "I'll just check to see if he's got hold of him."

CHAPTER 10

THE BLACK MONDEO turned into the roundabout. The car's interior was baking from the sun. From the passenger seat, Sanne observed the bustling activity on Halmtorvet, the public square in the Vesterbro district. She saw mothers' groups sitting in cafés, children playing around the sculptures and fountain. This wasn't exactly how people back in her native city of Kolding had imagined Halmtorvet. Where were the junkies, the prostitutes? The sex shops?

"Surprised?" Allan laughed in the seat next to her.

"No, it's just..."

"We'll be there soon."

The two uniformed officers in the front seat were silent. Still, she was sure they were laughing at her, at her accent. The innocent, inexperienced country girl in the big city. Her cheeks were burning. *We're almost there, we're almost there*, she chanted to herself. *Focus.*

She had spent the previous day on the streets, searching the area where Mira normally worked, questioning prostitutes and the staff in the corner stores. Had they seen her with the Bukoshi brothers? But she'd had no luck so far. On Maria Kirkeplads, the square in front of the Church of St. Mary where junkies scored, some of the girls recognized Mira, but no one had really spoken to her. And who could really expect a drug addict to remember what had happened on a specific date more than a month ago? Allan had worked the phones all day, trying to track down the Bukoshi brothers. He had gotten nowhere until this morning.

The car coasted out of the roundabout, drove up the alleys between the houses, and crossed Istedgade. They passed a sex shop, Private Corner. So there was still something left of old Vesterbro.

"They hang out at an Albanian basement club just up ahead. It's called Shqiptarë. It's number 10," Allan said to the officer at the wheel. "Just pull up to the sidewalk here," he said, pointing to the parking lot of an adult video store. "They'll smell us a mile away."

The officer nodded and pulled in behind a beaten-up Peugeot on the left side of Abel Cathrines Gade, just outside number 14 and the windows of Videokælderen. Private booths, the sign in the window promised. The heat returned to her cheeks. Why couldn't she just act natural? It didn't seem as if Allan had noticed her embarassment, though. He was giving last-minute instructions to the officers in the front seat.

Suddenly she realized what they were planning.

"It won't work," she interrupted. "If we all go barging in, they'll take off. They'll be heading out the back before we've made it down the stairs." She shook her head and pointed at Allan. "You get out here. We'll drive past the building and park a little farther ahead. The two of us —" she nodded at the officer in the passenger seat, "—will enter through the gate over there. When we get inside, Allan will go into the club. You stay here," she told the driver, "but be ready to back up Allan."

The officer in the passenger seat twisted around in his seat. "She's right. They normally have lookouts up there, in the apartments." He pointed at the windows on either side.

Allan leaned back. "That's not a bad idea," he conceded. "I'll give you one minute, then I'm going in." He opened the door and climbed out.

The Mondeo pulled away from the curb, found a parking spot further ahead, past a basement bar. Sanne nodded to the officer in the passenger seat, opened the door, and jumped out.

She went to the door and pressed the buzzer.

"It's the police," she said when the door phone picked up.

"It's about time you did something."

She heard the buzzer opening the gate.

In the courtyard, a couple of children were playing in a sandbox under a withered tree. The parents were sitting around a table with their coffees, watching Sanne and her colleague as they moved along the wall toward the staircase at the back of number 10. No one said anything. The sun was right overhead, turning the courtyard into a smouldering furnace. A radio was blaring from one of the apartments, mournful vocals over a primitive beat.

"I'm going in," Allan's voice crackled over the radio.

Sanne and the officer moved back against the wall. Sweat was trickling down her neck and from under her arms. She whispered to herself, *one, two, three, four*, but was interrupted by a loud clattering from the basement bar. Someone shouted. A door slammed. Immediately after, footsteps came up the stairs, the door flew open, and a large stocky man in a dirty tracksuit appeared in the doorway, squinting in the bright sunlight.

Her colleague stepped in front of him.

"Well, looks like it's the end of the road for you, buddy."

The officer raised his hand to place it on the man's shoulder but the man misinterpreted the move and struck out, hitting the officer on the temple. The officer fell to the ground without a sound. The man jumped over the officer, ready to run across the courtyard. Sanne instinctively stuck a leg out, and the man fell to the ground next to the officer with a hollow thud. She fumbled with the service pistol in her shoulder holster, then held it in front of her with both hands.

"Stay down!" she shouted.

Her heart was pounding; she was gasping for air. The parents at the table still hadn't made a sound. One of them held his coffee cup suspended halfway between the table and his mouth. One of the children was crying.

She heard more footsteps coming up the staircase.

"Jesus." Allan appeared in the doorway. He took two steps forward and managed to wrest the gun from Sanne. He glanced down at the other officer, who was groaning on the ground. Allan secured her weapon and stuffed it into his pants. Then he walked over to the suspect, forced one arm behind his back, then the other, and fastened them with plastic straps.

"It is now 9:37 a.m. and you're under arrest," he said. Only then did he return the pistol to Sanne.

"Sit down for a moment." He helped her over to a crate that was next to the building. "Put your head between your legs."

Sanne did as she was told while Allan helped the injured officer sit up. Her mind was swirling: the heat, the weapon in her hand, the sliding resistance of her trigger. Easy. So close.

The officer driving the car came racing into the courtyard with his weapon drawn.

"You can put that away." Allan said. He leaned over Sanne. "Are you okay?"

She nodded, spat between her knees.

"He—he's getting away." One of the parents was pointing. The suspect was on his feet again, running awkwardly toward a shed at the other end of the courtyard with his hands secured behind his back.

"Hey, you, hey!" Allan ran after the suspect. When he caught up with him, he got hold of his T-shirt but the man tore free. Allan caught up with him again and stuck his leg out. The suspect fell to the ground, but this time he couldn't break the fall with his hands and fell face-first on the asphalt. His face was battered and smeared with soil, blood, and grime. His eyes were half-closed and his T-shirt was torn to shreds. The pungent smell of sweat surrounded him.

Allan pulled him up, then motioned for one of the officers, and together they managed to drag the man back to where the others were.

"May I present: Meriton Bukoshi."

CHAPTER 11

ELENA WINKLER. Lars's eyes cast over the large sweeping letters on the glass door. *At least she hasn't changed her name yet.* Through the store window, past an opulent display of shoes, he saw her standing behind a large leopard-print armchair. Her back was turned to him. She was wearing a thin cream-coloured knit T-shirt, mocha-coloured slacks that were tight around the hips and wide through the legs, and a pair of high heels from her collection. Her dark frizzy hair was pulled back in a low, tight bun. The row of Chinese masks on the wall bore into him with their evil eyes.

He ran his hands through his hair and took a deep breath. This was it.

She turned around when the bell sounded.

"Hi Lars." They stood across from each other, uncertain. Two people with far too much history. Then she kissed the air by both of his cheeks and took two steps back, turned around, and continued arranging the display.

The scent of her skin and the light hint of perfume made his stomach tingle. He shut his eyes.

"Have you been to Milan again?" he asked after a while.

"Yes, I brought Maria with me. Just after . . . you left. We visited one of the factories and saw next year's collection. Those are this year's." She turned around and pointed at the shoes in the window. "Aren't they lovely?"

He had never really understood the concept behind the kind of shoes Italian women wore. Most of them looked like something from an adult movie. But he didn't get a chance to respond.

"I want to talk about Maria," Elena continued. She paused briefly, her dark eyes wandering.

"Elena—" he started, reaching out for her. She stepped back, turned, and began to rearrange the merchandise with quick, focused movements.

"I think that's enough of that. We've been through it all before." Her hoarse voice began as a whisper but ended with a firm and authoritative tone.

He observed the lines on her slender neck, the large, gold earrings. A heavy lump sunk slowly down his throat, continued past his lungs and entrails, to finally settle in his groin.

"I don't want to argue with you," he finally said. "If—"

"Lars." She turned around. A grey pallor had settled on her face. "We need to think of Maria now. She needs us, needs you."

The abrupt movements of her slender hands followed the rhythm of the sentences. Light brown skin with the beginnings of fine wrinkles. Even her hands were beautiful. They looked like—

Then came the longing, that sinking feeling in his body that never hit bottom. How long had it been since he had seen

Maria? One month? Two? He couldn't remember anymore.

"Is something wrong?" he managed to ask. His voice sounded wooden, hollow.

Elena ran her finger along a shelf, checking for dust. Then she looked directly at him.

"She's angry with you—no, not angry, furious." The corners of her mouth were twitching. She cocked her head slightly. "How could you be so stupid and just take off?" she whispered. "She needs you. More than you can imagine."

The air was quivering in the small store. Lars was about to reply when the bell rang and two women in their twenties stepped in, weighed down with bags from the nearby boutiques, Free Lance and Stig P.

"What about school?" he asked.

Elena went behind the counter and followed the two women with her eyes. She held her left forearm against her stomach, resting her right elbow in her left hand while she toyed with her earring. His gaze moved down to her breasts.

"She's moved over to Øregård."

He looked up again, hoping she hadn't noticed anything.

"She doesn't talk about anything," said Elena. "She just sits in her room with her homework. She sees only a couple of kids from her old high school."

"That's how teenagers are. And Simon?"

Elena bit her lip. "I think she broke up with him."

"Well, it's great that she's keeping in touch with her old friends." He moved around the counter, made sure it was between them.

Elena nodded, staring absently at the two customers.

"Excuse me." One of them turned to Elena, held up something that looked more like a spectacle than a shoe. "Do you have this in an eight and a half?"

Lars was about to say something but Elena interrupted him.

"Yes, one moment and I'll have a look." She turned to Lars. "That's all I wanted to say." She was already on her way to the storeroom. "And stop burying yourself in your work."

He whispered something; he hardly knew himself what he said.

"I know what you guys are like," Elena answered. Then she was gone.

Lars was standing outside the shop on Ny Østergade. He didn't know what he had expected of his meeting with his ex-wife; he only knew that nothing was as it should be. Apart from Maria — he would see Maria today.

CHAPTER 12

"**W**HAT THE HELL did you do to him?" The doctor snapped his bag shut. Meriton Bukoshi had submitted to the doctor's treatment without batting an eyelid. "I ought to report this."

Allan pulled the doctor aside, describing the arrest to him, while Sanne looked around Allan and Toke's shared office. It was a good deal bigger and brighter than the broom closet she had been assigned, but otherwise the layout was the same. Just two of everything: desks, telephones, computers, chairs, and filing cabinets. But what made all the difference were the two large windows facing Niels Brocks Gade, which let in the light from the clear blue summer sky.

Allan walked the doctor to the door, then turned to the suspect.

"Well, Meriton. How about we have a little chat now?"

Meriton gave him a surly look. *"Vetëm shqiptar."*

"What does that mean?" Sanne asked.

Allan folded his arms. "It sounded a bit like the name of their club, Shqiptarë. Does it mean Albania—or Albanian? No doubt he wants an interpreter." Allan looked at Meriton inquiringly, who nodded and looked away at the same time.

"There, you see. He understands perfectly well what we're saying. He just doesn't feel like speaking Danish, isn't that right Meriton?" Allan slapped the man on the shoulder.

Sanne flinched. Meriton smiled at her lewdly.

Allan looked at her. "Why don't you find us a translator?"

By rights, she should complain about being treated like a secretary, but she was new here and she certainly didn't feel like being left alone with Meriton Bukoshi.

A little while later, she returned with the translator, Shpend. He was tall and his eyes were constantly watery. His papers said he was in his mid-thirties but the guy looked at least ten years older.

She started coughing as soon as she opened the office door. The air inside was thick with cigarette smoke. Meriton was sitting bolt upright in the chair, hands on his lap. Allan sat on the windowsill. Hadn't the ashtray been empty when she left? They had to be on their second, maybe third, cigarette each. Meriton raised an eyebrow when she hurried through the office to open a window. Allan stubbed out his cigarette in the ashtray and, using his foot, pushed out a chair for Shpend. Sanne stood by the open window.

"Good." Allan rubbed his hands and winked at Sanne. "Let's get started."

Meriton dropped his cigarette in the ashtray, mumbling to himself.

"We'd like to know what Meriton did on the night of May 5."
Allan looked at Sanne, who nodded.

Meriton raised his eyebrows, probably suspecting that
someone had talked. They had to make sure they didn't expose
the girls. Sanne filled her lungs with a final mouthful of fresh
air and sat down on the edge of the table behind the interpreter.
Meriton followed her movements while he answered the questions, fixating on her breasts.

Meriton said he had been playing cards in their club,
Shqiptarë, until late, maybe 3:30 a.m., except when he had
gone to get some food around midnight. Afterwards, he went
upstairs to a small room on the ground floor that he and his
brother used for sleeping.

"Ask him to write down the names of the people he played
cards with that evening." Sanne placed a pen and paper on the
table in front of Meriton.

Allan pulled her over to the other side of the office and whispered, "Why? Their friends would pin aggravated murder on
their own mothers if the brothers asked them to."

"No doubt. But if we can place just one of these alleged card
players somewhere else, we have the first gap in his story."

Sanne returned, nodded at Meriton, and pointed at the paper
while Shpend translated. Scowling, the pimp started writing
down a list of names.

"Tell him we know that he knows exactly why he's here,"
Sanne said. "And then ask him where his brother is."

The interpreter translated; Meriton shook his head.

"He hasn't seen him since the day before yesterday," Shpend
said.

Suddenly there was a knock at the door and a large, bald
man in his fifties barged into the room. A considerable muscle
mass was hidden beneath a layer of body fat.

"Hi Kim," Allan said.

Kim A gave Allan a quick nod, then let his gaze fall on Meriton, who glared back at him. Then Kim A spotted Sanne. He pursed his lips and cleared his throat.

"Sorry," he said, to Allan. "I was told you were asking for me?"

Allan raised his eyebrows. "Really? Who told you that?"

Kim A pointed backwards, looked at Meriton, then out the window. "I just ran into..." He stopped. "It was probably just a mistake. Sorry for interrupting." Then he was gone.

"Who was that?" Sanne asked.

"Kim A. Former riot squad officer."

"Isn't he on the case that Lars is handling now?"

"That sounds about right." Allan snorted. Was that a laugh?

Meriton mumbled something and Shpend pulled out a cigarette, lit it for him. He inhaled, blew out two enormous clouds of smoke, one from each nostril.

Sanne pulled Allan into the corner. "He can't find out that we know they beat Mira. It will just get the other girls into trouble, and they'll probably get a beating too."

Allan nodded.

"Okay." Sanne crossed the room, looked Meriton hard in the eye. She tried to ignore the penetrating stench of stale sweat. "So you do admit that you knew Mira?"

Meriton puffed his chest out. "She was a—how do you say—girlfriend?" Shpend translated. "He has not seen her since the night of May 4."

Meriton took a drag on the cigarette; the ember flared up. He started speaking quickly, gesticulating; Shpend almost couldn't keep up. "Meriton and his brother Ukë had agreed to meet Mira at Burger Palace on Vesterbrogade at 11:30 p.m. But she never turned up. Some of their other girlfriends"—Meriton laughed at this point—"had seen her on Absalonsgade an hour before. They'd had people out looking for her, but the ground might as well have opened up and swallowed her whole. Until he saw her on the front page of today's paper." Meriton nodded at the open copy of the tabloid *BT* on Toke's desk.

Allan leaned forward in the chair. His stomach spilled out onto his thighs. "Do you know what I think? I think you and your brother discovered that she had a customer or two on the side."

Meriton looked away, took a drag on the cigarette. "You don't know shit. Danish police don't know shit," he said in Danish. "You need to find out who killed my friend Mira." The interpreter stared at him open-mouthed.

Allan started to get up, his face flushed. Sanne had to pull him back down into the chair.

She waved the paper with the list Meriton had made in front of his face. "We're going to check this list thoroughly. You'd better hope that one of your friends wasn't somewhere else that night. In a car accident, ticketed for running a red light, bar fight..." Meriton's gaze wandered. Sanne continued, "And when you see your brother, tell him we'd really like to have a word with him. Preferably today and at the very latest, tomorrow. If he doesn't show up, we'll make it our mission to destroy your business. Do you understand what I'm saying?"

Meriton spat out the cigarette butt.

"Danish police," he said getting up, then stomping toward the door. "You don't know shit."

A little later Sanne sat in her broom-closet-sized office. There were no windows and the walls were brown. The room smelled of linoleum and old paper. She twisted and turned a dirty envelope in her hand. The stamp was postmarked 22.4 BRATISLAVA, SLOVAKIA. One side of the envelope looked to have been opened with a knife.

She put the envelope down and sorted through the few,

modest belongings Mira had left behind: a fake Dolce & Gabbana purse, cheap lace underwear, a pair of tight H&M jeans, two very short dresses, three tops, a shirt, and a down vest. There were also a couple of books in some Eastern European language. Judging by the covers, they looked to be medical romance novels of some kind. She opened the purse: a lot of cheap, no-name makeup, probably bought in some backstreet shop, and a couple of curled-up banknotes. One kept rolling up every time she smoothed it out. Forensics would most likely find remnants of cocaine on it. Lip balm, condoms. And, in an inside pocket, a small folded-up packet containing white powder. Sanne stuck a finger inside, tasted it. The powder tasted metallic, hard. Speed or cocaine. The purse contained no phone numbers, no papers—in fact, not one of Mira's few possessions indicated anything about her as a person.

Apart from the one folded-up piece of paper and the envelope it was in.

Sanne took the letter out of the envelope. The words were incomprehensible to her, but it was signed by someone named Zoe, and Mira's full name was written on the envelope: "Mira Vanin, P.O. Box 2840, Copenhaigen, Denimark."

The least she could do was send an enquiry to the Slovakian police through Interpol.

Ten minutes later she was on the phone with Ulrik. She had to get his permission to get the letter translated.

"Sanne," Ulrik said in that preppy schoolboy Danish. "I can assure you that who Mira was as a person is not important. She was a prostitute who was killed by a customer or by her pimps. We're keeping our focus on her acquaintances in Copenhagen."

Sanne seethed. The condescending man and the sentimental woman? Not with her.

"On the other hand," he continued, "all the bleeding hearts and feminists as well as the press are coming down on us for not doing enough for female trafficking victims. Maybe it would be good to get to know Mira a little better, so if they start complaining again, we've covered that angle. You should know though, the letter won't bring us any closer to her killer."

CHAPTER 13

16 **SKYTTEGADE WAS** a corner property, constructed in grey brick sometime around the dawn of the twentieth century. The entire ground floor was painted rust red, and the front door was covered in graffiti. But the property was lined with neat rows of plants and white hollyhocks, and the double-paned window appeared to be well maintained.

"It looks like a housing co-op." Toke tilted his head back to look up at the top floor. Lars followed his gaze. Of course this guy lived all the way up on the fifth floor.

Lisa had finally managed to get hold of the Penthouse door-man's friend. He couldn't remember who the guy was that had been harassing Stine Bang, but he thought he worked in a music store downtown. Lisa went to a couple of record stores, but to no avail. Next she started visiting stores that sold musical instruments. Finally, in 4sound, on the corner of Åbenrå and

Landemærket, she got lucky. The store manager identified the man standing behind Stine Bang in the photograph as one of his employees, Mikkel Rasmussen. Mikkel hadn't been to work for a few days, but he lived at 16 Skyttegade in Nørrebro.

Nobody answered the door phone, so Lars buzzed the neighbour.

"Police," he said when someone finally answered.

"What do you want?" The voice was scratchy, like the man had just woken up.

"We need to have a word with your neighbour, Mikkel Rasmussen."

"Why don't you try buzzing him then?"

Lars took a deep breath. At least he hadn't hung up.

"Could you please let us in?"

The neighbour hung up. Ten seconds later, Lars heard a buzz. He pushed open the front door. These days, the police could not expect much help in the district. And he knew why. With the district's history of riots and fighting in the streets, Nørrebro held little love for the police.

Mikkel Rasmussen's neighbour opened the door a crack when Lars, Toke, and the two uniformed officers, heavily winded, arrived at the top of the narrow staircase. The neighbour was young and scrawny, with dark, medium-length hair and drooping eyelids above grey cheeks.

"I'll need to see some ID," he said.

Lars pulled out his badge.

"Thanks. And sorry." The guy nodded. "There are a lot of strange people around here."

Lars put the badge in his pocket. "I understand. We'd like to speak with your neighbour. Do you know where he is?"

The guy in the doorway looked surprised. "What did he do?"

"We just want to talk with him." Lars smiled in what he

hoped was a friendly way. "So you don't know where he is?"

Mikkel's neighbour shook his head.

"We're going to carry out a search, and by law we need two witnesses," Lars said. "Are you able to do that?"

"Well, actually, I'm studying for my exams. But hey, a little procrastination here and there never hurt. You need two people, right?"

Lars nodded. The guy disappeared inside the apartment but left the door ajar. He heard some murmuring from inside the apartment. *A student during exam time.* He shouldn't be so quick to judge.

Mikkel's neighbour came out with a young woman. She had spiky black hair and wore a short black tank dress over cut-off jeans. Tattoos ran all the way down one arm. She stared at Lars and the officers with a look of deep distrust.

The largest of the uniformed officers positioned a crowbar just above the lock between the door and doorframe of Mikkel Rasmussen's apartment, and forced the door open. The pungent smell of dank clothes, sweat, and rotten food filled the hallway.

There wasn't much room in the small apartment. Junk mail spilled across the entranceway. In the middle of the floor, on top of a supermarket flyer, was a half-full bowl of yogurt. A pair of underwear had settled into the thick, grey liquid.

They had to bend a little because of the sloping attic walls. Unwashed clothes were piled in every corner. In the first room there was a mattress on the floor with dirty sheets. A rectangular piece of chipboard rested on top of two plastic beer crates. Rolling papers, a week-old newspaper, coffee cups, a couple of beer bottles, and two ashtrays filled with butts competed for space on top of the improvised table.

"I'm sure Mikkel wouldn't mind if I smoked." Lars looked at the neighbour and his girlfriend, then lit a King's. He divided Toke and the two officers between the second room, the kitchen, and the washroom, then turned back to the neighbour.

"Were you home the night before last?"

The neighbour looked at his girlfriend, then nodded. "I was studying."

Lars flicked the ashes from his cigarette. The grey flakes fluttered through the dusty light and down toward the ashtray.

"What are you studying?" Lars asked.

The young man's face lit up. "Philosophy."

"That sounds a bit dry,"

"Well, yes and no. A couple of the courses are pretty crazy, so it can get quite interesting now and again."

"Really?" Lars raised his eyebrows. Then he continued, "How well do you know Mikkel?"

"Not that well." He shrugged. "We say hello and that's about it."

"The night before last, after 3:00 a.m., did you hear Mikkel come home around that time?"

The young man thought about it. "I must have been studying Merleau-Ponty around then. I'm afraid I was completely engrossed in it." He looked annoyed. Lars turned to the girlfriend, gave her an inquiring look. She shook her head, pointed at her ears. Only then did he see the white headphones and the wire running into the pocket of her cut-off jeans.

"She always listens to music," the neighbour explained. "The other night as well. She didn't hear anything."

"Come in here for a moment." It was Toke, yelling from the kitchen.

Lars went into the kitchen. Toke was holding a charcoal-grey denim shirt out in front of him with two fingers.

"Hello there," Toke said. "Doesn't this look like Mikkel's shirt?"

Dark splatters were spread in a speckled pattern across the chest.

CHAPTER 14

HE RAN INTO SANNE in the square just outside the main
entrance to the Copenhagen Police Department. Her sunglasses
were resting in her hair. The top buttons of her shirt
were undone. The two of them stood awkwardly, squinting in
the bright sunlight.

Lars was the first to speak.

"I'm sorry about yesterday. I was tired, and Ulrik—"

"Can we just forget about that?" She waved her hand.
"Where have you been?"

"On a search. It's the rape case. Actually I was going to go
for a walk. It's hard to think in there sometimes."

She smiled at him. "Do you mind if I join you?"

"Yes—I mean no, I don't mind. It's fine."

She laughed and slid her sunglasses on.

They walked across the square, turned down Bernstorffsgade,

and headed toward Kalvebod Brygge. Neither of them said anything. Lars walked with his hands in his pockets. Sanne turned
her head to the sun. Behind the dark glasses, her eyes were shut.

They crossed Kalvebod Brygge, passed the Marriott Hotel,
and stopped by the harbour. Across the water, they could make
out people swimming in the harbour baths on Islands Brygge,
tiny black insects swarming on the promenade on the far side,
dots popping up and down in the glistening water.

Sanne followed his gaze. "It looks lovely. Have you been in?"

He shook his head. "No, it's still too urban for me. I have to go
out to Amager Beach Park before I show myself in swim trunks."

Sanne laughed and followed him along the harbour. "There
ought to be a café around here. The view is absolutely fantastic."

"A little different from Kolding?"

"Actually we do have a harbour—your typical small-town
commercial harbour. Not as big as this one."

"I think we can get some coffee just around the corner
here." Lars led Sanne along the boardwalk, around the next
building to where a small café was nestled in a corner between
two buildings. He bought a latte for Sanne and a black coffee
for himself. They continued south along the water's edge with
their drinks.

The towering head offices of banks, the engineering union,
and the elite of the Danish corporate world cut off the view
to downtown Copenhagen. A broad, low tour boat shot past.
Gulls hung in the air above, squawking.

Sanne pushed her sunglasses up on her head and squinted.

"What is it with—?" She stopped herself. "No, just forget it."

Lars stopped. She had latte foam on her upper lip. She
looked lovely in the sunlight and by the glistening water. The
air smelled of salt and sea.

"It's just the two of us. We're far away from the station and
the others." He smiled. "Spit it out."

She took a sip of her latte and looked across the water.

"You can't get annoyed," she began.

"I'm the one who asked you."

"Fine. Nobody's said anything to me, but I can sense grumbling in the corners. From your team too, according to the rumours." She looked up. "What's the deal with you and Ulrik?"

His eyes wandered. He ran the bottom of the cardboard cup against his palm, coughed with his fist covering his mouth. There was only one way to say it. Quickly and to the point.

"A little over two months ago, my wife Elena came home and told me she was moving out, taking our daughter with her. To Ulrik's." Lars stared across the harbour. "He and I have been friends since the academy. We've been on vacations together, celebrated Christmas, birthdays." He shrugged. "Ulrik is more ambitious than me. I suppose that's what Elena was missing."

Sanne's smile stiffened. "If you don't want—"

"No, it's okay." He took another sip. The coffee tasted bitter. "We'd drifted apart—I just hadn't noticed it. Ulrik on the other hand—Ow, go..." He'd squeezed the cardboard cup so hard that the lid had popped off and hot coffee spilled onto his hand. Sanne grabbed the cup, started wiping the scalding hot coffee off his hand with her napkin. The touch sent a shock through him.

"It's not that bad," he said to Sanne. "It just surprised me."

She looked at his hand with a worried expression. "It's always bad when there are children involved," she said. "How old is she?"

"Maria's sixteen, starting grade ten." He pictured Maria. "She's going to stay with me for the next two weeks." He hadn't seen her for two months. How would she react when they met? Was she still angry at him? He was suddenly nervous about seeing her again. How well did he really know her anymore?

"Listen, if you'd rather just be with your daughter tonight..."

Sanne looked down. "But I was wondering if you'd like to come to my place for dinner? I mean, me and my boyfriend's place."

"That sounds nice. I think..." It should really be just him and Maria tonight of all nights. But what was he going to say to her? Where would he start? He threw the coffee cup into a garbage can by the promenade. "You know what, we'd like that a lot."

CHAPTER 15

THERE WAS A file from the translator in her mail slot when she returned. *Quick service. Impressive.*

She waited until she was inside her office before she placed the original and the translation side by side on her desk. She adjusted the lamp and started reading.

Dear Mira,

I hope you get my letter. I don't understand why I can't have your actual address? I promise I won't come to Copenhagen. I just get so worried.

Mira, I know you're just like me. You knew what you were getting into. But don't waste your life. Soon it will be too late. Soon you won't be able to have a normal job. The streets devour you. They chew you up and spit you out until there's nothing left. You know I've been there and God knows I never want to go back. I implore you, no I beg you: think carefully.

You were so beautiful when you were little. You babbled and laughed in my arms. It was just the two of us in the world. Can't it be like that again?

That was all I wanted to say. Hurry home, dear girl. Time passes by far too quickly and before you know it, it's too late. If it's money you need, then write. I'll see what I can do.

I love you.

Your Mom,
Zoe

Sanne put the letter down. Ulrik was right: its contents had not revealed much about Mira. The letter suggested that her mom had been a prostitute too. Had Zoe in some way passed her fate onto her daughter? She forced back the thought. Better to think about what she was going to cook for Lars and his daughter. Tasty but not too fancy. Everyday food, something along the lines of salmon, or fresh plaice. Something that tasted of Danish summer.

She had better call Martin and tell him they were having guests.

CHAPTER 16

A FLOCK OF pigeons flew up from the tracks and veered out over Lygten. The F-Line from Hellerup rumbled into Nørrebro Station.

Lars had a knot in his stomach; he was perspiring, afraid of meeting a sixteen-year-old high school student. It could hardly be more pathetic. But Maria was the person he loved more than anyone—and she was furious with him.

She had sent him a short text message earlier. She was arriving on the F-line at 4:18 p.m., and even though she'd said he didn't have to, he was waiting for her, just like he had after her first day of school. He remembered his little girl on a rainy day in the suburb of Mørkhøj—Maria standing on the road in a dress and sandals with her hair in braids.

Just before coming to meet his daughter, he had left Mikkel Rasmussen's shirt with Toke. Now it was on its way to Forensics.

Getting usable DNA wouldn't be a problem. They had him.

The crowd parted in front of him. A figure stood out. Then a body pressed against his, a momentary touch of a cheek before she pulled back, stood in front of him, waiting. Her pretty, deep brown eyes shifted toward the billboards, the people passing by—the light in their eyes had long since gone out—the departing train. Everything but him.

"Hey," he ventured.

Maria mumbled something in reply. He tried stroking her hair.

"Are we just going to stand here?" she said, pulling her head back.

When he laughed, he could hear how hollow it sounded.

"No, of course not. Come on, it's just over there." He speed-talked as he walked ahead of her toward the stairs leading to street level. On the first landing he stopped so she could catch up to him. She wore cut-off jean shorts, a black peasant top, Converse sneakers, and a backpack. Her hair was still long and dark brown like his. She had a small upturned nose and delicate eyebrows, and her mouth was slightly too big for her slender face. She was just as he remembered her. But had she lost weight? Did her cheeks look a little hollow?

She was already on her cell, texting. Her thumb passed lightning fast over the keys.

He glanced at her as they walked along the street under the tracks. She was somewhere else. Not here. Not with him. "Can't you wait a minute with that?"

She didn't answer, continued texting as she followed him down Folmer Bendtsens Plads.

When they got upstairs, Maria walked straight into the first room. "Is this supposed to be my room?"

"Er, we're going to paint it of course, but yes, that's what I was thinking."

"And where am I going to sleep? On that?" she said, pointing to the mattress that was leaning against the wall.

"Mom is sending all your things over tomorrow. Everything from your old room. Ulrik's bought new furniture for you, right?"

She dropped the backpack in a corner and sprawled in the old wicker chair, the only other furniture in the room apart from the mattress. The wicker creaked.

"And you can cut that out." She pointed an accusatory finger at the cigarettes he had just taken out. "You're not smoking in here."

He fumbled with the pack then put it back in his pocket. It was unbelievable how she could order him around. You could forget a lot in two months.

She kicked off her shoes and folded her legs under her. "At least it's not far from Caro's place."

"Caroline? Has she moved away from home?" Had it already begun?

"She's subletting an apartment on Ørholmgade." She looked up at him. "Relax. Her mom is so tough, and she knew someone who'd be travelling all summer." She began texting again.

So it was just a trial. And maybe that wasn't such a bad thing? With Caroline around the corner, the chances of Maria wanting to be here increased considerably.

"We're going to a colleague's for dinner tonight," he said. "I'm just going out on the balcony to — smoke."

"Fine," she said and rolled her eyes. Her phone beeped.

Lars closed the balcony door behind him, exhaled. The cigarette was already in his mouth. He struck a match and drew the smoke deep into his lungs.

An Audi streaked out of the roundabout, nearly grazing a rattling Opel. There was honking and a finger out the window. Lars looked back into the apartment. His home had just been subjected to something close to a hostile takeover and he had no idea what to do about it.

He looked at his watch. It was quarter to five. They had to be at Sanne's for six o'clock. He threw the butt down onto the street and went inside.

"I'm just going to take a shower," he shouted. "We're leaving in half an hour."

But the door to the bathroom was closed. When he tried the handle, it was locked.

Sanne answered the door on the third floor at Århusgade.

"Hi Sanne." Lars handed her the bottle of wine they had bought at Føtex on their way over. "Maria, this is Sanne." He pushed Maria in front of him. "It smells delicious."

"Thanks," Sanne said. "I hope you like fish. We're having plaice."

The evening went far better than Lars had expected. Sanne managed to engage his grumpy teenage daughter, and during the meal Maria laughed and told funny stories about her new teachers at Øregård high school. And as soon as Maria discovered that Sanne's boyfriend, Martin, was a Monty Python fan, she was sold.

Immediately after the meal, Maria and Martin disappeared to the room next door to watch an episode of the original BBC television show on the flat screen. Sanne and Lars cleared the table.

"How's it going with the case?" Sanne was rinsing the plates and putting them in the dishwasher. Lars came into the kitchen with the rest of the dishes. He told her about the search, the bloodstained shirt.

"That was quick," she said.

"The Internet helped." He explained how they had got on Mikkel Rasmussen's track by checking the club and bar web sites for photos at Penthouse from that night. "Unfortunately, it's as though the ground opened up and swallowed him whole. He's probably in hiding."

Sanne nodded as she rinsed the serving dishes.

They stood in silence. Lars turned his glass in his hands. "Is it a good idea to piss off your boss in your first week? I mean, by having me and Maria over like this?"

Sanne shook her head. "I'm here to learn, right? Frelsén said you were the best. Ulrik got annoyed about that too."

He laughed. So Frelsén had complained about him being dropped from the case. It must have been an interesting autopsy.

"Did you find out anything else about the girl—Mira, was it?"

"Hmm." Sanne nodded. "There was a letter among her personal effects, from her mom." Sanne was looking down at the sink. Lars followed her eyes. Scraps of plaice, potatoes, and parsley floated around in the cloudy dishwater, swirling toward the drain with a loud gurgle. "Another short-lived, sad life. She probably would have ended up like she did somewhere else anyway."

"You must never think like that," he said. "That's how the bureaucrats think, how Ulrik thinks." Then he caught himself. "Sorry. I shouldn't get you mixed up in my problems."

Sanne grimaced. "I think I'm starting to share your opinion of him."

"Cheers to that." Lars raised his glass.

They clinked glasses, then Sanne put hers on the counter.

"What about you?" she said. "Your wife ran off with your boss and you've got a teenage daughter. Who else is there? Parents?"

"Isn't that enough?" Lars looked out the window. "Well, my mom lives in a housing co-op in Sydhavnen. I suppose she's what you'd call a life artist."

"And your dad?"

Lars's gaze followed the ruler-straight line of hedges outside, the flowerbeds that framed the courtyard. Jungle gyms, sand-boxes. Benches for the stylish Østerbro parents.

"It's been a while since I saw him last. He's American. Absconded from military service and Vietnam in the late 1960s. He finally ended up in the hippie camp in Thylejren, where he met my mom. As she tells the story, she got pregnant almost straight away."

"And he's not here anymore?"

"In 1977, Jimmy Carter granted amnesty to ten thousand deserters. Among them was my dad. I was nine years old when he went back to the U.S. Now he's a professor of criminology at Columbia in New York," he said. "And you? You're from Kolding?"

"Another time." Sanne put down the sponge and went into the living room. Lars followed. From the TV room, they could hear Maria and Martin crying with laughter at "The Cheese Shop" sketch.

Lars sat down at the table, spun his glass by the stem. Sanne remained standing on the other side and pulled a file out of her purse.

"According to the autopsy report, Mira was shot with a nine millimetre Husqvarna P-40."

Lars whistled. "An antique?"

"It was originally manufactured for the Finnish army. During the war, when the Swedes couldn't get their standard weapon, the Walther P38 from Germany, they decided to start producing their own." She looked at him. "Ulrik is convinced Ukë and Meriton killed her. But would they use an antique gun?"

"Who else then?"

"A collector, or someone who has access to the weapon through their family? Of course it could have been stolen too."

Lars grabbed the file and began reading the report. "What

did Frelsén say? What about the eyes?"

"The same as when we found her. No scoring of the skull in the eye socket. It was a fine, almost surgical cut. And then she was injected with glutaraldehyde through the large vein in her thigh. Glutaraldehyde gives the tissue that yellowish tone we saw on the body. Formaldehyde, which is used today, doesn't cause discolouration."

"So you're looking for someone who uses an antique weapon and old methods of preserving bodies?"

Sanne nodded. Lars closed his eyes. He rubbed the bridge of his nose with his thumb and index finger until it hurt.

Sanne reached for her glass. She squeezed the stem until her knuckles went white. "One sick bastard."

In the cab, on their way home, Maria was in high spirits.

"'I'm keen to guess.'" Her bad imitation of John Cleese ended with her doubled over with laughter. The cab driver sent him a disapproving look in the rearview mirror. Lars shifted slightly away from her. Not everyone could tell that they were father and daughter.

Maria stopped laughing, pushed her hair back, and looked at him. Was that a smile? "She's sweet, Sanne. Too bad she's with Martin."

Lars cleared his throat. "She's just a colleague. I..." He didn't finish the sentence.

Maria looked at him. Then she turned her head and stared out the window.

CHAPTER 17

HE SITS AT the head of the table; the candles are lit. Sonja and Hilda are on either side of the long dining table. It's covered with Mother's best damask, her silverware and seagull dinner service. At the other end of the table, Karen's place is empty. He leans back, looks around the cellar. *This is how it should be in here. No complaining, no arguing. The soup bubbling on the stove.* The confusion, the bad times are over. He should have done something, taken action earlier; he should not have stood idly by. But he does love them, all of them. As you love your family. Something trembles deep down. An equilibrium is disturbed. Lorin Maazel and the Vienna Philharmonic with Agnes Baltsa are on the phonograph. *Kindertotenlieder.*

Oft denk' ich, sie sind nur ausgegangen,
Bald werden sie wieder nach Hause gelangen.

Der Tag ist schön, o sei nicht bang,
Sie machen nur einen weiten Gang.

He gets sad anyway. It's difficult to say goodbye like that. He does not want to punish. Tears press forth. And the trembling. Upstairs, the heavy floorboards creak. Is someone disturbing his peace? A Sten gun leans against the ammunition boxes in the corner. But there's nothing else. The sounds of an old house can make you crazy. *No, wait.* The creaking is inside him. His skeleton is creaking. The crack opens. Sonja and Hilda cower. They know what's coming. All the darkness, the black. Flames leap through the fissure. He shuts his eyes, tries to focus. Peace. That's all he wants. Is that too much to ask ? There's a throbbing behind his forehead, threatening to explode. He sways back and forth in the chair. The images come to him, images that he has long since banished: Mother no longer gets up; she lies in the small room in the attic. She must be delirious. The things she says, terrible things. It's wrong. And he is strong. Like Father or Grandfather. Not weak, not like her. He would really like some peace now. But the roar rises from within. It creaks and groans but eventually it gives way as he presses down, and the crack closes again. The flames are gone. Only a small bubble of darkness remains, floating around inside him. He follows it through his body, into the stomach, the chest, the right arm, down through the groin—then he's back. It's the soup that saves him. It boils over. The scalding hot liquid extinguishes the gas jet. He jumps up, turns down the temperature on the hot plate, scolding Sonja and Hilda for not warning him. Then he stops, takes a deep breath and looks at them. *You shouldn't pay attention to Daddy's little idiosyncrasies.* He takes their bowls and fills them using the old soup ladle. Dinner is served. He pulls out his chair, sits down. Cabbage soup, Mother's recipe. Then he has doubts. Was it really all Karen's fault that he had to let her go? Never mind. Everything is much better now, even if it hurts too. It's not easy when they fly from the nest. He swallows a spoonful of soup. It's as though the good atmosphere from before won't return, as though something is missing. Sonja and Hilda. They miss Karen, of course. But they'll have to get used to it. She's not coming back. It's only when he goes to place her eyes in the bowl in front of the empty seat that he realizes: one's missing—the green one. He must have dropped it when he returned her.

He sits for a while, forgets the soup. What if all Sonja and Hilda need is a little sister?

AUGUST 1944

SHE PLACES THE last plate on the dish rack. Tips the tub upside down and watches the filthy brown water gurgle down the drain with a loud belch. It speaks to her of the horrible thing that comes out during the night and climbs up the creaking stairs to her little room in the attic. The door's rusty hinges squeak.

She throws the brush into the tub and puts it under the sink. That's all in the past now. From the living room comes the clicking of Mother's knitting needles. Father is working on a couple of medical files. They'll both ruin their eyesight in the yellow light from the kerosene lamp. The blackout curtains are drawn. The three of them are prisoners here—the three of them and the patient downstairs in the cellar—while the spectres perform their *danse macabre* outside.

She doesn't mind the deluge of duties anymore. Now she

has something to look forward to. In the cellar, everything that makes life worth living awaits her. She washes her hands, dries them on her apron. The tray is already on the serving table, covered with a cloth. She pokes her head into the living room, nods to her parents. Father looks up with a grunt and returns the greeting.

She dances back into the kitchen, grabs the tray, and carries it over to the cellar stairs. At the foot of the stairs, she sets the tray on a small table and opens the secret door behind the vitrine to yet another staircase. He is lying down, at the very back of the labyrinth of bookcases and boxes, on a bed of ammunition, machine guns, and TNT. A wounded warrior surrounded by his weapons. He looks up when he hears her footsteps and his eyes light up.

"Hello, my blossom," he whispers, readying his lips for a kiss.

She blushes, places the tray on an ammunitions box, slaps the hand that slides up her thigh. She's not that kind of girl. She wants to hear him talk about his native land now. Glenridding on the shore of Ullswater in the Lake District. The pub down by the lake, the tall mountains that rise up on every side. Narrow, winding paths that cling to the steep mountainsides. His descriptions are so vivid she can picture it all. All that green, the vantage points by Heron Pike and Sheffield Pike, the long Z-shaped lake that meanders toward the northeast between the mountains. The snow-clad Helvellyn, which rises above the village, cold and unapproachable during the winter, warm and covered with grass during the summer. All of that is nice to have when the duties become onerous and it's a long time till dinner has to be carried down.

Above, the floorboards creak. And in the south, in Berlin and Hamburg, the firestorms melt flesh off bones.

"Tell me how things are in the outside world," Jack says. "I know you listen to the radio from London."

She shakes her head. Not now, not here. It is sacred down here; this place must not be defiled.

"You do know I have to get back, right?" He looks at her. The seriousness in his grey eyes colours them dark. "It is my duty. My country — your country — needs me."

She knows all of that, but he has promised to take her with him. They will flee to Sweden together and then live in England as husband and wife.

She bends over him, her breasts resting lightly on his chest — not too hard, his ribs are still healing — and presses her mouth on his cold lips. Then he starts to speak and his voice becomes warm and the deadly paleness leaves his lips. This, exactly like this. This is how she loves him best.

Again, the floorboards upstairs creak as she feeds him, spoonful after spoonful of the good, thick cabbage soup. It won't be long before he is fully recovered.

In the end she has to leave, but she promises to return tomorrow. He laughs at their little joke. Then he forms his lips into a kiss. She shakes her head firmly, but smiles as she walks up the stairs; she doesn't want him to think she is angry. She sends him a final melting look before crawling out through the secret entrance to the first cellar.

She closes the vitrine behind her with a small click, and grabs the tray on her way up. The figure hunched in the dark corner remains unseen as it follows her tiniest movement with eyes of burning coal.

TUESDAY
JUNE 17

CHAPTER 18

THE CELL PHONE snarled somewhere outside the dream. Lars opened his eyes, tipped his legs out of the bed. His hand groped in the dark, across the bureau. Maria was moving in the next room. Hopefully in her sleep.

"Yes?"

"This is Duty Officer Jørgensen. There's been another rape in Østerbro, at the star fortress on Fyens Ravelin. Toke and Lisa are on their way out there as we speak. There's a squad car parked on the corner of Folke Bernadottes Allé and Grønningen. The officer will give you directions from there."

"Thanks, I'll be there right away. Can you call Frank for me?"

"And Kim A?"

"And Kim A. Thanks."

Drowsy with a half-forgotten dream still lingering in his mind, Lars staggered into the bathroom, took a piss. He splashed cold water on his face and brushed his teeth before he went back into the bedroom to get dressed.

The sound of bare feet on the wooden floor behind him. He turned around. Maria was standing by the door.

"What's going on?" she whispered drowsily.

He pulled a shirt out of the closet, undid the top button, and pulled it over his head. "Work. Just go back to sleep."

"Is there—is there another one? I thought you'd caught him?"

"We have a suspect. We haven't caught him yet." He stroked her cheek. "But we will. Get some sleep, Maria. I'll call and wake you up at seven, all right?"

"Mmm." She rubbed her eyes, squinting in the light. "Promise me you'll catch him, Dad."

"Come here." He stepped toward her and she nestled up to him. A soft and warm baby chick. He kissed the top of her head. "We'll get him. And now it's time for you to get some sleep." He kissed her again, this time on the forehead. "I probably won't see you until this afternoon. This is going to take all night."

She waved at him, then slipped back to bed.

Lars shut the door behind him. A small, warm ball in his stomach radiated happiness throughout his entire body.

The streets of Nordvest were deserted and bathed in the dying orange glow of the streetlights. An occasional pedestrian was staggering home from the bars further down Tagensvej. A lonely ambulance. Otherwise nothing. The cab sped down Sølvgade, then turned down Øster Voldgade by the National Gallery of Denmark. He peered into the darkness through the trees where Stine Bang had been assaulted. Did they really have a serial rapist on their hands?

The cab stopped behind the police car that was parked halfway up on the sidewalk at the northwestern entrance to the star fortress. A uniformed officer he didn't recognize was leaning against the hood, smoking. Lars flashed his badge. The officer nodded, spat tobacco, and pointed at the entrance.

"In there and first path on the right. You'll be able to see the lights after a couple of hundred metres. The Crime Scene Unit has arrived."

Lars thanked him, gave him the names of the others on his investigative team, and told him to leave when they'd arrived. There was no reason to advertise their presence. The reporters would have to find out for themselves what had happened.

He disappeared into the darkness of the star fortress. A pale half moon shone, making the trees shimmer and casting dancing grey and silver shadows. The branches groaned; the leaves rustled.

He hurried on. The night was warm and he quickly started to sweat.

He heard the generator first; then he saw the gleam from its lights reflected faintly off the leaves, a pale glow shining on the bastion. He found the stairs, ran up, and stepped into the circle of light.

Bint and Frelsén circled around in their white outfits, their noses to the ground. For some reason, Frelsén had removed his hair net. Toke and Lisa stood outside the cordon. Lars walked over to them, pulled out his cigarettes.

He looked at his watch. Ten past three.

"The ambulance drove off with the girl less than ten minutes ago." Lisa stuck a match in her mouth. "She's at Rigshospitalet now."

"Did you get a chance to speak with her?"

Toke nodded. "She's in bad shape, but not quite as bad as Stine." He flipped through his notebook. Lisa shone her flashlight so Toke could read. "Louise Jørgensen, twenty-two years old, lives on Livjægergade, right here in Østerbro. She'd been to Penthouse" —Toke paused for effect— "and was cycling home down at Grønningen when another cyclist went to pass her. He knocked her over and dragged her off the bike path, through the moat, and up here. Lisa has been down to check it out. Louise's bike was halfway up the sidewalk with a buckled front wheel."

"I pulled it to the side, leaned it against a tree," she explained.

A shadow darted past, a dark silhouette against the blaze of lights. Then it disappeared into the darkness.

Toke gave a start. "What was that?"

"A fox," Lisa said.

Toke shook his head. "There aren't any foxes in the centre of Copenhagen."

"There are. They live off trash, get into garbage cans. I've seen a few of them on Østerbrogade at night," Lisa held her ground.

"If you think I'm buying that—"

Just then Frank came up the stairs.

"Kim A will be here in just a moment. He's bringing coffee." Frank shook hands with Frelsén and Bint. He looked tired. "Has she been taken to the hospital?"

Lars nodded. "Toke and Lisa were just bringing me up to speed." He asked them to proceed.

"So, Louise Jørgensen is riding her bike from Penthouse..." Toke said.

Frank whistled.

Toke continued: "She was knocked down on the bike path and dragged up here. He tears her clothes off on the way up, punches and kicks her repeatedly. He rapes her up here— anally." Toke pointed at Frelsén who was towering in the middle of the circle of light. "When he's done, he spits on her, kicks her in the kidneys, and takes off in the same direction he came from. Probably on bike."

"We'll call Forensics in the morning," Lars said. "Push for a quick response on the DNA analysis of the shirt. Who found her?"

"No one," Lisa said. "She called it in herself. Her purse and cell phone weren't far away and—"

Heavy steps came up the stairs. Kim A appeared with two white paper bags from 7-Eleven.

"Coffee's here." He crossed over to the small group and started handing them out.

"Frank, Lisa. Boss—?"

Just as Lars reached out for the steaming paper cup, Kim A handed it to Toke. After an awkward silence and with obvious unease, Toke finally accepted the cup. Frelsén and Bint came over and each got a cup. Finally Kim A handed Lars the last coffee.

"Did you think I'd forgotten you?" he laughed.

Bint grimaced, then turned to Lars. "There's leaves and dirt everywhere. I followed the trail halfway down the bastion. Presumably it continues all the way to the water and onto the street. As far as organic material—"

Frelsén took over. "Traces of semen and saliva and a single blonde hair—Louise is standard medium blonde. And then we have a set of footprints from a sneaker, between sizes nine and ten and a half. Surprisingly good coffee, Kim." Frelsén nodded at Kim A.

Lars drank slowly. The coffee tasted burnt and of asphalt. Filter coffee that had spent too much time on the hot plate. Exactly like the coffee at the station. It was almost too homey.

"Frank, Toke," he said, "talk to the cab drivers again. They must know you by now." He allowed himself a little smile. "Kim A, you stay here, help Bint and Frelsén. Lisa, we're going to Rigshospitalet."

He drained the coffee in one long gulp, crumpled up the paper cup with one hand, and threw it into the nearest garbage can.

Again it was Christine Fogh who had admitted the victim. Louise Jørgensen was still awake when they arrived. It had all happened so quickly; the only thing she could remember was the attacker's blue eyes.

On their way down from the Juliane Marie Centre, Lisa called in and requested a patrol car to drive them to Penthouse. Outside, day was rising. The golden glow rose, large and mighty in the sky above Copenhagen. The 3A bus drove past, heading toward Østerbro. Lars closed his eyes, but he couldn't shake the image of Louise's one arm, stiff and white above her hip, wrapped up in a thick layer of gauze; the shaking and far-too-thin body covered by a hospital sheet.

Lars's phone rang. It was the duty officer.

"Your suspect was arrested half an hour ago. An alert colleague filling up his tank recognized him at a gas station outside Roskilde. He's hopped up on a few substances. They put him in detention in Roskilde and will be bringing him in later this morning."

Lars clenched his free hand in a silent gesture.

"We've got him. We've got Mikkel Rasmussen." He put the phone in his pocket. The fatigue made his eyes ache. "Now where's that patrol car?"

Lars and Lisa caught the bar manager in the doorway of Penthouse nightclub. She was about to lock up but agreed to find the names and numbers of the three photographers who had been at the club that night. None of them were particularly enthusiastic about being dragged out of bed. One refused to give them his pictures until late the next morning. But when they rang his front doorbell ten minutes later, he still let them in.

By seven o'clock they were in a patrol car on their way back to the station. They were heading down Nørre Voldgade when Lars remembered that he had promised to call and wake up Maria. He pulled out his cell.

She didn't answer until the seventh ring.

"Time to get up, beautiful." He could hear how tired he sounded.

"Mmmm." Maria didn't sound like someone who was planning on getting out of bed any time soon. Didn't she have school? He suddenly went cold. Wasn't there something about an exam yesterday?

"How — didn't you have an exam yesterday?" He coughed, turned to face the window, away from Lisa's glare. He had a feeling that he had "Bad Father" painted on his forehead in bold letters. "Did it go well?"

"Yeah, it went all right." Did she hesitate a little? But it sounded like she was happy.

"All right? What does that mean?"

"Well, it was just a mock exam. But I did get a ten." Yes, there was no doubt. She was happy.

"Ten? That's great. Let's celebrate when I get home."

"We're going to Grandma's tonight. Did you forget?"

Apparently there was a lot he had forgotten.

"So we'll celebrate with Grandma." He sunk back in the seat. "But I'm going to need a couple hours of sleep when I get home. We're working straight through."

"Just catch him, Dad. See you later."

He was about to say goodbye, but Maria had already hung up.

"Did you forget about your daughter's exam?" Lisa shook her head.

Lars looked out the window. It had started to rain. A pouring blanket dragging across Rådhuspladsen and moving toward Tivoli.

CHAPTER 19

SANNE SAT DOWN as she had been told. She was fiddling with the zipper on her light summer jacket. The view from Ulrik's office was breathtaking, but the room was stuffy. Didn't any of those big windows open? A hint of a headache was sailing around the back of her head. She'd had a little too much to drink at dinner the night before. And then there was the argument she'd had with Martin afterwards.

But there was something else too. Her conversation with Lars had left her feeling sad and with a sense of unease. His hunch and their mutual, unspoken agreement regarding her case.

Ulrik was sitting across from her with his back to the window. His elbows rested on the desk, his head in his hands.

"So Meriton Bukoshi's alibi stands up?"

"Yes, and Ukë's. I've checked everyone who was at the club that night, but—"

Ulrik waved her off. "We have to let them go. I've already had their lawyer on the phone twice today."

Sanne decided to give it a go. "I don't think it's them anyway." The nails on her right thumb and ring finger started to click against each other. *Stop it.*

"What do you mean?"

"They paid money to bring Mira up here. Why kill her after such a short time?"

"But they did beat her before she went missing?"

Sanne put her hand in her pocket. Her fingers twitched once, then rested against her thigh. "As far as I understand, it's quite common. Beating and rape. It breaks the girls."

Ulrik shook his head, then swivelled in his chair. She couldn't see what he was doing; she saw only his thin hair sticking up above the back of the chair. Out by the reception, an elevator opened. The small ping reached them even through the closed door.

"It was easier in the old days," Ulrik said. "No trafficking, none of this callous violence." Suddenly the chair spun around. Ulrik was facing her again. "What do you think we should do?"

"Me?"

"Yes, you. Aren't you the sharpest investigator in all of Jutland?"

"Oh, that—" She was on the verge of telling him about her conversation with Lars the night before. But something stopped her. It probably wasn't a good idea to mention it right now. "As far as I've been able to uncover, glutaraldehyde isn't something you can buy over the counter. Hospitals and dentists buy it wholesale, and farmers use it for cleaning pigpens. But Forensics has assembled the remains of the glass eye. It arrived this morning."

"Yes?" Ulrik squinted, rested his fingertips on either side of the desk pad.

"It's green. In fact, it's a really bad fit, so it wasn't made for Mira. It was suitably large enough so as not to fall out as long as she was alive—" She swallowed. "We didn't find all the shards, so the reconstruction isn't complete, but you get a good idea of how it looked. They also pulled half a thumbprint from the back."

"And?" Ulrik got up halfway in his chair.

"Unfortunately, it's not on file."

Ulrik waved a hand in front of him. The apathy that had weighed on him only minutes earlier was gone. His gaunt frame suddenly exuded vitality and energy. Even his grey skin began to glow.

"Listen: the two brothers supply girls to a customer who wants something quite specific—girls with glass eyes."

Sanne's jaw dropped. "That sounds like something from a bad episode of *CSI*."

"You'd be surprised." Ulrik looked out the window.

"Then what about—"

"First and foremost, we need to follow up on that eye. That's the best lead we've got right now."

Sanne got up. She had better get hold of Allan.

"As for the Bukoshi brothers," Ulrik continued, "I'll get a court order for a wiretap. We'll put the club under surveillance too. It's vacation time, so you and Allan are going to have to take quite a few shifts."

Sanne nodded. Sometimes she regretted having left Kolding at all.

CHAPTER 20

MARIA WAS SITTING in the cathedral-like assembly hall below the giant copy of Thorvaldsen's classic sculpture *Jason with the Golden Fleece*. She was nervous, biting her nails even though that was frowned upon here. A pair of high heels attached to a pair of ridiculously long legs power-clicked across the marble tiles. An aggressive echo followed them all the way through the assembly hall. A couple of girls from her class sat at the table next to her, staring at an iPad. In less than forty-five minutes, it was her turn. Mock exam in oral Danish. *Yikes.* Mom said, "It's only a mock exam," but what did she know? And Dad? Did he even know she had another exam today? He hadn't mentioned it on the phone.

She started thinking about the cab ride the night before. Why did he act like such an idiot? It had actually turned out to be an OK night, and then he couldn't even give her a proper answer when she asked him about something important.

She tried concentrating on the photocopy in her hands. Søren Ulrik Thomsen's *Poetry in the Night*. One line read, "The Path of the Intoxicated." No wonder their teacher had chosen that poem. It had been a long time since she had seen such a well-kept drinker's nose.

Luckily none of her parents had problems with alcohol. Well, Ulrik might have a few too many sometimes, more than was good for him, but then again he wasn't her dad.

In a way, she understood why Dad had run away from everything. If only it hadn't hurt so much. If only she could have gone with him. But she had to think about school, her future, yada yada yada. They made her sick. Two months alone with Dad, with no stupid teachers, no overprotective Mom and her expectations. It could have been fantastic.

She heard a chair scrape the floor a few tables away. A couple of twelfth graders sat down. Christian and his friends. He was the one with the nice ass, the sandy hair, and the twinkle in his eye. Almost all the girls in the class, the entire school even, were prepared to open their legs for him if he even looked their way.

She glanced at his table from behind the photocopy. Was he looking over here? No, it was probably just her imagination. *Just concentrate on that crappy poem.*

> *sleep's ether seeps*
> *through the half-open mouths*
> *clings heavily to the bodies' dance*

What did that mean? It sounded creepy, almost like a horror film. And then the ending: "The way of the drunken to a dreamless sleep." A chill ran down her spine. She had to get up, move her legs a little. But maybe it also meant something else? The bodies' dance.

She glanced over at the twelfth graders again. *No. Stop it. Stop.*

"Oh my god, Maria. Isn't that your dad?"

"What do you mean?" She walked over to the other table. Leise and Christina were looking at her with their mouths agape. Two stupid cows with big tits.

She leaned over Christina's shoulder. Berlingske was on the iPad. There was a picture of Dad—not the best—and beneath it a short article.

ANOTHER RAPE IN CENTRAL COPENHAGEN. SUSPECT IN CUSTODY

Last night, another young woman was raped in central Copenhagen, this time at the star fortress. Police have detained a suspect in this violent case. The night of June 15, a 24-year-old Danish woman was raped at Püchlers Bastion in Østre Anlæg, Copenhagen. A man of similar age and Danish descent is currently remanded in custody and is due for questioning later this morning. Heading up the investigation, Lars Winkler from Copenhagen Police states, "It's a very unpleasant case, but we hope to soon have enough evidence for an arraignment." When questioned whether there was any concrete evidence, Winkler indicated that the case was still under investigation, and that he was therefore unable to comment.

"Isn't that your dad?" Christina repeated, pointing a long, pale pink fingernail at Lars's name.

"Uh, yes," Maria granted. She wasn't quite sure what kind of status it would give her, having a dad who was a police inspector. Probably only marginally higher than if he had been a garbageman. She had heard that Christina's dad, for instance, was a film producer.

"I hope he locks up that bastard and throws away the key." One of Leise's sandalled feet was rocking back and forth. "Soon everyone's going to be too afraid to go out anymore."

Had she heard that correctly? Was her status rising?

Behind her, a chair scraped the floor. Steps echoed through the assembly.

"Hey girls." It was him. He smiled. At her. "What are you reading?"

CHAPTER 21

MIKKEL RASMUSSEN SAT at the end of the table with his elbows resting on his knees and his head in his hands. A mop of curls covered his face. He groaned. Lars and Lisa looked at each other. They were both tired. Neither of them had slept, and it was already late in the morning.

"I told you, I don't know her," a voice said from behind the hair.

"I've got the police report from a former girlfriend, one Anne-Mette Møller." Lisa glanced at the report. "Assault and battery. Is that correct?"

"Dammit, I explained all of this a long time ago. She was just pissed off because I fucked one of her friends." He glanced at Lisa. "Oh, sorry."

Lisa raised an eyebrow. Lars kept his eyes on the report, pretending not to have heard Mikkel's explanation.

"These pictures are from Penthouse the night of June 15 at

1:45 a.m." Lisa banged her knuckles on a pile of photographs. "How do you explain these?"

Mikkel moved his hands from his face. He tried laughing but it came out as a strained cough.

"All right, listen. She was begging for it, the way she was standing there sticking those tits out. Those damn teases—"

"Are you saying she was begging to be raped?" Lars interrupted.

"I just told you, I don't know anything about that. I'm talking about this one." He pointed at the next photograph in the pile. It must have been taken right after he grabbed Stine Bang's breasts. The picture showed Stine Bang facing Mikkel. Her hand was raised, milliseconds away from landing on his cheek. Her face was distorted with rage.

Lisa was about to say something but Lars beat her to it.

"What were you doing that night between two and three in the morning?"

"I buggered off home, after this ice queen hit me. Dammit, I should be reporting her."

"And when did you get home?"

"It must have been about 2:20. Or 2:30. Listen, that report there—"

"Can anyone confirm that?" Lisa took over.

"I live on my own."

"That doesn't surprise me," Lisa mumbled. "And what were you doing last night?"

"One of your psychopath officers assaulted me at a gas station and threw me into his car. In handcuffs."

Lars looked out the window. "And before that?"

"I was with a friend in Lille Karleby."

Lars was desperate for a cigarette. Instead, he searched inside a drawer, pulled out an old pack of Ga-Jols. He offered them to Mikkel after taking one himself.

"Did you run away after raping Stine?"

Mikkel stopped chewing. "I already told you—"

"And then yesterday, you went and found Louise Jørgensen and gave her the same treatment?" Lisa broke in. She had gotten up and now stood with her arms crossed. Mikkel opened his mouth but no sound came out. "You were arrested in the convenience store at Borrevejle Camping," she continued, "on the way back to your friend in Lille Karleby. We're going to need a name and an address."

Mikkel shook his head. "I'm no rat."

"We're just trying to help. If it wasn't you, then your friend can provide you with an alibi."

"You wouldn't believe us anyway." Mikkel crossed his arms, imitating Lisa.

Lars opened a drawer and pulled out a small case. He opened it. Inside was a pair of rubber gloves, a mask, sterile swabs, and brown paper evidence bags.

"We're going to take a DNA test now, and—"

"I'm not taking any DNA test. As soon as I'm in the registry—"

"It's in your own best interest to help us." Lars proceeded to put on the gloves.

Mikkel crossed him arms. "Nope."

"Jesus, what an idiot." Lisa closed the door behind the two officers who had collected Mikkel to return him to lock-up.

"He did cool down again. And he didn't ask for a lawyer." Lars put the DNA test kit back in the drawer.

Lisa flipped through the pictures once more. "Why didn't you show him the shirt?"

"Let him sweat it until tomorrow," he said. "Then we'll try again."

* * *

Lars got off the 5A at Nørrebro Station. He fought through the swarm of people, then headed toward Folmer Bendtsens Plads. The sun was hidden behind a cover of milky white clouds. The bright light filtered through, stung his tired, sand-filled eyes. He had wanted to buy flowers for Maria, to congratulate her on the great result the previous day. But he had forgotten, and it was too late to go back and find a florist. He was ready to drop with fatigue.

He examined the flowers in front of the SUPER CORN R-STORE. Even he could see that the limp, half-dead stems were not exactly in their prime.

Still, he pulled two bouquets, the best of a bad bunch, out of the black plastic bucket. Water was dripping onto his pants as he walked inside the store.

The young, rather stout Dane greeted him with a nod. "Two packs of King's Blue?"

"You remembered." Lars said. "These too. Can you wrap them?"

The boy looked doubtful. "In newspaper?"

"Just leave them as they are." Lars shook his head, pulled out his bank card, and swiped it in the machine. He rocked back and forth on his feet.

"Are you a police officer?"

"Is it that obvious?" Lars punched in his PIN and pressed OK.

"Well yeah . . . Are you out at Bellahøj precinct?"

Lars grabbed the cigarettes. He picked up the flowers, holding them at arm's length to avoid the dripping water.

"Homicide." He managed to pull the cellophane off one pack with his teeth, and using his free hand, tapped out a cigarette.

"I see." The guy raised his eyebrows, gave him a light. Even in outer Nørrebro, in spite of the numerous riots in the district throughout the seventies and eighties, there was still a certain

119

fascination surrounding murder investigations. Slightly morbid, but better than having rocks thrown at you—or having your car destroyed.

"So you'd better stick to the straight and narrow." Lars laughed and raised his hand to say goodbye.

"Of course. See ya."

Maria wasn't home. When he finally got the door open, the kitchen looked like a war zone: dirty dishes, breadcrumbs, half-empty milk cartons in one god-awful mess. He didn't have the energy to do anything about it. He just opened the kitchen cupboard to find something to put the flowers in. But there were no vases. He gave up, put each bouquet in a pitcher of water, left one in the kitchen, and took the other into Maria's room. All of her old things had arrived. The bed was made; a couple of her old teddy bears were nestled in and among the pillows lined against the wall. There were posters of half-naked young men on the wall. Music? Sports? He had no idea.

He put the bouquet on her table. The flowers hung their heads. He was craving another cigarette. Instead he went into the living room, found a pen and paper, folded the sheet down the middle, and wrote.

> *To Maria, my clever, beautiful daughter.*
> *Congratulations.*
> *I'm proud of you.*
> *Love, Dad*

He rested the improvised card against the pitcher. She'd spot it as soon as she came in.

He went into the living room and stopped by the bookcase. His eyes searched for the tattered copy of *The Tempest* on the bottom shelf. With great effort, he managed to stop himself from looking at the row of LPs. Instead he walked into the bedroom and threw himself on the bed fully clothed.

Shortly after, he was asleep.

CHAPTER 22

ALLAN TURNED DOWN Nordre Ringvej and followed the road's curves. Sanne let her body follow the car's motion and stared out the front window. Low-rise apartment blocks, commercial buildings, residential neighbourhoods, and greenery—apart from the size of the city, they could just as easily be driving through a suburb of Kolding. But the monstrosity that towered above the patches of green farther ahead didn't look like anything they had in Kolding. Glostrup Hospital was a Stalinist architect's wet dream.

"Yeah, it's not pretty," Allan said as he turned into an empty parking spot and turned off the engine.

Sanne shook her head and looked at the map on her phone. "Well, let's hope it proves useful."

* * *

They got off on the fourth floor. Sanne grabbed a nurse, just as the elevator door closed behind them with a quiet sigh.

"Excuse me, where can we find Professor Lau?"

The nurse sent them down the corridor toward an orange door. Sanne thanked her and followed Allan under the fluorescent tube lighting, past a long painting of a verdigris green ocean and a light blue sky covered with wisps of cloud. Stylized terns were suspended in frozen poses on the flat canvas.

"It must be here." Allan stopped, pushed the door handle down without knocking, and stepped inside. Sanne followed.

"Professor Lau?"

A large man in a lab coat, hairnet, and face mask got up from behind a microscope and waved with gloved hands.

"Out!" he roared.

The door slammed behind them, but before Sanne and Allan had a chance to recover, the man stepped out. He was wide as a barrel, and his small, dark eyes flickered behind light-framed glasses. He took off the mask, let it hang around his neck. Red spots covered his cheeks and neck.

"Who told you that you could walk straight into my laboratory? It'll be pure luck if that sample isn't contaminated."

Sanne raised her chin. "Professor Lau? I'm sorry if we've spoiled anything. But we were told you could help."

The man was rubbing sanitizer into his hands as he looked over his shoulder. "I see. And you are?"

"Sanne Bissen. Copenhagen Police. This is my colleague, Allan Raben. Could we—"

"Follow me." Lau crossed the corridor and opened the door to a spare office with a view of the hospital's rear entrance and the barrack-like houses on the other side. He went inside and sat down behind his desk. The chair creaked under his weight as he gestured toward two plastic chairs by the door.

"Shoot." He folded his fleshy hands behind his neck, stared at Sanne through half-closed eyes.

She placed her purse on her lap, took out the small box she had gotten from Forensics, and placed it on the corner of his desk without speaking. The box practically disappeared in Professor Lau's large hands as he picked it up and opened the lid.

"Hmm." He returned the box to the table with the lid open. The glass eye was resting on a bed of cotton. It had a jagged hole above the pupil, half inside the iris, where a few shards of glass were missing. Thin lines in the milky-white glass revealed the fractures.

Professor Lau picked up the box again.

"May I?"

Sanne nodded. Professor Lau picked up the green glass eye with great care, placing the concave back on his right index finger.

"Where did this come from?" he asked.

"Forensics assembled it from fragments we found next to the body of a woman three days ago," Sanne said.

Professor Lau didn't move a muscle. Then he rested his glasses on his forehead, twisted and turned the glass eye, meticulously studying the concave back, the nuances from the pupil to the iris to the surrounding white. Then he placed it back in the box.

"Well, it's not from the mass-produced collections the opticians sell."

Sanne nodded. "We know that."

Professor Lau winked at her. "On the other hand, it's nowhere near the quality we normally see. I refuse to believe that any of the ocularists who work in this country would lend their name to it."

"Ocularists?" Allan leaned forward in his chair.

"The artisans who produce eye prostheses. Glassblowers. In this country, the only ones doing this work, as far as I know, are German."

"Sorry." Sanne opened and closed her purse, placed her elbow next to the box. "Does that mean that nobody in Denmark does this type of work?"

"As I mentioned before, mass-produced eye prostheses are sold at most larger opticians." The professor was smiling now, moving the box away from the edge of the table, away from Sanne's elbow. "But if you want quality, there's no avoiding an ocularist. A glass eye will last from one and a half to two years. Then you need a new one. The old one gets worn. The musculature around the eye, the eye socket itself, changes over time. Ocularists travel here a few times a year to make new prostheses for their regular clients. Either at the hospitals or at certain opticians."

Sanne placed the box back in her purse. "You work with a German...ocularist?"

The professor nodded. "Dr. Henkel in Mülheim. It's a shame— he was just in Copenhagen. Now you'll have to make do with his number."

"A German." Allan sat down in the driver's seat, turned the key in the ignition.

"I'll deal with him. In southern Jutland we grew up with German TV." Sanne closed the door and fastened her seatbelt. "I loved watching *Sesamstraße*."

Allan laughed. They were on the way out on Ringvejen again when Sanne got through.

"Hallo?"

"Hallo. Sanne Bissen. *Dänische Polizei*." She briefed Dr. Henkel on the case, got his email address, and sent him a series of quick photos of the eye prosthesis. The doctor got back to her before they had reached Politigården.

"I'd like to help you, Frau Bissen, but I'm sorry: I can

guarantee you that neither I nor any of my German colleagues produced this glass prosthesis. None of us would lend our name to such poor workmanship."

Sanne ended the conversation. "We drew a blank," she told Allan.

He clenched his teeth, just managing to brake as a 5A bus pulled out from its stop at Copenhagen Central Station without signalling.

"So we're back to the two brothers."

Sanne dropped the phone back into her purse. "But someone had to have made that glass eye."

CHAPTER 23

"THEY'RE ALL YOURS." Søren slipped into his leather jacket, flipped up the collar. The singing quality of the detective's accent indicated he came from the island of Funen. He was solid and broad shouldered, but the horn-rimmed glasses made him look like an academic. "The Bukoshi brothers haven't left the club all day."

"Anything happen at all?" Allan placed his pizza box on the table. Søren's colleague, Kasper, a small, thin man wearing a freshly ironed shirt and pressed pants, scrunched up his coffee cup and threw it toward the cardboard box in the corner. The box was overflowing with garbage. Sanne placed her Chinese takeout container and the box of spring rolls on the table next to Allan's pizza.

"Their crew stops by about every four hours to deliver the girls' earnings." Kasper grabbed his coat from the back of the chair. "The times are written in the book." He pointed at a lined notebook on the table. Columns with times and names were written in neat handwriting across the open pages.

Søren was already heading for the back door.

"I just put fresh batteries in the camera." He smiled. "Well, I guess all that's left is to say have fun."

Kasper acknowledged them by raising his fingers to his forehead. Then they headed down the staircase at the back.

"Well, this looks comfy." Sanne looked around at the table in the middle of the room, the three folding chairs, and the cardboard box in the corner. Other than that, the room was bare. Long strips of wallpaper had been torn off the far wall. The floor could do with being stripped and varnished.

"Mind if I let in a little fresh air?" Sanne wrinkled her nose. "That garbage..." She walked over to the window.

Allan stopped her. "Open the one in the kitchen. This apartment is supposed to be vacant, right?"

Oh, right. No need to advertise the fact that they were here. She walked to the other end of the apartment and into the kitchen and opened both windows. Hot air poured in. Asphalt, brick, the entire city had been soaking up the sun for several days; the pent-up heat was now surrendering to the night air.

Inside the front room, the camera was clicking and she hurried back. Allan was pressed against the wall between the two windowpanes, shooting a series of photos. The long, grey-white lens followed the movement on the street below.

"What have they been calling them?" He continued shooting. It was only when she looked in the notebook that she understood what he meant.

"Leather Jacket, Baldie, and Toilet Seat." She laughed. "Toilet Seat?"

"It must be this guy." Allan put the camera down on the

windowsill. "He's got one of those beards." Using his finger, he drew a circle around his mouth and chin.

Sanne continued writing in Søren and Kasper's neat columns, while Allan was shooting photos of people coming in and out of the club across the street. When Toilet Seat emerged from the club ten minutes later, Sanne jotted down, 8:45 p.m. exit Toilet Seat.

"What does your wife say about you doing stakeouts?" she asked Allan.

"She's used to it by now. It's worse with the little ones."

"I didn't know you had kids?"

"Two of them. Nine and three and a half. How about you?"

Sanne shook her head. How would it have been if she and Martin had…She must have seemed upset because Allan got that look on his face.

"Sorry. I didn't mean…Oh jeez." He grabbed the camera and held down the shutter release. The small clicks merged into one long salvo.

"What's happening?" Sanne got up, positioned herself behind him. She had to stand on her toes to see over his head.

Meriton and Ukë Bukoshi were heading up the street. A dark-haired girl was walking between them, smoking. The expression on the girl's face was impossible to read, but everything about her looked strained. The glowing cigarette shook in her hands. Allan continued shooting. Sanne checked her watch. It was 8:59 p.m.

Meriton removed the cigarette from the girl's lips, threw it into the gutter. Then he walked over to a black Audi, opened the central locking, and got into the driver's seat. Ukë bundled the girl into the back and climbed in next to her.

"Do you think…" Despite her skepticism about Ulrik's theory that Meriton and Ukë were killers, she quivered.

"We'll get the other officers to follow them." Allan rang the duty officer, submitted a report and licence plate number as the Audi drove toward Viktoriagade. "There." He returned the cell to his pocket. "We've got a car on Vesterbrogade. They'll take over from there." Allan got up. "Do you want a cup of coffee?"

Fifteen minutes later they were sitting in Sanne's car, each with a latte to go. Sanne had parked on the right side of Abel Cathrines Gade, the section leading down to Halmtorvet and the former meat-packing district. Vesterbro hipsters, tourists, and the few remaining alcoholics and drug addicts passed them in a steady stream. Allan's phone rang.

"They're in Gentofte, 16 Søtoften." Allan switched off his cell. "Meriton and Ukë are waiting outside."

Sanne stared across Istedgade, down at the club. "What do you think is happening out there?"

"Well, I assume someone's getting the royal treatment."

"But why did they drive her there themselves? And why are they waiting?"

"An important customer, maybe?" Allan stared at the clock on the dashboard.

Sanne bit her lip. "What if Ulrik's right?"

They looked at each other. Sanne turned the key. Allan reached into the glove compartment, found the flashing light. He rolled down the window and clamped it onto the roof. Sanne backed up, cut around the car in front, and took the sharp right onto Istedgade at high speed, racing toward Copenhagen Central Station.

Their colleagues were parked on the right side of Søtoften in a green Opel, across from number 22. Meriton's Audi was parked farther ahead. In the driveway, at number 16, was a newer model red Toyota. A light flickered behind the closed blinds. Allan contacted their colleagues on the police radio.

"What's up? Anything happening?"

"Nothing." The voice was metallic but clear. "They haven't budged."

Sanne was restless in her seat. Allan fumbled with his seatbelt.

"I don't like it." He cracked his neck, looked up and down the road.

"What if it's just a normal transaction?" Sanne had her hand on the door handle.

"And what if he's about to surgically remove her eyes?" Allan clicked his seatbelt, and opened the door in one quick movement.

Just then the radio crackled. Ulrik's voice came through loud and clear. "Do you know who lives there?"

How did he know where they were?

"That's what I thought." Ulrik paused. "The chief executive officer of Gentofte council, Mathias Langhoff. Do you know what kinds of problems he can give us? Don't go barging in there just because he's having a little fun while his wife's out."

Allan inhaled, slumped back in the seat. Sanne closed her eyes.

"Have you got anything—anything concrete, I mean?" Ulrik had lowered his voice. "Something to warrant you going in?"

Neither of them answered.

"I see. Just stay put."

Something yellow and warm was reflected in the side mirror then disappeared again. A door opening and closing. Sanne leaned forward, squinted.

"Here she comes." The girl scurried down the stairs with her head bent forward. A cigarette was glowing between her lips. The back door of the Audi opened and she climbed in.

"There, you see," Ulrik said.

The Audi slipped away from the curb, passed them as they turned around at the end of Søtoften, then drove back. Sanne looked down as they passed. Out of the corner of her eye, she saw Meriton looking at her.

"So. No harm done." Ulrik was still on the radio. "Back to Abel Cathrines Gade, you two. You've got a long night ahead of you."

There was a click, then the radio went silent.

CHAPTER 24

"**D**AD. DAD. WAKE UP.**"

Maria was hovering over him.

"It's late. We're supposed to be at Grandma's in an hour."

"A dream," he whispered. "It was just a dream." He grabbed her. Held tight.

"Dad, stop it. You're hurting me."

He let go and Maria stepped back. She sat down on the bed.

"Sorry." He raised himself on his elbows, looked down at his wrinkled clothes. Maria rubbed her upper arm; her face was drawn.

"Did you find him?"

He looked at her. What did she mean? "Oh. No. Well, we have a suspect in custody, yes." He rubbed the sleep from his eyes. "Did you see the flowers?"

She laughed. "Thanks, Dad. That was sweet of you." She

gave him a quick peck on the cheek. "You're itchy." Then she got up and danced into the living room.

Lars sat back, followed her with his eyes. A kiss. Maybe there was a way back after all.

"You'd better hurry if you're going to have time for a shower." Her voice came from the living room. There was a clattering: Maria was trying to open the door to the balcony. The roar of engines poured in.

Lars took off his clothes. As he turned on the shower, he realized that he was whistling.

"You shaved," she said when he emerged in the living room dressed and with dripping wet hair.

"Yes, if it means getting a kiss, then..."

"Oh, Dad. If you only knew." She smiled, looking secretive.

"What's with the look? Do you have a boyfriend?"

She was swinging her purse. "Don't you think it's time to get going?"

Forty-five minutes later they were standing outside Anna's house in the Mozart Community Garden. Maria knocked.

"Good Lord, the two of you already? Is it that late?"

Anna was a tall woman in her mid-sixties, with piercing grey eyes that matched silver, tousled hair cut in a long bob that fell just above her shoulders. It seemed to Lars that her face had gotten more wrinkled from all the years spent outdoors in the community garden. Lars and Maria both got a hug before Anna led them through the house and out onto the terrace. A loose black pantsuit fluttered around her wiry frame.

"I've got white wine and elderflower cordial."

The house consisted of two old portables positioned at right angles to each other so that they formed a large V. On one side were the bathroom and the sleeping area; on the other side were the kitchen, the dining room, and the study. The house had always seemed small but cozy to Lars. Like a summer cottage. The terrace filled the space between the two sides of the V-shaped house. Anna had arranged for a glass roof to be constructed over the innermost corner of the terrace with windows from floor to ceiling, so the house had become a good deal wider at the intersection. The terrace itself was built from used railway ties that were placed directly on the ground. The levels were uneven and standing there felt a little precarious. The rickety, rusty garden furniture went well with the comfortable, crooked house.

"It's so nice seeing you both again." Anna filled their glasses and they toasted. Lars ran his eyes across the small garden, which was wild and unkempt, just as his mother wanted it.

"It's nice to see you too, Grandma." Maria's eyes had a completely different glow to them.

The sun was about to set above the rooftop of the neighbouring house. The light dripped from the leaves of the gnarled birch that leaned over the terrace. The pale summer cloud cover had disappeared while he slept. The air smelled of grass and flowers. Somewhere in the vicinity, a barbecue was lit. A little further away, someone tried to play the guitar. Whoever it was, he or she couldn't play. It sounded awful.

He suddenly realized that Maria and Anna had gone silent. They were both staring at him.

"What?" he asked.

"Don't mind him," Maria said. "Dad's been working all night. He only managed a couple of hours of sleep this afternoon."

"Is it that rape case?" Anna asked.

Lars nodded, took a sip of wine. He had to be careful. He shouldn't have too much, considering how little he'd slept.

"Unfortunately, yes. We had a new incident last night. We have someone in custody, but we're waiting for the lab results before pressing charges."

Maria shuddered. "I think it's horrific."

"Well," Anna said, "that's not something we should talk about anyway. What do you say to chicken and new potatoes and my nice bean salad?"

After they'd had dinner on the terrace, Maria went inside to look through Anna's bookcases. Anna had an infinite number of eclectic bric-a-brac: figurines from Turkey, North African pottery, and empty soda bottles from Mexico and India, as well as a small army of sculptures she had made from materials she had discovered on her many travels. Anna was also a keen photographer. Her photographs were cherished by some galleries. And then there were all the books. Maria could spend hours going through it all.

Lars and Anna were sitting at the table. He lit a cigarette while Anna sat with her elbows on the table, staring into her wine glass.

Suddenly she raised her head. "Do you have any idea how much she's missed you?"

Lars twisted the end of his cigarette in the ashtray, then moved the knife on his plate. "She's been busy."

"She's been busy trying to figure out what's actually going on."

"I've had this discussion with Elena already. I don't—"

"It's your child we're talking about. And you just disappeared."

He didn't want to argue, especially not with Maria in the other room. But the anger bubbled up inside him.

"Elena left *me*."

"But you're the grownup—or you ought to be. Your daughter, on the other hand..."

There it was: the anger. A surging storm that threatened to wash everything away. His fist hit the table before he realized it was moving. Cutlery and plates clattered, his glass tipped over.

The wine flowed out, dripping onto the railway ties through the cracks in the table. For a while, they were both frozen. Lars was about to continue, to shout something he would come to regret, when Maria suddenly appeared.

"I got asked on a date today," she said.

Something broke, soaked up the anger, the harsh words.

Anna reached out her arms, pulled her granddaughter close. "That sounds wonderful, my girl. You could do to be spoiled by someone."

Maria kissed her on the cheek.

So that was it. Not the light, not him. Not Anna. He took a drag on the cigarette, which had been resting between his index and middle fingers, forgotten.

"When?" he asked.

"Tomorrow." She looked happy.

He hated himself for it, but he had to continue. "Who is he?"

"Does it really matter?" There was a pleading tone in Anna's voice. She looked up at Maria. "Is he ni—"

"I—" he interrupted, then stopped himself. He lowered his voice. "Right now I need to know who you're with."

Maria, still standing, looked first at Anna, then at Lars. She fiddled with her napkin, which was crumpled under the edge of the plate. The wine ran from the broken glass.

"It's someone from school. You don't know him."

"What grade is he in?"

"He ... grade twelve."

Something singed; there was a burning pain in his hand.

"Ouch, goddammit—" The smell of burnt flesh. The forgotten cigarette caused the skin right between his index and middle fingers to bubble and burst. He threw the cigarette down, quickly dipped the napkin in his water glass, and dabbed the burn.

"Okay, but stay away from Penthouse nightclub."

"Dad, do you really think I go to places like that?" Maria grimaced. Then she disappeared into the kitchen.

He looked over at his mother. "What?"

She stared at him with dark eyes, shook her head.

MIDSUMMER'S EVE, 2006

THE SPARKS FROM the bonfires around the lake leap up toward the bright evening sky. Voices ring out across the water. Drunken shouts. Laughter. The noise from the traffic a heavy, incessant roaring over the water.

> *Every city has its witch,*
> *and every parish has its trolls.*
> *With our merry bonfires, we will keep them from our shores...*

He slips in through the bulrushes, leaving the summer solstice celebrations behind. Dad's face is scarlet from highballs and red wine and an entire day spent looking at porn; Mom is the perpetual pale shadow in the corner—you're never quite certain if she's really there or not. The smell of burnt steaks, booze, and perfume fills the air. Someone tells a joke, and Dad laughs longer and harder than the rest. They're flying to Nice the next day to spend three weeks at Uncle's house. When they return, he'll be in grade seven. Soon he'll have to think about high school. But tonight is different; tonight there's a tingling inside him.

He looks back. Then the rushes close around him and he finds himself in a world of shadows and great stillness where everything is open. He slips forward, a shadow without scent or sound.

He steps onto the floating bridge, treading lightly across the pale boards. His blood is pumping. He turns away from the lake, onto the network of paths that lead to the back of the gardens. It's darker here under the brush. Leaves rub against each other, whispering; branches reach out for him.

The moon rises, its white beams sharp blades that cut through the thicket and force him to shield his eyes with his hand. He's drawing closer now.

He moves along the elder thicket, toward the fence by the big rotten tree stump—the one he'd discovered when he went to bury the cat and dug up a large bone—then squeezes through the gap in the decayed, peeling boards.

At first he sees nothing. His passage through the thicket has made green and red spots dance in the darkness in front of him. But slowly his sight returns and the old garden opens up before him. It's an enchanted, chaotic world, completely different from the straight-ruled, landscaped gardens and flower-beds he knows from home. This place hasn't been looked after for years; everything grows wild. The red-brick house with the black half-timbering build on a low rise in the back of the garden. It is secluded from the road and far from the neighbouring houses. Is it lonely and abandoned?

No, he knows better.

He settles in the thicket at the back of the house and pulls out the pack of cigarettes he'd nicked earlier that evening. They were the neighbour's smokes, the one with the long tits, the one he saw Dad fucking in the sunroom last summer. She had squealed like a stuck pig. Dad had to cover her mouth. Long and hard, until she stopped shaking.

He fumbles for the lighter, holding one hand in front so the flame won't be seen from the house. He keeps the cigarette and the ember hidden behind his palm. It's only a matter of time now.

The nicotine seeps into his bloodstream, nausea and dizziness spreading. He leans back. A branch cuts his skin. The blood trickles from the wound on his arm, heavy, black drops against his white skin. He brushes the blood off with his index finger and sticks it in his mouth. The warm, salty taste of himself.

There is life around him: the nocturnal insects crawl in the undergrowth under the cover of darkness, the birds' black shadows cross the sky. He inhales once more; his head swims.

A streak of light escapes by the stairs leading down to the cellar. Now's the moment. He holds his breath. Then the light disappears. He leans back, annoyed.

He counts to ten. He's about to take another drag on the smoke when he hears something passing through the long grass. Is it a sound or a flash that makes him react? At once he sits bolt upright, all senses alert. He looks forward, following the lines between light and shadow.

A figure floats out of the shadows, dragging something behind it — a rolled-up carpet. He sees the white in its eyes; he doesn't dare to breathe. Right in front of his hiding place the figure stops and clutches its back. Something heavy falls to the ground. The figure stoops down and picks up a shovel that's been left in the grass by the old elder tree. As the shovel is raised, the handle knocks aside a corner of the carpet.

A blurry white face. Dark empty eye sockets stare straight at him.

The figure lifts the spade.

He is still holding the cigarette by his mouth, in full view. With a silent movement he turns it, conceals the ember in his hand. The figure twitches, barely twists his body. The stroke of the spade changes direction, shoots across the ground and into the thicket toward his face.

Without a sound, he crawls backwards, away. The edge of the spade passes millimetres from his face. His back, neck, arm are grazed. He presses himself further back. The abandoned cigarette is still glowing on the ground. Only when he squeezes through the gap in the fence and feels the boards behind him does he turn around. Then he starts running, back the way he came. Blood pumps in his head, pressing against the back of his eyeballs in hot, throbbing rhythms. All he hears is the sound of snapping branches, the hissing of his pursuer, right on his heels.

A blurry white face, dark, empty eyeballs.

Out of the thicket. He jumps up, runs back along the path. The moon is cold and clear just above him; everything vibrates. Then come the footsteps from behind.

He runs onto the floating bridge. It bobs up and down beneath him, gives way on the water as the other reaches it. A swan looks up startled, takes off noisily across the water. He barges into the rushes on the other side. He can no longer hear the pursuer behind him. He tries to speed up but the reeds clutch at him with their tough stalks. The soggy earth sucks his shoes. And now he hears the man barging through the rushes behind him. Hissing, swearing.

Then he's out.

The bonfire is no more than fifty metres away, forty metres to the circle of light and the adults standing around it with their backs turned to him. They're singing. Dad stands out. His right hand is on the neighbour's wife's ass. The other rests lightly on Mom's shoulder. There is something about the neighbour's wife's posture. It's rigid, unnatural. There's a rustling behind him. The pursuer emerges from the rushes. He throws the shovel down when he sees the group by the bonfire.

The figure catches up just before he reaches the circle of light and grabs him by the arm.

"You."

Narrow yellow slits hover centimetres from his face. He senses the hand rising behind the contorted face that glows in the light of the bonfire.

Sudden sounds behind him.

"Christian?" It's Dad.

The eyes narrow even more, scan the row of adults between him and the bonfire. The hand drops limply, but the grip around his arm tightens.

The pursuer hisses, "Your parents are next, if…"

He tightens his grasp one final time. It hurts so much he thinks he is going to pass out. Then the man lets go, turns around, and disappears through the rushes with one last piercing glare.

"What was that?" Dad is already on his way, craning his neck to follow the movements in the rushes.

"Nothing, Dad. Come on. Isn't it time to go home?"

WEDNESDAY
JUNE 18

CHAPTER 25

LARS WAS EXHAUSTED. A great, inner void was sapping all the energy from his brain and body in small, continuous drips. More than anything, he wanted to lie in a corner, fold his jacket under his head, and settle in for a good nap.

He'd had three glasses of wine and a single beer yesterday. Too much to drive, yes. But a hangover? He wasn't that old. The disapproving look he got from his mom would give anyone a migraine.

The voices around him drifted together, deep, distorted. Drawn out consonants, deep vowels. Roaring predators in slow motion. Then the sound sped up. Toke's voice:

"Are Frank and Kim A on their way?"

Lisa walked through the door balancing a tray from the canteen, five cups and a Thermos of coffee. She placed the tray on the table and poured the coffee, first for Toke and Lars, then for herself. Lars took the plastic cup then sat down in his office chair.

Lisa looked at her watch. Toke grumbled, grabbed a pen from Lars's desk, and started working on a crossword.

Another five minutes went by, then the two men rolled into the office. Frank was in the middle of telling a story; Kim A was laughing boisterously. He placed his fleshy backside on the desk with his back to Lars. Lisa took Frank's usual place on the windowsill. She was hanging on Frank's words.

"And so the guy says, 'You're not pulling that one on me' and sits down." Frank shook his head. Kim A's shoulders were bouncing.

"Fucking unbelievable," he gasped.

Lars cleared his throat. Toke looked up, expectantly. Kim A and Frank didn't seem to have noticed. Lisa caught the look of annoyance on Lars's face; she continued laughing but more quietly and to herself.

Lars cleared his throat again. "If I could get—"

"Two seconds. I'm just..." Frank began. Then he spotted Toke staring at him. He went quiet.

Kim A turned to Lars. "Just something we needed to finish." He gave Frank a sly smile.

"Yes, so I hear." Lars took a sip of coffee. "If you're done, maybe we could get started?"

"Of course, boss." Frank nodded, leaning back against the door.

Lars glowered at them. Kim A, he could understand. Their relationship had always been strained. But Frank? Lars knew that his past raised a red flag for most police officers, but was it really only his friendship with Ulrik that had kept them from falling upon him?

He placed his cup back on the table. A couple of months. This case, maybe one or two more—then he was gone.

He gestured to Lisa. "Lisa, can you give us an update on Mikkel Rasmussen?"

Lisa straightened up. She brought everyone up to speed on their interrogation of Mikkel. Lars took out a photograph of Mikkel's shirt.

"Toke?"

Toke dropped the newspaper and pen on the desk. "I sent a sample to Forensics. We should have the results in a few days."

"Let's hope it's positive." Lars got up. "We have to place Mikkel Rasmussen near Nørregade or Nørreport at the same time as Stine. You know what needs to be done. Toke, the two of us are taking Rasmussen."

"Have a seat." Lars kicked a chair across the room to Mikkel Rasmussen. He did his best not to sound unfriendly.

Mikkel shook his head, stared at them with bloodshot eyes. "I'd rather stand."

He probably didn't get much sleep in detention. Lars looked down at a random report, then directed his attention back at the suspect.

"We searched your apartment."

Mikkel shrugged.

"We found this under the kitchen sink."

Lars nodded at Toke, who pulled out the grey denim shirt they had found in the apartment and laid it out on the table.

"Is this your shirt?" Toke asked.

"If you say so." Mikkel was staring at a point just above the table.

Lars recognized the resignation in the suspect's face; he'd seen it a million times before. Now it was only a matter of coaxing a confession out of him. A smile spread across Toke's face.

"This stain here, what is that?" Lars pointed at the spot on the front of the shirt.

Mikkel shrugged. "What do I know? Salad dressing? Dish-washing detergent maybe?"

"I've seen this kind of stain so many times I don't need a for-ensic analysis to tell me it's blood."

Mikkel shrugged again.

Lars continued. "What if I told you that it was Stine Bang's blood?"

Mikkel looked pained. He sat down. Lars almost felt sorry for him. Then he thought about Stine Bang and Louise Jørgensen at Rigshospitalet.

Mikkel leaned back in the chair. "Okay, I did it. I hit her."

Toke winked at Lars.

"Listen, let's take it from the beginning. When Stine left Penthouse, how long did you wait before you followed her?"

"What do you mean? I didn't foll ...? Ah." Mikkel's face collapsed. "You think I beat and raped that girl?"

"That bloodstain is pretty convincing."

"I had a nosebleed." Mikkel had his face in his hands. His voice sounded hollow from behind the layers of flesh and bones. "You showed me the pictures yourself. You saw her hit me. And yes, I hit back."

Lars and Toke exchanged looks.

"It doesn't matter what I say," Mikkel mumbled. "You still won't believe me."

"Okay." Lars rested his elbows on the table. "Let's say it did play out the way you say it did. Did anyone see you at the club with blood on your shirt?"

"No idea. I just left and walked straight home. Don't they have surveillance cameras in that club?"

"Why didn't you tell us all of this yesterday?" Lars was doodling on the back of a printout of one of Ulrik's emails.

"I don't know, maybe because that police lady was so damn pissed off." Some of the aggressiveness from the previous day was returning. "If I'd told you I hit her but didn't rape her, you wouldn't have believed me."

"We still don't believe you," Toke said.

Lars folded the shirt. "It would be a good idea to get a lawyer now, Mikkel. If you don't have one, or can't afford one, the Crown will appoint you one. The state will pay."

"Whatever. Can I get some coffee?"

"He doesn't seem to care." Toke closed the door after an officer had taken Mikkel away.

Lars scratched his head. "Listen, I've got a bad feeling about this."

"In rape cases, there's almost always previous contact," Toke reasoned. "Two out of three cases. You know that."

"Well, yes and no." Lars turned to the window. It needed cleaning. In the courtyard below, a group of civilians on a guided tour tilted their heads skywards. He turned around.

"Call Forensics. Get them to speed up the analysis."

Toke shook his head. "Mikkel isn't going anywhere. There's no reason to put pressure—"

Lars's cell rang.

"Hi Lars. It's Simon."

"Simon?" He didn't recognize the voice.

"Maria's Simon. Do you know where Maria is? She's staying with you now, right?"

He liked Simon, but he knew better than to get involved. "She's probably at an exam. Listen, I'm sorry, but I'm in the middle of something here. I'll make sure to tell her you called."

Toke stood with his hand on the door handle.

Lars put the phone down, then exhaled. "There were two days between Stine and Louise getting raped. If it wasn't Mikkel, then the perp might strike again tonight."

Toke sighed. He was already searching for Frelsén's number on his cell.

CHAPTER 26

AN INFERNAL RUMBLING shook the packed cabin. Sanne grasped the armrest, leaned her head back, pressed her neck against the headrest. *It's going to be all right,* she chanted to herself. But she wasn't able to convince her body. Cold sweat ran from her armpits and between her breasts, beaded on her upper lip.

Takeoff and landing were always the worst.

She was the one who had half threatened, half persuaded Ulrik to approve the official trip to Bratislava to return Mira's body. Not exactly a dream assignment. But she needed to meet the mom, Zoe Vanin, to better understand Mira as a person. But there were no direct flights from Kastrup to Bratislava, so she had been forced to book a seat on a LOT Polish Airlines flight that stopped in Warsaw. Two takeoffs and landings outbound, two takeoffs and landings inbound. Same day. And down below, a mother was waiting with the Slovakian airport police for her daughter's casket. As a representative of the country where her daughter had been murdered, Sanne was responsible for conveying the official condolences. This was definitely not her day.

Directly beneath the plane, the large, black hole of Bratislava's M. R. Štefánik airport was pulling her in.

She was in a bare, windowless room with the airport police. Sanne placed her purse on the sticky plastic table and looked around. Two chairs. Dirty grey walls and a single exit. The wall opposite the door was adorned with a calendar of Slovakia's most popular tourist destinations. The month of June showed pictures of Bojnice Castle and Čachtice.

Her purse started vibrating on the table. Diana Ross's "Upside Down" echoed through the room. She pulled out her cell phone. It was a Danish number, Copenhagen Police headquarters.

"Hi, it's Allan. You've landed?" He sounded agitated.

"Yes, just now. Any news?"

"You were right."

"How so?"

The sound of rustling paper filled the receiver.

"Elvir Seferi. Meriton claimed that Elvir had played cards with him and Ukë in the club the night Mira disappeared."

"And?" She clutched the back of one of the chairs.

"Our colleagues in Middelfart had him in lock-up all night. He was drunk, pissed on a seat while travelling the Intercity train from Århus to Copenhagen without a ticket. The train left Århus at 8:01 p.m. and arrived at 11:18 p.m. at Copenhagen Central Station."

"And he was arrested on the train in Middelfart at...?"

"9:16 p.m. The trains were running on time, down to the minute."

She sat down. "Why haven't we heard about this before?"

"Provincial policing." Allan laughed, then the phone went quiet. "Sorry. I didn't mean—"

"Never mind."

Allan continued: "The officer who arrested him—his computer went down, so he filled in one of the old forms by hand. He was meant to enter the details into the central registry the next day but the following morning he got sick."

There was a knock at the door.

"I have to run." Sanne hung up just as the door opened and a woman with short, bleached hair walked into the room.

Zoe Vanin wasn't very tall. Her grey skin was etched with deep lines and she had a severe look on her face. The dark roots of her hair spread out toward dry, bleached ends. Her hand shook as she opened her purse and took out a cigarette and lighter. A Slovakian policewoman followed her in and closed the door behind them.

Sanne smiled and nodded at the chair on the other side of the table. The woman lowered her gaze, then sat down. She lit her lighter. The flame flickered, shook in the stagnant air in the room. She couldn't hit the end of the cigarette.

"My name is Sanne Bissen. I'm from the Danish police. You're Zoe Vanin, Mira's mother?"

The woman looked up at the Slovakian policewoman who translated. Zoe nodded.

"*Áno*," she answered. Her voice was the creaking hinges of an old door being forced open for the first time in years.

"Yes," the interpreter translated. "Mira was her daughter." Then Zoe collapsed into thin, shrill sobbing. Her shoulders shook. Tears dripped down on the unlit cigarette in her hand. The Slovakian policewoman stared at her, unmoved.

"My condolences, Miss Vanin." Sanne leaned forward.

The woman nodded, dried her nose on the sleeve of her jacket, and tried to light the wet cigarette again, but she had to give up and pull out a new one. Sanne held her wrist steady until she'd managed to get it lit.

"Did she suffer?" Zoe looked up, held Sanne's gaze.

"She was shot. She went quickly." The image of the naked body by the edge of the water with flies buzzing out of the empty eye sockets surfaced in Sanne's mind. She shook her head. "Her eyes were removed, but we believe that happened after she died. No, I don't think she suffered." There was no reason to tell her about Frelsén's assessment of the probable sequence of events, the autopsy report. The glass eye. How would that benefit Mira's mother?

Zoe breathed out. Then, eventually, she began to tell her story.

She was twenty in 1989, when the rumours of the demonstrations in East Germany, of the borders to the West opening in Czechoslovakia reached her hometown of Borisoglebsk, which was halfway between Moscow and the Caspian Sea. Like so many other young people, she was adventurous. She wanted to get out, to find a better world, the world all young Russians dreamed of. So together with a friend, she set out to the West, to Czechoslovakia. When they arrived, the wall had fallen, but neither Zoe nor the girlfriend made it across the Iron Curtain, which was now gone. Instead they were in a foreign country, with no money and a nationality the Czechoslovakians detested. After almost two weeks had passed, hunger and hopelessness drove them into prostitution. Mira was born before the first year was up. Life had gotten somewhat better after the separation of the Czech Republic and Slovakia. Suddenly the Czechs were the enemy. But Mira was rebellious; she also dreamt of a better life, a different world. And one day, toward the end of February, she had left without telling Zoe. Zoe had received a letter from her daughter, from Gdańsk, Poland, then another from Copenhagen. After that, silence.

Sanne had to ask Zoe one final question, then she would leave the grieving mother in peace.

"And you only heard from your daughter the one time, just after she arrived in Copenhagen?"

Zoe didn't answer, lost in the haze of the cigarette smoke.

"Miss Vanin?"

Zoe looked up, so ashen that Sanne was sure something had died inside of her.

"Yes?"

"Did you hear from Mira in Copenhagen? After the first time?"

"She called one other time. She had just gotten my letter." Zoe curled the letter up in her hand, lowered her voice. "She was very scared. She said the men who controlled her—"

"Her pimps?"

"Pimps, yes. They had killed a girl. Mira saw them carry the body away." Zoe grabbed Sanne's wrist. Her frail fingers had surprising strength. "Were they the ones who killed my Mira?"

Sanne placed her hand over Zoe's, patted it, then loosened her grip.

"Did Mira say when that was?"

"She didn't say—I think, between when she got my letter and when she called."

"Your letter is postmarked April 22. When did she call?"

Zoe shook her head. "I don't know. Maybe the thirtieth? I remember it was a Friday. I was busy." Her eyes hardened.

Sanne got up, went over to the calendar, and flipped through it. The month of April was illustrated with a dramatic photograph of Modry Kostolik, the Blue Church. She quickly found the thirtieth. *Piatok*, it said.

The Slovakian policewoman followed her finger and translated with a flat, toneless voice.

"Friday."

Friday April 30—four days before Mira had disappeared. What had she been doing over the weekend and at the beginning of the following week? At some or other point, Meriton and Ukë had killed one of their girls, if Mira had been telling the truth, and disposed of the body. There was no denying it shed new light on the case.

Sanne sat down in front of Zoe again. "Do you know how she came to Denmark? Who helped her?"

Zoe shook her head, sniffled.

"In the neighbourhood around Krizna," the policewoman said. "That's where most of the prostitutes hang out, also where the human traffickers find the girls."

Sanne gazed uneasily at the woman sitting in the middle of the room. She had become a mother far too young. Now she had to bury her grown-up daughter before she had even turned forty.

Sanne held out her hand.

"*Vd'aka,*" Zoe whispered, taking her hand. She didn't look up.

THURSDAY
JUNE 19

CHAPTER 27

"**D**AMN," **LISA MUMBLED** and threw yet another picture on top of the hefty pile on the desk.

"It's not all that bad." Frank aligned the pictures so the piles were in order again.

"Knock it off," Lisa snapped.

The answer had come from Forensics early that morning. The blood on Mikkel Rasmussen's shirt was his own. And neither it nor the remains of skin and hair that had been found on the shirt matched the perpetrator's profile. Or Stine Bang's. Mikkel was released less than fifteen minutes after they had received the result of the test.

They had received more photos from Penthouse, from the evening Louise Jørgensen was raped. Photos from both evenings were handed out yet again and passed around the room. Everyone had to go through every single picture again.

"We're looking for a male, around five foot eight, possibly with blonde hair, who was present on both nights." Lars grabbed another pile, let his eye wander across the prints. Happy kids posing, posturing. Sex and booze and a kind of desperate hunger permeated the atmosphere of the photos and gradually became more and more pronounced as the night proceeded. Both Louise and Stine appeared in many of the photos. Both were tall, slender girls with long hair, dressed in skimpy outfits that didn't leave much to the imagination.

"Stine and Louise actually look quite similar," Toke said.

The room was quiet for some time. The only sound came from fingers flipping through photos and laboured breathing. They passed the pictures around again.

"It's hopeless." Lisa threw her pile of photos on the table. "He has to be there, but I just can't see him."

"I know it's not something we normally do," Toke said, crossing his legs. "But isn't it about time we called the shots?"

"What do you mean?" Lars supported his head with his hand on his forehead. He could guess what Toke was driving at, and he didn't like it.

Frank straightened up in the windowsill. "You mean a trap?"

Toke nodded. No one spoke.

When Toke opened his mouth again, he only addressed Lars. "This guy has done it twice now. We have his DNA. If he takes the bait, we've got him. Not even the best defence lawyer in the country would be able to get him off."

Lars looked out the window. "And if something happens to her?"

"She'll have people covering her. We'll be right on her heels. Plan her route in advance, have people stationed along the entire track."

"Well, at any rate it shouldn't be you, Lisa." Kim A laughed loudly. "You're not really his type."

Lisa stuck out her tongue. Then she laughed. "And you'll never be mine either."

"I don't think it's a job for a probationer." Lisa was sitting backwards on her chair. She buried her chin between her arms, which were folded over the back of the chair. Lars looked down at his papers.

"Kim A—can't you put some pressure on Forensics to get that report on Stine Bang?"

Everyone in the room stared at Lars.

"What?" he said.

Lisa was the first to answer. "Kim got the report two days ago."

Two days ago? And it seemed that Lisa and Frank had already examined the results. A pattern was beginning to emerge. Or was he being paranoid?

Just then the door opened and Toke escorted a tall, busty blonde into the room.

"This is Lene. She's agreed to act as bait on the sting operation."

Kim A and Frank nodded. Lars tried to smile. Lene had blue eyes and summer-brown skin. There was no doubt that she would be noticed at Penthouse—and everywhere else.

"Of course the operation's not without some risks," Lisa began.

"Toke has briefed me on what you want me to do," Lene said. "I'm not scared."

"She's perfect," Frank mumbled to himself. Then he said, "It's either her or we forget about the whole thing."

Lars ran through Lene's record in his head. She was a third Dan in judo, an outstanding runner, mentally stable, and she had proven that she could handle pressure during the demonstrations at the Copenhagen Climate Change Conference a few years back.

Frank was right. It was her or no one.

"Okay, if you're sure?" Lars said. She smiled. "Good," he continued. "That's settled then. Let's review the operation."

An hour later they had been through all the details. Toke left with Lene, and Lisa and Frank went to get some lunch. Kim A got up and was about to follow when Lars cleared his throat.

"What's all this about the report from Forensics?"

Kim A raised his eyebrows. "Which one?"

"You know what I'm talking about."

"What do you want me to say?" Kim A shrugged. "I must have forgotten about it."

What was he going to do? Speak to Ulrik? He couldn't imagine anything worse.

"What's the problem?" Kim A asked. "It doesn't say anything we didn't already know."

Lars waved him off wearily. Kim A slipped out of the office.

Maybe he was just imagining things. Maybe Kim A had forgotten all about their past. He leaned back, opened the window, and lit a forbidden King's. And if not? The office chair creaked under him as he put his feet up on the windowsill. If he leaned back, he could just about catch a ray of sunshine on his face.

CHAPTER 28

"**A**REN'T YOU GOING to offer me a cup of tea?"
     She walked right up to him. The heavy scent of perfume overpowered the lilacs from the hedge behind her. They were at the back of the high school by the empty parking lot. The school was empty as well. Everybody had gone home. They were all alone.

Maria was going out to a girlfriend's; she wouldn't be getting home till late that night. He hoped to see her then. Until then the evening stretched out empty before him. Christian looked down at Christina's blue eyes and blonde hair.

"I have to work out first." He shut the passenger-side door of his convertible for her, and walked around the front of the car.

She lowered her eyes, giggled. "That's okay. I can watch."

He was bored already.

* * *

Three sets of fifteen squats and then the bench press. Twenty-eight kilos on each side. Not too much, not too little. The sun shone in through the cellar window. She sat on a plastic chair under the window, pretending to read. She stole a glance at him when she thought he wasn't looking.

He should be able to do fifteen reps, but it suddenly seemed so trivial, easy. The burning sensation in the muscles just wouldn't come.

She had undone the second button of her thin turquoise blouse. He could see the curve of her plastic tits, her tiny, pink sixteen-year-old nipples quivering in the dim light.

He let the barbell fall back onto the rack; the metal sung and he sat up with a groan. The book fell into her lap. She didn't even try to hide it: she devoured him with her eyes.

"I'm just going to take a shower."

She got up, toying with the third button on her blouse.

"You don't have to," she said.

He wiped the sweat off his face, avoided looking at her. "How about that tea?"

She spotted the jar by the window. The last amber rays of sun shone through its contents; long, mushroom-shaped shadows danced on the opposite wall.

"What's that?"

He curled his lips behind the towel. Maybe the evening would turn out to be interesting after all.

He carried the tray with tea and toast up the stairs, her gaze at his back just above the buttocks. She closed the door behind them.

"The tea can infuse while I'm in the shower. Why don't you make some honey sandwiches in the meantime?"

She picked up the jar and turned the glass in her hand. "What is it?"

"My own recipe. It's good."

He disappeared into the bathroom. While he lathered up, he thought about the trip to the golf course last fall. Dad, so wrapped up in his six over par and X-18 iron, hadn't noticed that Christian had spent most of the day with his ass in the air. There's no better place to pick psilocybin mushrooms than a freshly mown golf course after a good rain.

He came out of the shower with dripping hair and a towel around his waist. She sat staring at a piece of toast. She had spread a thick layer of honey on it. It was dripping everywhere.

"What's that?" She prodded the mushroom with her knife.

"Eat." He let the towel fall to the floor. He couldn't be bothered to put underwear on; they were going to come off soon anyway. He found a pair of loose linen pants in the closet and pulled an old T-shirt over his head. "Is the tea ready?"

He threw the towel on the bathroom floor and sat down next to her. Firmly but gently he pushed her hand with the honey sandwich toward her mouth. She looked up at him, held his gaze as she took the first bite, and swallowed.

"You can't even taste it," she said.

"Of course you can't. They've been infusing since fall." He buttered a piece of bread with his concoction, and poured tea into the thin, green porcelain cups.

They drank in silence, munched on the honey toast. Outside night descended. The house was quiet.

Then he lay on the bed, yawned. He could tell by looking at her that all he had to do was pat the bedspread beside him and do his usual routine. Then she'd come to him.

She swallowed. "So what is it?"

"Psilocybin mushrooms. Liberty cap. Acid." He looked up at the ceiling, followed the car headlights that swept through the window.

"Acid?" Her voice trembled a bit.

He sat up, swung his legs over the edge of the bed. "It's a little like LSD, or Ecstasy. Don't worry, it's going to be good."

Christina got up and reached for the teacup. She walked carefully across the room and sat down on the bed next to him.

"You have to take care of me." Her eyes had that familiar glassy look. He put his arm around her. She took small sips of the tea.

"Of course." Then he took the cup from her hand and placed it on the floor. He crouched over her, then pushed her onto the bed. Her mouth was warm from the tea; she tasted of Ceylon. A door opened somewhere in the house. Footsteps moved up the stairs, faded away. His hand was under her blouse now, stroking the little hairs on her belly, then moving farther up. She wrapped her arms around his neck and kissed him greedily.

He didn't know how long they had been lying there. His hand moved toward her jeans. He undid one button, then another.

She sat up, smiled. "I just have to go to the bathroom."

When she disappeared into the bathroom, he removed the bedspread and threw it on the floor. Then he rolled the comforter up against the wall and leaned back. The moon was dancing somewhere outside; its light shone in through the window. Out there, the night shadows were alive.

From the bathroom, he heard the sound of denim on skin. She flushed the toilet. His fingers were so thick, they started tingling. The sheets exploded against his skin. The window frame buckled, collapsed, melted into large drops that slid onto the floor. Branches passed through the glass, stretched toward him. The smell of topsoil and rotting leaves filled the room. It was very hot; still, he could see his breath, a pale cloud suspended in the middle of the room.

She came out of the bathroom, whispered, as she crawled

into bed with him, "I don't understand what you see in her. Her dad is a cop..."

Maria was his. He pulled her down to him, stopped her with a kiss. His entire body quivered. He was one great mouth. Her lips were so hot, and he could feel her tongue between his teeth. She began unbuttoning his pants.

Flames licked the walls; the wallpaper curled as it disintegrated into brown flakes. Burnt confetti and embers sprinkled onto the bed, settled on their hair. He must have been gone, for now she had taken her blouse off and was sliding up his chest. He was naked, lying on his back, staring at the ceiling, following the lines between light and shadow.

A blurry white face floated above the bed, a face with the mouth open in a muted scream. Empty eye sockets looked directly at him.

He sat up with a start, slid out of her.

"Shh," she said, pushing him back onto the bed. She tried to pull him inside her again.

With a sudden start, he pushed back. She tumbled backwards, hit her face on the edge of the bedframe. She winced, looked up at him from the floor. Her eyes were two white slivers. A dark line ran from her nose down toward her Cupid's bow. His hand trembled with excitement as he wiped the blood that was black in the moonlight from her lip and stuck his finger in his mouth. The salty taste of iron on tongue and palate.

Her legs wobbled as she got up. He picked up her clothes and threw them out onto the landing, then pushed her naked body out the door and shut it in her face. She scratched at the hollow doorframe a couple of times and whispered his name. But he knew what he had to do. He was already grabbing his clothes. A faint sobbing trickled through the crack under the door. Then she slipped quietly down the stairs.

Only when the house was silent again, and he was certain

that she was gone, did he open the door and bound down the stairs.

It was time for a night out.

CHAPTER 29

THE HARD, POUNDING beats worked his organs into a tangle while drumming his body into the collective movement, an obscene bacchanal of swirling bodies, hungry lips, and greedy gazes. The meat market.

Lars's gaze swept across the dance floor. Girls, far too young to be let in, held their hands high over their heads, bounced up and down in time with the music. Was that how people danced now? He used to pogo at punk concerts when he was young, but this? He shook his head, turned to the girl at the bar, and raised a finger. Another club soda. In the dim light, the girl leaned over the rows of beer and water, allowing Lars to see all the way down her top, and shouted something in his ear. He nodded, even though he couldn't hear a single syllable. The girl walked down the bar, pulled out a Coke, opened it, and placed a glass and the bottle in front of him. He held out forty kroner, but she shook her head. At least the staff was helpful.

Toke appeared next to him. "Have you spotted him?"

"No idea."

Toke looked at his watch. It was almost 1:30 a.m. One hour to go.

Lene stood in the middle of the dance floor, at one with the mass of moving flesh. Lars had to admit, he was impressed. She actually looked like she was enjoying herself. Sweat ran down her face. She was completely lost in the music. A large group of guys was watching her, and not all of them were undercover officers.

They had spent most of the afternoon planning every last detail of the operation and reviewing every possible outcome. They had set up scenarios, experimented with surveillance posts in different locations. Lars, Toke, and Lene had even walked the route a few hours earlier to judge visibility and points of orientation in the dark. Officers with night-vision goggles and communication equipment had taken their positions in the stairwells, on roofs, and at other discrete corners. They couldn't be more prepared.

But the careful planning also had its downside. Maria had initiated a somewhat serious conversation over dinner that evening, a conversation which, as far as he could remember, had dealt with her sense of loss and her feelings about the divorce. And now that he thought about it, hadn't she also mentioned the date she had been on? Had she been happy? He couldn't remember; his thoughts were buried in the evening's operation. In the middle of dinner, Maria had screamed at him and slammed her fork onto the plate, sending spaghetti sauce everywhere. Then she locked herself in the bathroom and refused to come out until he was gone.

"Hey, look who's here!"

Toke's exclamation tore him back to the high-octane atmosphere of Penthouse. A familiar face was moving along the bar, carrying a half-empty glass of beer, glazed eyes fixed on Lars's. Beer splashed onto the pants and shoes of random guests by the bar as he made his way toward them.

"What are you doing here?" Mikkel Rasmussen practically spat out the question while tipping the glass in his hand. He spilled the rest of his drink all over himself, without seeming to notice.

"Hey, watch it, dirtbag." A blonde guy in a hoodie and brightly coloured T-shirt grabbed Mikkel.

"Easy." Lars got between them. He pulled Mikkel aside. It looked like he hadn't washed his hair since he had been released, let alone changed his clothes. When he got close, the smell of stale sweat and damp, stained textiles overpowered the club's mix of cheap perfume and banana oil.

"Aren't you two finished harassing innocent people?" Mikkel was wailing so loudly that people around them turned and stared.

"We have to do something," Toke whispered. "Before he ruins everything."

Lars nodded, put the Coke down, and took a firm hold of Mikkel's arm. "Come with me."

"I'm not fucking—"

"You'll do what I tell you." The low pitch, the abrupt choppy syllables, the sudden vehemence worked as intended. Mikkel Rasmussen was in such shock that he went along with no further protest.

Lars leaned over the end of the bar and shouted into the girl's ear. "Do you have a back door?"

The girl nodded, pointed over her shoulder, and let Lars and Mikkel go behind the bar. A bright red door lit up a matte black wall. Lars opened it and pushed Mikkel in front of him.

"What the hell are you doing? You can't just—"

"You're obstructing a police operation. I can do whatever I like. Let's go."

He gave Mikkel a shove. Rasmussen was swaying from side to side, then he took a tentative step down the steep flight of stairs. Lars was right on his heels, forcing him to continue. About twenty steps further down there was an open door leading to the courtyard. The night air was fresh after the nauseating stench from the club's smoke machine.

Stacks of empty soft drink crates were piled up just outside the door, and three large dumpsters were pushed against a low wall in the back of the courtyard. The dull thumping from the club made the summer night vibrate. He grabbed Mikkel by the arm, dragging him through the gate and around the corner to the unmarked car parked on Vestergade alongside Gammeltorv. The square had been a central meeting point of the 1980s Copenhagen punk scene. He had sat on the low wall framing the square so many times back then. Lars shrugged off the past, opened the rear door, and pushed Mikkel inside.

"Mind holding onto him until I give word?"

The officer in the passenger seat sent Mikkel a disinterested look, scrunched up his face, then gave Lars the thumbs up.

"Thanks."

Lars slammed the door and made his way back to Penthouse and his place by the bar.

"He very nearly ruined everything," Toke shouted in his ear. After the brief reprieve outside, the noise inside the club seemed deafening.

Lars took a sip of the Coke. It had already gone flat. "Did anyone notice anything?"

"Nobody left the bar," Toke said. "I've checked with our colleagues at the door."

"So we wait."

* * *

Lene went to the bathroom. Lars looked at his watch. It was 2:25 a.m. It was at this time that Stine Bang and Louise Jørgensen had left the club. He nodded to Toke who positioned himself halfway toward the exit. The door to the women's washroom opened. Lene came out, looked at him, and sent a quick smile. Then she pushed her way through the lineup at the bar toward the coat check.

Lars gave her a one-and-a-half-minute head start before following. He walked along the bar and then up the stairs. She wasn't in the lineup at the coat check. He couldn't see Toke either. He made his way out to the street and spotted Lene further up along Nørregade. She went past Vor Frue Kirke, pushing a vintage bike.

"She shouldn't walk so quickly," Toke whispered in his ear. "Give the guy a chance to follow her."

"He'll follow." Lars moved a few steps away from the crowd by the entrance. It was good to get outside. They strolled up Nørregade, two friends on their way home from a night out, checking out the home decor display in the window of Notre Dame and strolling past Vester Kopi print and copy shop.

"There, she's easing up a bit now," Toke said.

"Relax. We're not the only ones watching her. See if you can spot our guy instead." Lars stuck a hand into his jacket pocket and put the small earpiece into his ear. He heard static, then muffled voices. Contact.

Toke pulled a package out of the bag he had collected from the coat check, and handed it to Lars. He checked the magazine on his service weapon, a Heckler & Koch USP Compact, then stuffed the gun into his pants. He shivered as the cold steel pressed against his thin shirt.

"We're the only ones here. Another unit is up at Krystalgade. She's passing them now." Toke kept a constant eye on her. "There. Who's that?"

A figure came staggering toward them, past the old KTAS building across from Hotel Skt. Petri.

"Just somebody on a night out. He's coming from Nørreport. Remember, we're looking for someone who's following her." Lars patted him on the shoulder. Toke snorted, stared at the guy as he sailed past them in a blissful drunken stupor.

Lars turned around, took a look at the guy after they had passed each other. There was no one else behind them. Reports from various surveillance posts flowed in: Nørreport, all quiet. Farimagsgade, nothing to report. Dronning Louises Bro, empty.

They continued through the city. Nørregade opened up toward the blaze of lights in front of the 7-Eleven at Nørreport. Lene was already walking down Frederiksborggade. Lars and Toke ran across the crosswalk at Fiolstræde, ducking through the construction at Nørreport Station and breezing through the penetrating stench of piss before reaching Frederiksborggade. There were more people on the streets now, lone figures or couples, on their way home from a night out. On Queen Louise's Bridge, the neon signs of Irma supermarket reflected on the black surface of the water. The bridge glowed under the orange and yellow of the streetlights. Out toward the district of Østerbro there was a permanent glow in the sky. The white nights. It was so beautiful Lars had to stop. The older he got, the shorter the early days of summer felt. Another heyday was about to die.

As planned, Lene turned down Peblinge Dossering. Lars and Toke followed, cutting past the old air-raid shelter. A family of ducks bobbed by the shore, their beaks tucked under their wings. Lene continued along Baggesensgade, Blågårdsgade, across Blågårds Plads. On Korsgade, Lars and Toke looked up at Hellig Kors Kirke's massive spire, which ripped through the sky at the end of the street. Here, along the narrow streets, they could move in without fear of being exposed.

They passed the church.

"It's got to be now, if it's going to happen," Toke mumbled.

Lars nodded. The hair on his arms stood on end. Hans Tavsens Park opened up to the right, disappearing into the shadows of Assistens Cemetery. There wasn't a soul to be seen. Down toward Struenseegade, loud music drifted out of open windows. Lights shone from the odd apartment. Up ahead Lene was a white figure in a sea of shadows.

Lars's earpiece crackled.

"There—what was—" The excitement in the voice levelled off. "Sorry, probably just a false alarm. Bravo here. All quiet. Wait—"

Just then the shadows in Hans Tavsens Parken sprung to life. Something moved in the grass, darted past them, and knocked Lene over. As her bike hit the ground the metallic clatter echoed through the night.

"This is it." Lars started running. His service weapon was already in his hand. Toke rushed after him. The streets around them were filled with the rapid pounding of boots. Everybody was moving in. Lene was rolling around on the ground with her attacker, then managed to get up. The shadow took a swing at her, but she grabbed his clothes and pulled him on top of her, planting a foot in his stomach and sending him flying. He fell into a roll and was on his feet in one swift movement. The assailant took a swing, striking Lene on the temple with something in his hand. She staggered back, falling to the ground near a bench.

"Stop! Police!" Lars shouted. He was now less than thirty metres away.

Only then did the assailant notice that they weren't alone. He looked steadily at Lars before breaking into a run toward the cemetery. Lars swore. Lene's fingers were groping for the bench, then her hand dropped limply to her side. She mumbled something. A thin line of blood ran from her temple.

"Call an ambulance," he shouted at Toke. Then he shot past her.

The shadow was already by the cemetery fence. He jumped up on the chainlink and swung his legs over the top. A small thud broke the silence when he landed on the other side.

When Lars got to the fence, he took three quick steps and was halfway over before he slid headfirst down the other side of the fence. He managed to soften the landing with his hands, but stabs of pain radiated in his leg and torso when his hip hit the ground. The service weapon flew out of his hands and clattered onto the path. He forced himself to his feet, lunged for the pistol, and popped up with one knee on the ground and his weapon raised in front of him.

It was completely still. No sound, no movement. Then came the voices from Hans Tavsens Park, the shouting on the radio, the baying of the dogs. Lars tried to block out the noise and focus on the cemetery. There. A bush moved. He approached with the pistol raised. Then he heard steps running in the opposite direction, toward Nørrebrogade. Lars abandoned the footpath and ran in between the gravestones where the soft grass deadened the sound of his steps. The steps ahead of him slowed down; the assailant was getting tired. Lars listened for the sound of breathing. He peered forward but the shadows were alive here — dead things with fluid, bobbing movements, a world under water.

During the day, nursing mothers, children, and people living in the area used the cemetery as a park. They had picnics, smoked, drank coffee, kissed. But during the night something else took over, something primal.

A shadow broke away from the darkness and slipped between two trees only to melt into the shadow of an imposing headstone. Lars felt a light splatter on his forehead and on the back of his hand. He blinked, wiped the raindrop from his forehead with his sleeve. He crouched down, ran in a wide arc across the lawn, and circled around to the other side of the headstone. No one was there. The pistol was shaking in his hand.

Then the sky opened and water came pouring down.

The noise was deafening. Leaves screamed under the downpour. In an instant, his visibility was reduced to a couple of metres. Everything was a pale grey, moving carpet.

But what was that? It sounded like someone was whistling.

Lars headed in the direction of the sound, toward the dense thicket of trees at the other end of the cemetery. He slipped on the wet asphalt but recovered his balance. His hair clung to his forehead and water ran into his eyes. He tried to ward off the blows from the branches. The hissing sound of tires on wet asphalt. They had to be near Jagtvej.

He could hear it through the rain now: the sound of a body ploughing through the bushes. Lars began running in the direction of the noise. He kept wiping the water from his eyes but it was futile: a second later and his sight was again blurred by the rain. Suddenly the wall was there, towering in front of him. He was going too fast; he couldn't stop on the soft, wet surface, and crashed into the wall. Pain exploded in his nose, knees, and elbows, and his forehead and hands were cut. Dammit. Where was he? A little to the right was a mulberry tree. The bark had been stripped away, and the exposed trunk shone in the dark. Lars flung himself up the tree, one metre, two metres, three metres above the ground, until he could see over the wall. Sure enough, Jagtvej was on the other side. He stepped off the tree and onto the wall, jumped down on the other side, landing on both feet. He looked up and down the street. Shiny wet asphalt, puddles teeming with raindrops, a cab's headlights, engine noise, pizza joints and bars. But nobody was on the street.

He closed his eyes and tilted his head up toward the sky. He wished he could be swept away by the rain. Forget and be forgotten.

AUGUST 1944

"LAURA? WE HAVE guests." Father's voice rises up through the stairwell. She hides *Family Journal* under the pillow, straightens her hair, and hurries downstairs. Who could it be? The evening sun shines through the window of her parents' bedroom, warm and red. The soft call of a blackbird rises and falls through the gardens. It is almost time for her daily trip to the cellar.

On the landing, she looks down, stops suddenly. A pair of long black boots is waiting just inside the door, the brim of a black cap.

"Welcome. It's been too long." Father and Arno shake hands.

What is he doing here?

"It is an honour to be received in your home!" Arno slides the cap under his arm and stands at attention.

"Come down here, my girl." Father motions for her to come

downstairs. The steps glide away beneath her. The black uniform, the boots float up toward her. She doesn't want to, and yet she must. Arno holds out his hand. She sees herself from the outside, watches as she places her hand in his and lets him help her down the last steps.

If he's come for Jack... She doesn't want to finish the thought. She takes the final step, looks down, and curtsies deeply. She can be nice. For Jack.

"I've made coffee." Mother wrings her hands, then shows Arno into the living room. Father places a hand on Laura's shoulder, steers her after him. Arno smells of leather oil and horse. There are sweat stains on the collar of his uniform. His long neck is white as a sheet from the collar up to the short strands of hair peeking out at the edge of the black cap.

Now they are sitting on the sofa beside each other, Father in the chair opposite them. And outside in the garden, the evening is so beautiful that it hurts. Mother pours coffee and offers Arno the tray with the war macaroons, the ones she baked for Jack in the morning. It's so quiet, the few sounds grow. Arno champs the milled barley oats with lateral movements of his jaw; his boots squeak. Father breathes with a quiet whistling.

She breaks a little piece of the war macaroon on her plate. The slightly nauseating taste of the cake grows in her mouth; she hurries to swallow before she has to throw up. She hopes Jack is sleeping down there, that he doesn't hear Arno dragging his boots across the living room floor.

"The rumours say the resistance will attempt to sabotage the weapons factory in Ordrup." Arno smiles. "But they will fail, as they failed with the labour strikes last month."

Father and Arno stare at each other for a long time. She holds her breath. *Good God, it's over now.* In a moment, they'll be pounding on the door, then forcing their way inside with their dogs and guns. Then Father smiles. He shakes his head and wipes his mouth.

"Laura? You're not saying anything? You've been so distant. Are you keeping secrets?" Father's still smiling at her. But his gaze stings, burns into her. She can't catch her breath. All those things that can't be said. Everything they mustn't touch upon. The little fish is doing somersaults behind her navel; she can almost hear Jack groaning in the cellar below.

Arno takes off his cap, turns it in his hands, then places it on the sofa between them.

"Laura." He grabs her with his cold, clammy hands. "I have work to do now, for Denmark. For you."

Father leans back in the chair, satisfied. Everything has been turned upside down, out of joint. What are they up to?

"Come." Arno gets up, attempting to pull her up with him. "It's a beautiful evening. Let's go outside."

She doesn't want to go, her knees are shaking. But Arno has a firm hold and she is forced to her feet. Father and Arno. And Jack trapped in the cellar. She can't go on, it's too much. She breaks away, dashes up the stairs, and hides under the blanket in her small room in the attic while Arno and her parents call from downstairs.

When Arno has left, Father forbids her to take food down to Jack. He has to manage as best as he can, he says. With her head buried in her pillow, she cries herself to sleep.

CHAPTER 30

THE SLAM OF the tailgate cut through the dogs' barking. They continued baying behind the windows of the truck, their eyes large in frustration at the abortive pursuit. Lars sat with a blanket around him on the tailgate of Forensics' Toyota HiAce. Someone had placed a warm cup of coffee in his hand. He patted his jacket pocket, took out the pack of cigarettes. It was drenched. He threw the pack down, looked around for someone to bum a smoke from.

Toke approached, handing him a pack without asking. Lars pulled out a Prince and leaned toward the lighter that Toke held out. Hans Tavsens Park was filled with flashing lights, colleagues, and curious onlookers. Somewhere out there, on the other side of the cordon, a couple of press photographers flashed their cameras. Lars inhaled, let the smoke filter out through his nose. It burned.

"The ambulance has just left. With Lene." Toke put the cigarettes back in his pocket. "They say she's suffered a concussion. Lisa went with her."

Lars nodded. He was far away. Why had the assailant whistled? And he had come through the park, not along the streets. That meant he'd been behind them. He had known that they were tailing Lene. That it was a trap.

He inhaled again, narrowing his eyes. A short distance away, Bint was bent over Lene's bicycle. A crime scene investigator Lars didn't know was examining the area for fingerprints.

"What does Bint say?"

Toke followed his gaze. "It doesn't look like there are any fingerprints. A little saliva but that could also belong to Lene — or someone else altogether. And they've found a bludgeon. That must be what he hit her with. Bint says it's sheer luck her skull wasn't crushed."

Lars drew the last of the cigarette into his lungs, threw the hot butt on the ground, and stubbed it out with the tip of his shoe. He was about to collapse with fatigue.

"Can you take care of this?" He got up, pulled the blanket off. "I need to ..." He patted Toke on the shoulder and left him.

Lars stepped over the barrier tape and started walking down Hans Tavsens Gade, past the journalists that had gathered there. One, two photographers fired off their flashes in his face. Someone asked him a question, but he kept walking.

On Jagtvej the scene had not changed in the half hour that had passed since he last stood there. Car lights, puddles, pizza joints, pubs. No pedestrians. He walked slowly toward Nørrebrogade, made note of the spot where the assailant had jumped over the wall separating the street from the cemetery. There were far too many streets the perp could have run down. Stairways, courtyards. Back into the cemetery, even. It was futile. He continued toward the roundabout at the intersection of Jagtvej and Nørrebrogade. He couldn't let go of the thought that the perp had known it was a trap all along. He pounded his fist into the wall in rage, clenched his teeth as the pain crippled his breathing. He stuffed the wounded hand deep into his jacket pocket and started walking faster. He should have stopped the operation; he shouldn't have allowed it to happen. He'd had a bad feeling right from the beginning.

Now the perp knew that they had discovered where he found his victims. Lene was in the hospital, and the investigation was left in ruins.

There was life on Nørrebrogade: buses were filled with people on their way home from a night out, and the morning bars had begun to open. He just wanted to go home. At St. Stefan's Church, he hailed a cab. The driver shot him an angry glance in the rearview mirror when he climbed into the back in his wet clothes, then streaked along Nørrebrogade. He tore down the short stretch by Nørrebrohallen's sports facility, where cars were forbidden. Lars was too tired to protest.

He crawled up the stairs to his apartment, threw his wet clothes in the hallway. Then he turned on the shower and let the scalding water pour over him for several minutes. The headache had returned. He brushed his teeth in the shower, wrapped the towel around his waist, and went back into the hallway. A squeaking sound was coming from Maria's room. It was rhythmic, rough. The sound of two bodies...

He wanted to grab the handle, tear the door open. But just as he put his hand out, he heard her moaning. His hand dropped to his side. His hand opened and closed. then he turned, slunk off to his bedroom. Raising his head, he caught sight of his reflection in the dark window. A burnt-out, middle-aged man with loose, grey skin, bags under the eyes, and cuts on his nose and forehead. He leaned his forehead against the windowpane.

He got dressed, slipped into the living room. Grabbed

The Tempest from the bookcase, and let it fall open to the familiar place. He found the secret pocket in the bright-red knitted bookmark and took out the small, square sachet. He poured the white powder onto the table and used his bank card to form a line. He rolled a two-hundred-kroner note into a tube, stuffed one end into his right nostril and snorted, pressing his index finger against his left. It burned inside, near the bridge of his nose and in his throat. Steel and ice. He had to sneeze but managed to hold back, licked his index finger, dragged it across the remains of the fine powder, and rubbed it into his gums. More steel. Blood.

He returned the book to the bookcase, folded the paper and the banknote, put both into his pocket and disappeared down the stairs.

CHAPTER 31

ABEIUWA PULLED THE leopard-print fur tight around her shoulders, tugged at her tiny, pink, plastic skirt, and peered up and down Vesterbrogade. It was so cold in this country, even though they said it was summer. She was tired. Her whole body ached. She took a final drag on her last cigarette and threw the stub into the gutter. On her corner of the public square of Vesterbros Torv, car lights darted across her slender body and neon signs reflected on chrome trim and shiny hoods. The pedestrians she tried to forget. Most avoided her; some stared. People here were surly, angry. Not like at home in Porto-Novo. She longed to return, missed her mom and her siblings, her father who worked on the other side of the border.

One more customer, then she would call it a night. She hoped they wouldn't beat her when she returned with the money. But why wouldn't they? They always did.

A car drove through the puddle by the sidewalk. The murky water splashed the curb and Abeiuwa sidestepped the spray. She bent down, squeezed her arms against her breasts to push them up and out. It was a trick she had learned on her first night in Torino.

The window rolled down, she smiled into the darkness.

"Fucky fucky?" Abeiuwa winked, puckered her pink lips.

"How much?" The voice was rusty. An old man's. It didn't bother her. As long as he didn't smell.

She smiled again, this time a little broader. "Two hundred, no condom."

"Too much, black whore." The car accelerated, skidding on the pavement. Again a hard jet of water shot up from the puddle, this time hitting her fur.

"Asshole." She gave him the finger and looked down at the damage. She wouldn't be able to wash until she got home. A little methylated spirit would get the worst off. But for the rest of the evening she would look terrible.

Over on the other side of the street, a young couple was staring at her. People had so many opportunities here; so few needed to work the streets.

She turned around, began to walk toward Justine who worked a corner further down Vesterbrogade. Maybe she had a smoke?

Justine had both North State cigarettes and gum, and five minutes later Abeiuwa was back on her corner. She was already feeling better, chewing gum and blowing smoke rings into the night air. She swallowed the pill Justine had given her, dextroamphetamine. Now she could manage a couple more hours.

An old vintage car pulled up to the curb. She repeated her routine—she bent down, squeezed her breasts together, puckered her lips, and whispered hoarsely through the window.

"Fucky Fucky?"

The man in the car shook his head. "Sucky sucky?" The voice was neither young nor old.

Abeiuwa smiled, opened her mouth, let the tongue slip across her lips. "Two hundred, no condom."

The door opened and she got into the passenger seat.

"Go to Fisketorvet. Behind."

The customer was an older man. It was dark inside the car and she couldn't see more than his shadow. Glasses, sharp nose, high forehead. Heavy breathing. The front windshield was messy. She placed her hand on his thigh, let her fingers slide upwards. He was breathing heavier now. They crossed Istedgade, turned down Halmtorvet, and out along Skelbækgade. The festival of lights from the Fisketorvet Shopping Centre twinkled at them from the other side of the train tracks. He drove down Kalvebod Brygge, into the parking lot and down among the blacked-out properties behind. He'd been here before.

They parked in the shadow of an apartment block where the lights from Fisketorvet didn't reach them. He turned off the headlights. Her fingers found his zipper. There was a sudden smell in the car. Piss? No, something else. Something chemical? She smiled at him so he could see the whites of her eyes and her teeth in the dark.

Then she filled her mouth with saliva, bent over the gear-shift, and took the limp, wrinkled dick in her mouth.

He mumbled something; it sounded more or less like what they all mumbled. She assumed it was Danish; it sounded stupid at any rate. But she froze when he started stroking her hair as he stiffened in her mouth. If only he would stop. The ones who touched her tended to force her head all the way down, until she was about to choke. She was used to it now, she could manage. But not this. This terrified her. She sucked her cheeks in, moved her head more quickly, up and down. Her tongue ran in circular motions around the head of his penis. Come on. Get it over with.

His hand stopped stroking her hair. He was doing something by the windshield. Now the hand returned; a finger caressed her right eyelid. She shivered.

A wet and pungent cloth was pressed over her nose and she was pulled up by her hair. Then the cloth was forced over her mouth and the world dissolved.

Abeiuwa came to, dizzy, dazed. She had no idea where she was or how much time had passed. She sat on a concrete floor that was rough against the skin of her bare buttocks. Her hands were bound behind her back. Carefully she opened first her right eye, then her left.

Blurry shapes, shadows in the twilight. A tiny bit of light filtered in through an opening high above. The shapes accumulated into shadows, bodies. One on a chair, the other on a sofa sitting in front of a dark television. They were completely still. One body's head was slumped against its chest; the other's back was against the sofa, its head bent backwards.

"Help," she whispered. There was no reaction.

"Help me," she tried again, this time louder. Neither of them moved.

For a long time, she watched their eyelids. They didn't move: no twitching, no trembling arms. She tried lifting her head but was far too weak. The small movement made her nauseous and she threw up. Her vomit splashed down on the concrete floor between her legs and fear took hold of her.

"*Nana Buluku,*" she whispered. "*Mawu et Lisa.*" The silent figures didn't react. "*Aide moi,*" she continued, this time a little louder. Still no reaction, no answer.

"*Aide moi,*" she shouted. Her voice echoed between the concrete walls.

The sound of footsteps came from above. Then came the

cutting sound of metal on metal. A bright light forced her to shut her eyes. Something creaked. Someone was on the way down—a staircase? Heavy, slowly. She opened her eyes again, blinking until she had adjusted to the light. And then she screamed.

The two shapes were naked white women. Their skin had an oddly yellowish hue, like the beeswax from her uncle's village. But it was not the unnatural hue, nor the fact that they didn't move that made her scream.

It was their eyes. They stared blankly forward, cold and stiff, glasslike. Like doll's eyes. Each had one green and one greyish-blue. Dead faces. Like the Vodun her grandmother had told her about.

"*Nana Buluku*," she whispered again. "*Mawu et Lisa. Aide moi, aide moi.*" Again and again, she rocked back and forth.

High above, a figure emerged through a small door at the top of a steep staircase. A thickset, older man walked down the stairs, one step at a time, humming while keeping an eye on her. She screamed again, but the man continued his descent, smiled as he passed her, and walked over to a bookcase. He turned his back to her. His arms were moving; he took something from a shelf, operated a device. Music spilled out from hidden speakers. Strange, slow, creepy music. A woman sang words she didn't recognize. Then the shape stepped toward her carrying something, shutting out the light.

"Sucky sucky?" she whispered.

The man didn't answer; he just kept smiling. The sharp chemical stench surrounded her again; she couldn't stop him from forcing what he had in his hands against her mouth. It burned her eyes. The room, the man, and the two Vodun disappeared into the darkness.

* * *

The crude wooden bookcases, the ceiling high above her—everything was swimming as she came to. She remembered the image of the two naked female figures. Abeiuwa opened her mouth to scream but no sound came out. She couldn't speak. Something had been stuffed into her mouth. She tried spitting it out, but the only result was something tightening around her neck.

She was lying on a table, freezing and naked. A chemical stench penetrated the air. Something was stuck to her right eye. Above her, she could hear him mumbling, humming cheerfully to himself. The music was very loud now. She tried opening her eyes, but could only see out of the left one. Something was pressing down on her right eye.

She couldn't move her arms or legs. Her right eye started twitching, the pain radiating all the way from her head down to her feet. The soft tissue was stretched like one of the fish eyes she had played with as a child. The pain was a fire burning in her head. She tensed her body, arched her back. The man standing over her continued humming to the strange music but didn't speak. And then she heard a soft pop. The pain momentarily vanished, only to return worse than ever. She managed to slip her left hand free; she fumbled over a rough surface, hit something. It fell, clattered. Abeiuwa's hand closed around a jar and she struck, upwards and to the right with all her strength. The soft humming stopped and a large body tumbled to the floor.

Driven half-mad by pain, she reached over, fumbled with the buckle around her right hand, then her feet. Seconds later she was free. She tried to get up, then wailed as her right eye twitched. A low table had been overturned in his fall, instruments and jars with liquids were scattered across the floor. Behind him, out of the corner of her left eye, she caught sight of the foot of the staircase. She hurried across his body to the staircase. As she raised her foot toward the first step, a hand grabbed her ankle. She kicked backwards, struck. The grip relaxed and she tumbled up the steep staircase. Now heavy steps creaked on the staircase behind her. She pushed through a small door, slammed it shut in her pursuer's face and slumped onto the floor. Bewildered she tried to get her bearings. Another dark room, another staircase. She scrambled up the stairs on all fours, heard the door squeak behind her. He was clawing his way across the floor below her. His hand grazed her heel before she managed to pull it away. Wailing, she dragged herself up the stairs, through the door. A small bureau stood on the other side. She tore at it half blindly, managed to move it to the doorway, and pushed it down the staircase. A curse from down below, the sound of something heavy falling, the staircase creaking. She tottered down a corridor. A door. *Out?* She entered a room with windows on all sides, fumbled along the walls and the window frames. Gasping and half-blind she felt for the latch on one of the windows, listening for steps all the while. The window flew open and she plunged headfirst out into the cold night, somersaulted down a soft hill, hit her back against a metal object, and pulled herself up.

A blaze of white lights burned her eyes. The right one still hung from the socket and dangled on her cheek. She turned, looked back toward the house and the pale outline of a Vodun in the open window.

She let out a long scream and ran into the nearest thicket, away.

FRIDAY
JUNE 20

CHAPTER 32

THE DUTY OFFICER called Sanne at 3:37 a.m. Martin was furious at being woken up; he slammed the phone against the wall. Sanne didn't have the energy to explain. She apologized on the phone. Her boyfriend had accidentally knocked the phone off the nightstand; no, there was nothing wrong.

The officer didn't buy it, but what was he going to say? He gave her the address and signed off with a "Have fun."

Now she was sitting in a room at Gentofte Hospital. A young African woman was lying in bed, staring into space. The terror in the woman's healthy eye didn't disappear when she introduced herself. The woman had no papers and wouldn't declare an address. She spoke limited English.

The woman had a patch over her right eye. The duty nurse told them that when she had been brought in an hour earlier, her eye had been dangling on her cheek, attached only by the optic nerve and something-or-other that Sanne couldn't remember the name of. They had now more or less managed to get it in place, but they doubted they would be able to save her sight.

Sanne leaned closer. "What happened? Who did this to you?"

The woman shook her head. She tried to speak but nothing came out.

"Where are you from?" Sanne tried again. This time the woman lit up.

"Benin," she answered. "Dahomey."

The ambulance had picked her up on Brogårdsvej, by the roundabout. Several local residents had called and complained; one had shouted that a black whore was standing in the middle of the road screaming. That was more or less how the words had come out. By and large this was the sum of what the police knew. But Sanne had no doubt why the duty officer had called her. A prostitute with eye damage, likely done forcibly. A victim that had succeeded in getting away? Was this the mistake they'd been waiting for?

Benin. Sanne got up, smiled at the woman, and hurried out to the corridor. She called the duty officer on her cell.

"I'm going to need an interpreter. Yes, for whatever it is they speak in Benin. Yes, Africa. Thank you."

Half an hour passed before a patrol car arrived with the interpreter. A large man with a gentle face introduced himself as Samuel. He started talking with the woman, but after a couple of sentences he turned around.

"We don't speak the same language."

"But I asked for an interpreter from Benin?"

Samuel smiled. "We speak many languages in Benin. I speak Yoruba, she speak Fon Gbè. I can hardly understand. She speaks only a little French. I think she comes from the slum in one of the large cities in the south. Cotonou or Porto-Novo."

Sanne nodded. They weren't going to be that lucky after all.

"Could you try anyway?" she asked. "Don't you understand any of it?"

Samuel shrugged. "I understand a little but it's difficult. I'm not sure it's correct."

"Let's try anyway. Ask her what her name is."

Slowly, over the next half hour, Samuel managed to draw out the woman's story. Her name was Abeiuwa and she was nineteen years old, from Benin, and, as Samuel had guessed, from the slum in Porto-Novo. She had been lured to Europe with the promise of a well-paid job—the classic story. She had arrived by plane from Nigeria to Torino, where she had been given her first rough introduction to her new profession. After several months in Torino she was sold again, this time to Rotterdam. Next stop was Copenhagen. She had been here for two months now. Sanne went cold inside, as she saw the realization in Abeiuwa's face. She would soon be sold off to another city, other men. The young woman knew it; she had long since accepted that this was what life had to offer her.

Her last client had picked her up on the corner of Vesterbrogade and Gasværksvej. Sanne tried getting a description, but all Abeiuwa was able to tell her was that he was old, wore glasses, and had a strange, strong smell.

Abeiuwa was about to perform oral sex on the customer when he drugged her with a cloth. When she woke up, she found herself in a dark room on a concrete floor filled with wooden boxes.

"And the dead were sitting there, on a chair and a sofa," Samuel translated, furrowing his brow. "They had dead eyes." Samuel pointed at his eyes. Abeiuwa started, pulled the comforter over her eyes.

"Botono," she whispered, terror stricken.

Sanne tried reassuring her with a smile. "What did she say?"

"Botono. It's Vodun."

Sanne sat back in the chair.

"Vodun? I think you'll have to explain that."

"You call it voodoo but really it's Vodun. Vodun is one of our old religions. In Vodun, there is a creator, Nana Buluku, and there are many spirits, good and evil, who we call Vodun. And witches. Botono. They invoke bad spirits. She say the dead were Botono, or that the man who took her is a Botono and has invoked the dead who then are bad Vodun."

Sanne nodded, pretending to understand. "What happened next?"

"This Botono drugged her again. When she wake up, he's removing her eye. She get away...I can't quite understand how." Samuel shrugged. "She came out on the street. The lights hurt her eyes—her eye. She thought the lights were evil Vodun too, so she ran the other way. There was a lake. Suddenly she was standing on the road and the ambulance was there."

"Can she tell us a little about the house? What did it look like?"

But Abeiuwa couldn't remember anything. She just wanted to get as far away as possible.

"Can you stay a little?" she asked Samuel. "The doctors will most likely want to talk with her afterwards."

Samuel looked at his watch. "I can stay another hour, then I need to go to work."

Sanne nodded and smiled at Akeiuwa, who was still lying in bed with the blanket covering the bottom of her face.

"Thanks," she said. "I'm going to speak to the doctor. Could I have your number in case I need you again?"

Samuel scribbled his cell number down on an old bus ticket and sat down next to Abeiuwa's bed. Sanne hurried out of the room and down the corridor, asked for the doctor who had treated the girl.

While a nurse went to find the doctor, Sanne found a water fountain and filled a plastic cup. Fatigue slowed her down; her eyes were gritty with exhaustion. She took a sip of water, scanning a row of bright portraits on the wall above the fountain. Was that Professor Lau? She read the text on the small paper sign next to the picture. Professor Lau, Head of Ophthalmology at Gentofte Hospital from 1978. In the photo, he was younger, more slender. His hands were folded on his lap, almost feminine. She recalled his fleshy paws from the other day, the glass eye that nearly disappeared between his fingers.

"Ah," the voice came from behind her. "I see you've met Professor Koes?"

Sanne only just avoided spurting water all over the younger doctor when she turned around. He was tall, with horn-rimmed glasses and a side part in his thick brown hair. He had a slightly arrogant bearing.

"Koes?"

The doctor nodded at the picture next to Professor Lau. An older man with a black comb-over, the sides shaved above the ears. He had bushy eyebrows and an impressive moustache.

"Koes founded this department back in the 1930s."

"No, the one next to him, Lau. I met him on Tuesday." She cleared her throat. "You received Abeiuwa?"

The doctor nodded, put his hands in his pockets. "Someone performed a very delicate enucleation on her only a few hours ago."

"What exactly does that mean?"

The doctor looked over his horn-rimmed glasses. "Enucleation, in layman's terms, is the removal of the eyeball. The muscles that enable the eye to move are severed. Lateral rectus, inferior rectus..."

Sanne held up a hand. "Okay, thanks. The muscles are severed?"

The doctor sighed. "There are four. After that, the eyeball is attached only by the superior oblique and nervus opticus."

"The optic nerve. But none of them were severed?"

"No. If we assume that the plan was to remove the entire eye, she got away before he got that far. I must add—it's wonderful work. The incisions in the muscle tissue are neat and clean."

CHAPTER 33

DEBRIEFING IN LARS'S office. Yesterday's catastrophe was imprinted across the ashen, exhausted faces. Toke walked in, just back from the hospital where he had been to see Lene. He looked around the circle, despondent, and then slumped into the only available chair.

Lars allowed silence to descend. He had worked all night and morning with a restless energy unleashed by the amphetamine's release of noradrenaline and dopamine into the nerve tissue and of serotonin into the synaptic vesicles. But without any kind of usable result. The perp had gotten away. At some point over the course of the morning, sitting with a cup of coffee in the canteen, it had dawned on him. It wasn't enough that the rapist had worked out that it was a setup, that Lene was bait. In Assistens Cemetery, he had whistled to make sure that Lars wouldn't lose his trail. The only saving grace was that

Lene hadn't suffered any serious injuries. A mild concussion, a gash on the eyebrow that had been stitched. That was it.

He'd be held accountable, he knew that. It was his responsibility. His team waited for him to say something, get the ball rolling, but his reserves were depleted. Even the amphetamine was useless now; it only sucked him dry. His legs bounced up and down at an insane pace.

"Okay," he finally said, forcing his legs to calm down. "A police op that goes wrong is always front-page news. We have to expect that the press is going to be all over this now. Be careful who you speak with and what you say. If you're contacted by the press, refer them to me."

No one spoke. Kim A scratched the back of his ear, smiled to himself. Toke's eyes were glued to the floor between his feet.

"Why doesn't a club like that have cameras recording people leaving?" Lisa asked.

Frank shrugged. "The entrance is where you get trouble."

Something flashed through Lars's mind, an electric impulse that sent a shock through his tired, beaten-up body. He attempted to block out the conversation around him, the scraping of the chairs against the floor. Cameras. Video surveillance. Light. He looked up.

"There are no cameras filming people leaving Penthouse, but the 7-Eleven on the corner of Nørregade and Nørreport... I wonder, wouldn't there be a camera there?"

"How would that help?" Frank stared out the window.

"Yes, dammit," said Lisa. "Both Stine and Lene walked down Nørregade past Nørreport. If the perp followed them from Penthouse..."

Lars headed down to the canteen. It was empty at this time of the day. Just inside the door, a female officer he didn't recognize was sitting with a newspaper and a cup of coffee. They nodded to each other. The rubber soles of his Converse stuck to the linoleum floor, producing a small, soft smack every time he raised his foot, a series of kisses following his every step. It couldn't be later than ten in the morning, and with the amphetamine in his bloodstream, his hunger was suppressed, but he thought he should have something. He hadn't eaten much the previous day. At the counter, he chose a greyish hamburger patty with potatoes and caramelized onions. He paid, poured a glass of water from the pitcher by the counter, and sat down at one of the tables at the very back. An abandoned copy of *Ekstra Bladet* had been left open on the neighbouring table.

He tore open the small blue and red salt and pepper sachets and sprinkled them generously over his food, vacantly studying the vegetable of the day. The two gherkins glistened under the fluorescent lights.

He started eating, grabbed the paper. The front page was filled with a large picture of a girl in a very low-cut dress. A black bar covered her eyes, but her clothes and surroundings revealed her profession. The headline in bold, black type: "Hookers on Vesterbro: 'The Sandman can come and get us.'" He flipped to the pages the cover story referred to. A large spread summarized the case, describing Mira alongside a huge picture of the most recent victim in her hospital bed at Gentofte Hospital. She was nineteen years old and came from Benin in West Africa. The girl in the picture didn't look a day over seventeen. Her right eye was covered with a large white dressing. She looked scared and in shock.

When he folded up the paper, he realized he had finished eating. Using his tongue, he removed the last strands of meat from between his teeth. No flavour remained, just a greasy feeling running all the way down his throat. He emptied the glass of water in one go. How was Sanne doing? He really should thank her for that dinner. Was that on Monday? Five days ago already.

Ulrik appeared, walking toward him through the canteen with firm, purposeful steps. Some people just knew when their presence was unwanted.

Ulrik nodded, pulled out a chair, and sat across from Lars. "Mind if I sit here?"

He didn't want to speak to Ulrik. Today least of all.

"I heard about yesterday," Ulrik began.

Lars pushed the cutlery around on the empty plate. His legs bounced up and down under the table. He nodded at the paper. "I see he's been at it again? And the papers have already given him a name: The Sandman."

"What?" Ulrik glanced at the *Ekstra Bladet* next to Lars's plate. "Oh, yes, poor girl. But we were..." He leaned across the table, lowered his voice. "I've read Toke's report from yesterday and..." He stopped, fidgeted in the chair. "Why don't we go up to my office?"

Lars took a deep breath, forced his heart rate down. Was he going to take him off the rape case too? "I've got nothing to hide."

"I see. Well, the fact of the matter is..." A single drop of sweat trickled down Ulrik's temple. "A complaint has been filed against you—your way of leading the investigation." He went red, lowered his voice. "There are people on your team, people with seniority, who believe the case is crumbling. Leads not being followed up on..."

"Kim A," Lars mumbled. "You know what this is about. You were there."

"It's actually not that simple. Frank and Lisa have signed it too. Kim A isn't stupid. I have to respond to this."

Lars clenched his fist under the table. Strictly speaking, it wasn't Ulrik's fault. Still, he had this urge to hit somebody right now. Hard.

"Lars, I'm trying to help you." Ulrik put his hands on the table, his palms open.

He had to get out, get some air. He got up, sent the chair backwards with a violent kick. It slid across the floor, clattered into the table behind him. The female officer by the door looked up, startled.

"Do whatever the hell you have to do."

Then he strode toward the exit without looking back.

CHAPTER 34

LARS STAGGERED INTO his apartment. His heart was pounding in his chest. He was trying to suppress the memory of the sounds from Maria's bedroom the other night, but the creaking and moaning kept on going in the back of his head. The hyperactivity was abating. His head ached, his jaw was tender. And he was tired. Every single fibre in his body screamed for rest, oblivion. Speed comedown. He needed a piss; his bladder was about to burst.

Lars threw his jacket down on the floor and went into the bathroom. He lifted the seat. A splashing in the toilet bowl. He caught sight of himself in the mirror and almost took a step back in shock. His skin was ashen, and the large dark bags under his eyes gave him a hounded look. His hair was flat and lifeless. He needed a shave.

Lying on the edge of the sink was an exhausted toothpaste

tube; the screw cap, with its hardened rim of grey paste, stood on the other side of the faucet. When would she learn to clean up after herself? He put the toilet seat down, and washed his hands. Then he grabbed the empty toothpaste tube, and stepped on the garbage can pedal.

Nestled in among rolled-up toilet paper, toothpicks, and crumpled Kleenex smeared with makeup, was a used condom.

He had to lean against the wash basin with both hands; the tiles buckled. This was not something he should get involved in; it was her life. But his body didn't agree. He chucked the toothpaste tube into the garbage can and let the lid drop. Then he turned on the cold water, splashed water on his face, and spat in the sink: a viscous, bloody glob slowly ran down the drain. His throat tasted of iron. The fatigue returned. There was a hammering in the back of his head and then everything went black.

"You have to wake up, Dad. Now." Maria was tugging at him. Were those tears in her eyes?

The blanket of fatigue wouldn't lift. The headache hit him. His mouth tasted of blood, metal. Bad breath.

"Hmm?" He pulled his arm back, drew the comforter over his head.

It was torn off again. Crimson light penetrated his eyelids.

"Dad!"

He sat up and rubbed his eyes. Somewhere in the apartment, someone was quietly and persistently sobbing.

He opened his eyes, saw Maria in front of him. Mascara and eyeliner drew grimy lines down her cheeks. But it wasn't her crying?

"What's going on?" he mumbled.

"It's Caroline. She was raped. Last night."

"Has she been to the hospital?" Wide awake, he got up. The blood drained from his head. He swayed back and forth, but his calves tensed against the edge of the bed and kept him upright until the blood returned. He picked up his pants and a sweater from the chair by the wall and got dressed.

Maria was shaking. She had moved to the edge of the bed, collapsing as he pulled the sweater over his head.

"We have to take her to Rigshospitalet. Does she know the person who did it?" Lars buttoned up his pants.

"Could it...be him, Dad?"

That one sentence was like a blow to his body. Lars had to lean against the wall so as not to double over.

"Where is she?" he managed to stammer.

Caroline was curled up on the couch in the living room. His daughter's friend was almost unrecognizable. Her long blond hair was matted. She kept moving her fingers through it, scratching, messing it up. She stared out the window, rocking back and forth. Her green eyes were vacant, the skin around them bruised and swollen. Her nose was crooked. She sobbed, wiping the tears on her sleeve.

They sat down on either side of her.

"Caroline?" He placed a hand on her shoulder. "You have to go to the hospital. I'll call for a patrol car." Caroline didn't answer; she just rocked back and forth, staring into space. Lars looked at the dense pattern of wounds and gashes across her scalp, the caked blood in her hair. "She hasn't had a shower, has she?"

"I don't know," Maria answered. "She didn't call me until noon..." She bit her lip, then glanced at her friend. "But the skin on her fingers was all wrinkled when I arrived."

Lars got up, patted his pockets. Where did he put his cell?

"Stay with her. I'll call."

It had to be in his jacket in the hallway. He was there in

two bounds, picked up his jacket, and pulled out the cell in one motion. Lars asked the duty officer to send a patrol car to his address and returned to the living room.

"Has she had anything to drink?" he asked. "We need to get some water in her."

Maria nodded, got her friend to stand. Lars could hear the tap running while he put his socks and shoes on.

Four minutes later they were down on Folmer Bendtsens Plads, Maria with her arm around Caroline, Lars half a step ahead of them. He tore open the back door as soon as the patrol car pulled up and helped Maria get Caroline into the back before he climbed in after them.

"Rigshospitalet. Centre for Victims of Sexual Assault," he said. The tires screeched as the officer behind the wheel pulled out sharply and shot across Nørrebrogade. It had started to drizzle.

The duty nurse took one look at Caroline, now leaning on Maria, and said, "I'll get a doctor. Two seconds."

Christine Fogh emerged almost immediately. She nodded at Lars, then smiled at Caroline and Maria.

"Hi, my name is Christine. I'm your doctor. Could you please follow me?" Her voice was soft and calm. Subdued. She helped Maria with Caroline, held her on her other side. They went through the first door on the left and into the windowless room where he had interviewed Louise Jørgensen on Tuesday morning. Christine directed Caroline to an examination table covered with a sheet of paper and fixed with two stirrups at one end.

A young nurse entered with a trolley.

"I'm going to examine you now," Christine said. "And Line is going to take some tests. We'll be careful. Have you been in the shower?"

"I scrubbed and scrubbed and scrubbed," Caroline whispered, "but it wouldn't go away."

"That's okay." She stroked Caroline's hair, gave Lars a pointed look over the rim of her glasses. His gaze wavered. What did she want?

"Dad, really. Get out." Maria shoved him toward the door.

Of course. He mumbled an apology and hurried out.

Inside the reception room on the other side of the corridor, he sat down on one of the low pine chairs with a light green cover. The ceiling light had a cold, yellowish tinge, making it difficult to make out any details clearly. On the way here, he had been able to concentrate on Caroline, on what needed to be done. But now, the thoughts descended on him. Caroline would never have set foot in Penthouse. She would never have met him if they hadn't come up with the idea of using Lene. He'd chosen that exact route through the city.

He closed his eyes, leaned his head back. Let it wash over him.

He had no idea how much time had passed when Maria opened the door a crack.

"Do you want to ask her some questions, Dad? She wants to speak to you."

He got up but couldn't look Maria in the eyes.

"No more than a few minutes," Christine said when he walked in. She was leaning against the wall.

He pulled up a chair, sat by the headboard. Caroline turned and looked at him. She attempted a smile.

"I've given her a sedative," Christine said. Maria went to the other side of the bed, grabbed Caroline's hand.

"Caroline, I know this is difficult," he started, "but I have to ask you a few questions about last night. Do you think you can manage that?"

"Yes," Caroline nodded. The movement was hardly noticeable.

"Good." He tried smiling. "Where did it happen?"

"In Nørrebro Park." Her voice was hoarse from hours of crying. "I was going to get some cigarettes…"

He noticed Maria's ashen face out of the corner of his eye.

"Nørrebro Park—where exactly?"

"Behind the playground with the airplane, by the side street Bjelkes Allé. He pulled me into the trees by the basketball court."

Lars nodded. He knew the place.

"I'll send someone to check it out." There wouldn't be much to find. After an entire day, the crime scene would be contaminated by children, dog walkers, and joggers.

"What did he look like? Did you get a look at his face?"

Caroline shook her head. "He was wearing a cap. And black clothing. It looked like a tracksuit."

"Can—" He cleared his throat; he had to force the words out. "Can you remember what time it was?"

"Twenty past three?" She looked at Maria. "Maybe 3:30 a.m.?" Her voice was almost gone now, her eyelids kept dropping. Lars caught his breath. No more than five minutes after he had escaped Lars on Jagtvej.

"Okay," Christine said. "I think we should let Caroline get some sleep. I'll let you know when you can speak to her again." She nodded at Lars.

It was time for him to leave, but would he be able to get up?

Caroline forced her eyes open, grabbed him by the sleeve, and held tightly.

"He hummed—during. Like this." Slightly off-key and in a staccato shuffle, she tried reproducing the tune. But the bloody lips, the gap between her front teeth, made everything come out as spit and air. She started crying. On the other side of the bed, Maria tightened her grip on her friend's hand.

"Okay." Christine moved away from the wall, placed a hand

on Lars's shoulder. "She needs some rest now."

Lars got up. Everything tensed.

"Can Maria stay with me for a bit?" Caroline forced the tears back. "Just until I've fallen asleep?" Her voice lingered.

"I'll be out in a minute." Maria waved. Lars followed Christine out, closed the door behind them. He had found the strength from somewhere after all.

"You know her?" Christine looked at him with her probing grey eyes.

"Caroline is my daughter's friend."

She held out her hand, bit her lip. Then she let her hand drop. "I just have to complete her chart, so if you have any more questions then come by my office."

Lars nodded. He just had to make a call.

By the elevator, he rang the duty officer and asked him to get in contact with Frelsén and Bint and tell them to go out to Nørrebro Park. Then he called Toke to brief him.

"I should have caught him." Lars massaged his temples with the thumb and middle finger of his free hand. A chair creaked as Toke sat down. It sounded like he was preparing himself for a long conversation.

"You're not going to catch him by blaming yourself," Toke said.

He cleared his throat. Toke was right. "You'll have to go out to Nørrebro Park. Kim A, Frank, and Lisa have filed a complaint against me with Ulrik."

Toke cursed. "I heard."

"But Lisa? I didn't think she was that tight with Kim A?"

"They worked together on a couple of cases while you were gone."

There wasn't much more to say. They hung up. Lars looked at the door to Caroline's room. Stine Bang and Louise Jørgensen. How many more victims were going to end up here?

The door to Christine Fogh's office was stuck. Lars gave it a hard push and it flew open with a crash. She looked up from behind her desk, startled.

"Sorry." Lars mumbled, looked around for a chair.

"Yes, the door sticks a little. One moment and I'll be right with you." Christine concentrated on the screen, punching in the final details of what had to be Caroline's chart.

"Well," she said, pressed Enter, and looked up at him.

Lars took out his small notebook and a pen, flipped to a blank page. "How . . ."

She pushed her chair back, straightened her back. "Raped anally, several blows to the head and face. Caroline has a concussion, a broken nose, and several gashes on her scalp. Also several loose teeth, and one upper front tooth is broken."

"Any bodily fluids? Bite marks?"

"I took a very small sample of semen from the rectum. It appears to be mixed with soap and water, but we might get lucky. I've sent it over to Forensics."

"So it appears to be the same person who raped Stine Bang and Louise Jørgensen?"

"Her injuries resemble those of the other two victims." Christine jotted something down on a notebook by her computer. "But there are differences too. The wounds on her scalp, for example. Fewer blows, but harder."

Lars looked away, closed his notebook. "He was excited. He'd just tried attacking someone else."

"I saw the newspaper," was all she said.

Maria was waiting for him in the corridor. "Thanks, Dad. I didn't know what to do."

Lars wrapped his arms around her. Maria snuggled up to him.

"They say she'll sleep until late tomorrow morning," she said.

"Come on." He held her tight, wallowing in the self-loathing and melancholy of a severe speed comedown. "Let's go find a cab."

Upstairs in the apartment, Lars put out bread and cold cuts, but neither he nor Maria was hungry. They both picked at some bread and liver pâté in silence; it was all they could manage.

Maria ended up breaking the silence.

"I saw on the Internet that you had an operation last night? Did you try to catch him?"

Lars nodded. "He attacked a police probationer. I chased him into Assistens Cemetery, but he got away from me." It was now or never if he was going to tell her. He took a deep breath but couldn't begin. Maria placed her hand on his. They looked at each other.

Then he looked away, tried changing the subject. "You went on a date the other day. How did it go?"

She smiled. She looked beautiful like that. "It was fine."

"What's his name? Where did you go?"

She had that secretive look that he couldn't quite decipher. Then she shook her head. "It's not good for you to know everything, Dad."

He was suddenly back in the hallway the previous night, standing in front of her door, the bed squeaking inside.

"You're right about that." He drank some water, hoping it would hide his flushed cheeks.

Maria didn't notice. "I don't think we should talk about it. Not with Caroline lying in the hospital."

"I'm sure Caroline would want you to be happy." He could hear how stupid that sounded.

"Yeah, but still." She changed the subject. "You didn't make it home last night?"

He nearly choked on his water. So they hadn't heard him, despite his having had a shower.

"I worked straight through. I only got home this afternoon and went straight to bed. Then you woke me up."

She stared down at her plate, pulling her sweater tightly around her.

He woke up in the middle of the night. Maria had come in his room. She hadn't done that since she was a little girl. She brought her comforter with her, curled up underneath it, and nestled next to him, half asleep. He put an arm around her and pulled her close. Then he fell back to sleep.

CHAPTER 35

A STEADY STREAM of cars cruised down Gasværksvej from Vesterbrogade toward Istedgade. Single men were cruising for flesh under the dusty orange and purple glow of the streetlights. The evening air tasted of gasoline and rubber. A greasy layer of hydrocarbon settled in the throat.

Sanne held the photo of Abeiuwa in her outstretched hand.

"Have you seen her before?" The young girl, wearing a denim jacket, black skirt, and ankle boots, blew a bubble, then carried on chewing her gum.

"Maybe."

"She was assaulted last night." Allan stared down the street. He was sweating. "A customer attempted to surgically remove one of her eyes. We're actually trying to help you and the other girls."

The girl tried to make an effort. "Let me see. It might...No, I don't know." She handed the picture back. Her jaw churned again. "I have to work." She stepped away, looked out at the incessant flow of cars. A blue Fiat Punto signalled to pull in.

Sanne moved next to the girl; Allan did the same on the other side. The Punto switched off the signal, then slipped back into the flow of traffic.

The girl turned to Sanne. "I'll get beaten if I don't make enough money. You know that, don't you?"

"Take a proper look at the picture. You were saying something before?"

"One of the black girls stole my corner up on the square a few weeks ago." Something flashed in her eyes. "I've still got bruises." She started rolling up the sleeve on her denim jacket, but Sanne stopped her.

"That's not necessary. Is this her?"

"I don't know her name or who her pimp . . ."

Sanne's cell danced in her pocket to the chorus of "Upside Down."

"Hey, I think we've got something here." Søren sounded excited. "We're with someone out by Copenhagen City Museum. She says she knows her."

"What's up?" Allan stood next to Sanne, trying to catch his breath. Søren stood on the sidewalk just off Absalonsgade, while Kasper sat on a bench next to a long-limbed girl wearing tight satin shorts and stiletto heels. Both had their backs to a small fenced garden that was decorated with a miniature version of Copenhagen as the city must have looked several hundred years ago. Sanne was able to recognize some of the churches, the harbour.

"Justine says she knows the girl in the picture." Søren hadn't learned to pronounce Abeiuwa's name. "Tell my colleagues what you told us."

Justine looked up. "She is — all right?"

"She's scared." Sanne tried to smile. "But under the circumstances, she's doing well. Would you like to visit her?"

It was clear that Justine wanted to, but she shook her head, hardened herself. They were kept on a tight leash, the girls on the street. Sanne sat down on the bench next to her.

"We were standing here together yesterday." Justine fiddled with the strap of her top, which twisted over her bare shoulder. "I'd just given her a smoke and some gum. Then she went back to her corner." She pointed toward Vesterbro Torv, at the corner of Gasværksvej. "A customer picked her up a little later."

"Do you remember what time it came, the car?"

"I looked up at the clock on Føtex. It was around midnight."

Sanne turned her head. Behind them, on the other side of Vesterbrogade, a concrete wall rose up above the surrounding rooftops, carrying the department store's blue and white logo. A clock shone at the very top.

"And the car?"

"It was a dark colour, black or dark blue. Red maybe. Purple."

"Did you see the licence plate?"

Justine started shaking her head but stopped. "I think...it ended in fifty-six or fifty-nine. There might have been a C or a G? I'm sorry, I can't remember." She got up. Her legs shook beneath her. "I have to...work."

Sanne caught her eye. "We can help you get off the street. If you want."

Justine turned and walked away. In the middle of the sidewalk, she stopped and rummaged through her purse. When she straightened up again, she had lit a smoke.

Kasper shook his head. "They always say no."

"If she takes off, they'll bring her fourteen-year-old sister over here instead." Sanne leaned back. Her limbs were heavy. "What's she supposed to do?"

Justine walked to the curb, planted one leg in front of the other. Her stiletto heels clicked on the cobblestones. The first car signalled to pull in.

CHAPTER 36

IT CREAKS AND trembles inside. The continental plates are shifting. Soon there is a glimpse of the Urgrund. The roar rises through flesh and sinews, tears tissue and bone fragments apart until the nerve endings flap in the bloodwind and a roaring chaos reigns. Primordial soup. He staggers down the stairs. He's lived here for so long that the two—the soul's house of flesh and bones, the body's of stone and wood—have gradually become one. His blood flows through the pipes; the stairs and rafters are his skeleton, the breaker panel and the ingenious network of power cords his neural network.

Upstairs, in the bed beneath the roof, Mother screamed about all the forbidden things her father did to her, about Father who is both Father and Grandfather. The long months alone in the cellar before he was born. And after. Why couldn't she just die?

She was weak and now she is gone. He is strong. Only he and Sonja and Hilda remain. But deep down, there is turmoil, rebellion. It is not just the crack inside him. Down there it tears and toils, trying to break free and rise. He tumbles through the kitchen, downstairs to the cellar, and tears open the secret door. Thank God. They're still there, sitting on the chair and the sofa in front of the television. Waiting for him.

Ihr wolltet mir mit eurem Leuchten sagen:
Wir möchten nah dir immer bleiben gerne!

She got away. He tried to catch her—or did he? The body and the house, it is not easy to differentiate. He cannot get out. The door is shut. Their little home is shaken. Sonja and Hilda had also been looking forward to it—to their little family being complete again. And now she has run away. The primordial soup is sloshing about. He vomits in a corner. Only greenish slime and fatty bile come out, splattering over his shoes and onto the floor. He leans against one of the ammunition boxes. What is that sound? Are they laughing at him? Are they sitting there mocking him? The bloodwind rages. He reaches the portable phonograph, places the needle in the groove. The built-in speakers crackle. He breathes deeply. The serene prelude begins. Then Agnes Baltsa's mezzo-soprano springs up from the accompaniment, towering above the dark horns.

Nun seh' ich wohl, warum so dunkle Flammen
Ihr Sprütet mir in manchem Augenblicke.
O Augen!
Gleichsam, um in einem Blicke
Zu drängen eure ganze Macht zusammen.
Doch ahnt' ich nicht, weil Nebel Mich umschwammen.

Then he walks over to the table and starts to hit.

Primordial soup.

Bloodwind.

O Augen!

SATURDAY
JUNE 21

CHAPTER 37

SANNE STRAIGHTENED UP in the chair as Allan came storming through the door. She tried to shake off the daydream. She hoped her cheeks weren't too red. Loose sheets of paper from the report on Abeiuwa's interview were spread across her desk. Allan was sweating profusely in the stagnant air. Large patches were spreading under the sleeves of his white polo shirt.

"I've just read the transcripts from the last twenty-four hours of wiretaps." Allan went quiet. She had gotten to know him quite well in the short time they had worked together and knew he had to be urged on.

"Yes?"

"Yes, well"—Allan was far too excited to notice her feigned enthusiasm—"something's going down. The Bukoshi brothers have spoken to someone in Germany several times now.

They've got a new delivery coming on Monday."

The daydream evaporated at once. "A new delivery? Are they talking about girls?"

"That's what they do, right?" A broad smile spread across Allan's face. He sat down on the corner of her desk. The legs creaked. "This is starting to look like a major human trafficking case. If we can bring them in for that, we'd have time to unravel everything. Mira's murder, Abeiuwa…" He put his hand on the scattered sheets on the desk.

Sanne bit her lip. She still wasn't convinced that the brothers had anything to do with Mira and Abeiuwa. But human trafficking—that she could believe.

"Where are they meeting?"

"Well, they didn't mention that. But if we put the brothers under twenty-four-hour surveillance, then it's only a question of time."

Ulrik waved Sanne and Allan into his office. He was on the phone. A worried look was spread across his face.

"No, I will—"

He was interrupted by a metallic female voice. Sanne figured the connection was bad; either that or the woman was very worked up. It was impossible to make out what she was saying. Ulrik shut his eyes, rested his elbow on the desk.

"But Maria is fine, and Lars—"

The piercing voice broke through once more. Ulrik listened, nodded.

"I'll see if I can find him," he said. "But promise me you'll stay calm. The last thing she needs right now is for you to overreact, okay?"

The voice on the other end quieted, allowing Ulrik to end the conversation.

"Take a seat," he said as he hung up, pointing at the two chairs in front of his desk. "My stepdaughter's friend has been assaulted."

It wasn't as stuffy as her office, but Ulrik was wearing a shirt and tie. That couldn't be comfortable. And what was that about his stepdaughter? Was that Maria?

Allan cleared his throat. "The wiretap on the Bukoshi brothers' club has revealed that they're receiving a new shipment the day after tomorrow. Sanne and I think they're bringing in new girls."

Ulrik got up from his chair and began pacing back and forth in front of the window, a thin, trembling body filled with pent-up and nervous energy. Behind him, the empty gondolas of the Ferris wheel in Tivoli Gardens continued to spin.

"And do we know where they're going to pick up the shipment?" Ulrik said.

"It could be anywhere," Sanne said. "A rest stop by the freeway, a warehouse in the city. Or they could drive them up here in ordinary cars and drop them off on Abel Cathrines Gade in broad daylight."

"Unfortunately, yes." Ulrik nodded. "So what do you want to do?"

The Ferris wheel stopped turning.

"We can assume the driver is coming from Germany — via Rødby or Gedser — and that they're going to meet somewhere between the ferry and Copenhagen. None of these guys are interested in too much attention, right?"

A minute later, Ulrik's computer was out of sleep mode and a map of Zealand filled the screen.

"It has to be somewhere within this triangle." She drew an imaginary triangle, with its points covering the towns of Fakse, Næstved, and Vordingborg.

They looked at each other.

Allan stood with a hand on the back of the chair. "So from here on out it's going to be ...?"

Ulrik looked at them in turn. "The three of us," he said. "Plus the two cars that are already monitoring the brothers. So three unmarked cars." He turned to Sanne. "Where are we at with the glass eye?"

"Negative, I'm afraid." Sanne could see Professor Lau, his large fingers around the small eye prosthesis. "But we're still investigating."

"And the neighbours on Brogårdsvej? Did they see or hear anything? This Abu ... Abuiwa ... The black girl. Are they ...?"

"Abuiewa." Sanne sighed. "Gentofte Police are canvassing today."

Allan put his hands into his pockets. "Kim A called an hour ago," he said. "I don't know how he got wind of it, but he wanted me to ask if he could come along."

Ulrik's brow lifted into a series of wrinkles. "To South Zealand? Why?"

"Maybe things are starting to get a little strained on Lars's team? After the complaint, I mean. He was very eager."

"I'll deal with that," Ulrik said. Then he started packing up the papers on his desk. "That'll be all."

Sanne got up and walked out of the office with Allan, so many thoughts milling around in her head. What had happened to Lars's daughter?

CHAPTER 38

LARS HAD GONE to Rigshospitalet with Maria in the morning. Caroline was still asleep. He'd spoken with Christine Fogh for a bit, just as she was finishing her shift. She was unusually quiet. She promised to keep an eye on Maria, who wanted to stay until Caroline woke up. Now he was standing by the coffee machine in the reception area of the Violent Crime Unit, pouring what promised to be the first of many cups.

Before leaving, Maria described how she had found Caroline hiding behind the sofa in the corner of her apartment, just inside the open door. She was squeezing an old teddy bear, her arms locked in front of her chest, rocking back and forth. How long she had been sitting like that, Maria didn't know.

"Lars?"

A hand rested on his shoulder. He started, turned around. Ulrik. Again.

Lars's gaze wandered along the walls as he looked for an escape. But the reception desk was empty. There was no help to be found. Ulrik leaned against the wall, searching his eyes.

"It's terrible about Maria's . . . about Caroline. I understand it was you and Maria who brought her to the hospital?"

"I have absolutely no interest in discussing this with you." He clenched the plastic cup, squeezed the sides until the lukewarm coffee rose to the edge.

"But we have to . . . I care about Maria too. And Elena—"

"Just stay out of this." Lars took a deep breath. "What you do at home doesn't concern me. What I do—" He started walking toward his office. "Just stay away."

Over far too many cups of coffee, Lars had pored over the reports on Stine Bang and Louise Jørgensen once more, hoping to find something new. He got up, swore, then kicked the wastepaper basket, sending it rolling toward the door. Crumpled up handouts, apple cores, paper cups, and broken pens spilled out onto the floor.

The door opened, hit the basket. Toke poked his head in.

"Everything okay?"

Lars sat down on the windowsill. Bits of food and waste paper were spread across most of the floor.

"Come in." Lars remained on the windowsill, staring at the wall.

Toke pushed the door open and stepped inside. "What have the departmental wastepaper baskets done to you now?" he joked. He started picking up the garbage. "You know these cases can be hell. It can take years to catch the perp. And then it's most likely by chance."

Lars didn't respond. Toke gave him a blank look, then put the wastepaper basket back in its usual spot next to the desk.

"Listen," Toke said. "About an hour ago, a journalist from *Ekstra Bladet* cornered me outside. She wanted a little background info on you. I think something's brewing."

Just then the door opened and Lisa walked in. She shook her head before either of them could manage to open their mouths. No good news, then.

"Caroline is doing better," she said, taking off her jacket and leaning against the doorframe. "Fortunately she's suffered less damage than the other two."

Lars leaned the back of his head against the windowpane. *So now all she needed was a few too many hours with a psychologist.*

The door opened and Frank stepped in with Kim A, who was waving three DVDs. He nodded at Lars. Curtly, but still a nod.

"So we got lucky," Frank said.

Everyone straightened up. Frank grabbed the DVDs from Kim A and slid the first disk into Lars's computer. The office was filled with the sound of scraping chairs and shuffling feet. The entire investigative unit gathered behind Lars's desk. Only Kim A stayed back, taking over Lisa's position by the door.

The screen showed an image of a 7-Eleven and a particularly well-lit stretch of Nørregade, Nørre Voldgade, and Nørreport. The time stamp in the upper right-hand corner showed 02:11:55.

"That can't be from the 7-Eleven," Toke said.

"No," Frank said. "They don't have any video surveillance outside. But Danske Bank, across the street, they do. They were kind enough to make a copy of the videos from each of the nights in question. Look at this."

On the screen, Stine Bang appeared pushing a bike. A group of kids in front of the convenience store stopped her; one girl gave her a hug. A guy handed her a can of beer. They clinked cans and kept talking. The time stamp ticked away in the corner.

"Well, that explains the minutes we couldn't account for," Toke said.

"She stays here for quite a while, a quarter of an hour. It's not very interesting but check this out—" Frank wound the video forward to 02:24. Stine waved and pushed her bike to the crosswalk at Nørregade, headed toward Fiolstræde, then disappeared from view. Immediately after, a person in dark clothing hurried across the street after her.

"Try playing that last bit back in slow motion." Lars's heart was pounding in his chest. It was him: the shadow he had chased through Assistens Cemetery.

Frank's fingers danced across the keyboard and the film rewound. Stine waved goodbye again and began pushing her bike across the street at a deadly slow tempo. Then the figure followed in slow motion.

"That could very well be a black tracksuit," Lisa said. "And he is blonde." Her voice was about a quarter of an octave above her normal pitch. She was also amped up from the adrenaline. Her jaw was moving, her eyes shining.

"Look how oddly he's walking." Toke leaned toward the screen. "Is he trying to avoid the camera?"

"Hardly. He's ducking his head so the group of kids doesn't see him." Lars cocked his head. He tried to see what was below the cap, but it was no use: he couldn't make out the person's face. "Okay, freeze there. That's probably the best we can get?" He looked at Frank who nodded. "Good. Print it and let's see the two other DVDs."

"How are you going to find him?" Toke nodded at the face on the screen, a grainy white blob.

Lars slumped back in his chair. What now? He wound Media Player back. Stine's hand lifted the beer can to her face. Over and over and over again.

"Stine has to know the guy who gave her the beer. Maybe he saw something?"

Lisa shook her head. "We asked. She can't remember anything."

Lars tugged his lower lip. "The beer, there." He paused. "Frank, Kim A, you're going back to Nørreport. We need the surveillance videos from inside the store."

Kim A rolled his eyes. "How's that going to help?"

"We need a picture of whoever bought a can of beer right around that time. We'll have to hope that the person in question paid with a credit card."

CHAPTER 39

SANNE CLOSED THE door behind them. Allan remained standing by the filing cabinet.

"Right, so I guess it's just a matter of waiting until there's news from the wiretaps?" He tapped his fingers on the filing cabinet, producing a hollow and metallic sound in the small office. Sanne sat down. She gathered the papers she had left behind when they went to see Ulrik.

"Hey, I was thinking about what Justine told us yesterday."

"It's too vague," Allan said.

"But let's just suppose that what she saw was correct?"

"Do you realize how many licence plates end in fifty-six or fifty-nine? And even if it was a C or a G..." He slammed the filing cabinet with the palm of his hand. "I need a coffee. How about you?"

Sanne was consulting the Central Registry for Motor Vehicles.

"Come here." She waved him over. "Abeiuwa was found on Brogårdsvej. What if we limit the search to Gentofte—what's the postal code?"

"Twenty-eight twenty." Allan closed the door, positioned himself behind her.

She keyed in numbers and letters, filling in the postal code. They looked on in silence while the computer searched the system.

Nothing.

"Try it with fifty-nine." Allan was excited now; his eagerness rubbed off on her. She replaced the fifty-six with fifty-nine in the search field and pressed Enter.

A list of licence plate numbers appeared on the screen. One jumped out. Margit Langhoff. 16 Søtoften.

"Bastard," Sanne whispered. "He's using his wife's car to pick up hookers."

"We have to go about this rather delicately." Ulrik was sitting in the back seat, observing the Saturday traffic on Lyngbyvej drift idly by. "He's chief executive officer of Gentofte city council. He could give us a lot of trouble."

"Should we turn around?" Sanne caught his eyes in the rearview mirror. Small beads of sweat were glistening on his upper lip. This clearly was not something he enjoyed. Still, he had insisted on coming along. The political animal had taken over.

"No," Ulrik said, considering it. "No, the correct thing to do is check this out. We just have to tread carefully."

Sanne signalled to turn onto Brogårdsvej, reduced her speed.

* * *

"Sorry for disturbing you on a Saturday, Mrs. Langhoff." Ulrik smiled, showing his badge. "But we have some questions we were hoping you and your husband might be able to help us with."

Margit Langhoff was an anorectic woman of about fifty. Her long hair was damaged from too much bleaching, and her tanned, wrinkled face set off the dark circles under her eyes.

"We're having lunch." She led them through the kitchen and out onto the terrace. "Mathias, it's the police."

Mathias Langhoff started to get up from his chair. He was tall and lanky and his scalp was red from too much sun. He wore chinos and a checked shirt. Flower beds and stone circles flowed down the terrace to the bottom of the garden. The lawn was tidy and well kept; not a blade of grass was out of place.

Margit sat down opposite her husband. A Danish lunch filled the checkered tablecloth between the married couple: herring, liver pâté, eggs, salmon, and cold cuts. They each had a beer.

"How can we help you?" Mathias asked.

"There are a few dates we'd like to ask you about," Ulrik said. "Can we go into the study, Mr. Langhoff? That is where you keep your calendar, isn't it?"

Allan remained outside with Margit Langhoff. Ulrik and Sanne followed Mathias into the house.

"Well, what is it you wanted to discuss?" Mathias Langhoff shut the door behind them. "I'm sure you're aware that my secretary manages my calendar."

Ulrik smiled. "Sanne?"

So this was Ulrik's idea of being diplomatic? Palming off the interview on her? She wet her lips, looked Langhoff in the eyes.

"You drive a silver BMW?"

He nodded.

"It's not in the driveway?"

"It's in the shop. The muffler went on Wednesday. I'm getting it back next week."

"On Tuesday, between 9:15 p.m. and 10:30 p.m., you had a visit from a prostitute at this address," Sanne said. She sensed Ulrik catching his breath.

For a few long seconds, Mathias Langhoff stared at her. Then he folded his arms across his chest. "And?"

"The night before last, another prostitute, a young African woman, was found on Brogårdsvej. With one eyeball hanging out. A client attempted to remove it with a scalpel."

Mathias Langhoff rested his hands on the desk. He went white. A yellow stain glistened on his collar. Curried herring?

"I heard about that. It's awful. And here, in our neighbourhood."

"Sanne?" Ulrik must have been in shock, otherwise he would have stopped her long ago. But she wasn't paying attention.

"Where were you on the night before last?"

"Listen, I don't need a secretary or a calendar to answer that. But just out of curiosity: why are you asking me?"

"A witness saw the African girl being picked up in your wife's car on Vesterbro."

Mathias Langhoff smiled broadly. "I sincerely doubt that. You see, Thursday I was at a meeting for the Association of City Councils in Fredericia. The meeting finished late. I spent the night at Kronprinds Frederik Hotel and only returned last night."

Sanne cleared her throat. "But your wife's car—"

"Neither myself nor my wife's car were on Vesterbro the night before last. You see, I drove it to Fredericia. I'm certain that the toll booth at A/S Storebælt can produce a photo of both my outbound and return journey over the bridge. You're also welcome to see the hotel receipts."

Sanne went hot and cold all at once. She tried to avoid Ulrik's gaze; he was seething next to her.

"That—I think that's everything, Mr. Langhoff. We're sorry for disturbing you. Enjoy the rest of your day."

Mathias Langhoff opened the door for them.

"No need to apologize. It's been—entertaining. By the way, the girl you asked about?" Sanne stopped in the doorway as Mathias Langhoff continued: "I thought you should know, I wasn't home alone that evening. My wife took part in our... ah, ménage à trois."

Sanne banged her forehead against the steering wheel when they got into the car. Ulrik was silent.

Allan looked from Sanne to Ulrik. "What happened in there?"

"Sanne learned a valuable lesson." Ulrik sat stiffly in the back seat. "Can we leave now?"

CHAPTER 40

EVENING. PEACE. FREE from the grumpy faces at the station. Toke—and Sanne—were probably the only two he could really trust. He skewered the last tortellini, moved the fork to his mouth, and let his molars grind away. There was next to nothing Italian about it, the ham inside even less so. He chewed, raised his glass. At least the Ripasso was from Valpolicella.

He turned on the TV. One feel-good news feature after another, only to be replaced by an in-depth feature on the price difference between plastic bags. What was it his mother had said? That TV is society's appendix, a useless part of a system whose only function is to release shit.

Maybe the patient wasn't going to kick the bucket straight away, but it definitely looked inflamed.

He poured more wine, then turned off the TV. He squatted

in front of the old boxes on the floor and started flicking through the LPs. There was only one medicine, one thing that would help ease this melancholy: loud music, old school, the type that made Maria shake her head and think he was beyond redemption.

She had sent him a text. She was going to meet her boyfriend in town and he shouldn't wait with dinner. An infinitely long and solitary evening stretched out before him.

He had reached Lou Reed's *Transformer*. "Perfect Day" was probably the right track for the moment. He hesitated, chose the compilation just behind it, "Sad Song." He found a crumpled pack of King's in his pants pocket and lit up. He tilted his head to one side to avoid getting smoke in his eyes while he took the record out of its inner sleeve and placed it carefully down on the record player. Once the needle was in the groove, he leaned back and tapped ash on the plate. The first bass tone, Mick Ronson on the piano. And then that voice. Lars would have gotten goosebumps if that weren't so banal.

The doorbell rang.

The music wasn't that loud, was it? He flicked the ash off the cigarette, went to the entrance and opened the door.

A young man stood there, well dressed and holding a large bouquet of flowers. He was wearing a graduation cap.

"Good evening. Is Maria home?"

Good evening? Did anyone really speak like that anymore? Lars took a drag on the cigarette and scrunched up his eyes. The boy was probably a couple of years older than Maria. His sandy hair hung down over eyes so blue that the colour seemed to spill out.

Lars shook his head. "I'm sorry. She's meeting someone in town. I'm not sure when she'll be back."

"That's all right." The boy stepped forward with a self-assured gait that forced Lars to step aside. The next thing he knew, the boy was inside. "We agreed to meet here instead. She'll probably be here soon."

Lars scratched the back of his neck and stared at the kid in disbelief. Although it was a warm summer evening, he wore a brightly coloured trench coat. The dark red shirt underneath looked freshly ironed and expensive.

In the living room, Lou had launched into "Sad Song."

"Do you want a glass of wine?" he heard himself asking. "And congratulations." He nodded at the cap.

"Thank you, that would be great. Would you mind taking these?" The boy handed Lars the flowers, which were practically exploding yellow and blue. He just managed to grab the bouquet before it fell to the floor, then followed the boy into the living room. Lars put the flowers down in a corner. The young man was hunched down in front of the LPs and the stereo.

"Rega P1? And an NAD 3020? Cool." He nodded. "Low-end classics."

"I didn't think anyone of your generation listened to LPs anymore."

"Well, actually I listen to MP3s mostly. But I do have a Pro-Ject Xtension, a Marantz PM-11S2, and a couple of B&W 804 Diamonds at home."

Lars had heard a demo of the 804 Diamonds a few years back. The speakers were undoubtedly a sound engineer's wet dream, but the sound they produced was far removed from what he would call music. Wooden and dead. He pictured a teenager's room, piled with ridiculously expensive hi-fi equipment. But Maria's boyfriend didn't look like someone who lived in the stereotypical dank basement. Presumably he had an entire floor of his parent's villa in Hellerup at his disposal.

Suddenly the boy turned around, held out his hand.

"Christian. I've just graduated from Øregård High School."

Lars rolled his eyes. Yes, thanks very much, he knew where

his own daughter went to school. He shook the outstretched hand. The boy had a powerful handshake.

"Lars." He nodded. "Sit down. I'll get a glass."

Christian grinned, pulled out a pack of Benson & Hedges. It was the kind the yuppies and the really stylish fashion punks smoked back in the 1980s. Lars suddenly had a flashback of himself as a seventeen-year-old at Floss. Depeche Mode and Bowie videos blaring on the TV behind the bar. Happy hour — strong beers and lines in the washroom.

"Do you mind if I smoke?" Christian asked.

Lars nodded at the ashtray and disappeared into the kitchen with his plate of half-eaten tortellini.

When he came back with a glass for Christian, the boy was on the floor flipping through his record collection.

"Not exactly the latest stuff, eh?" Lars was about to protest but Christian waved his hand. "It's cool. You have some great stuff. And old Stones," he exclaimed, holding up *Beggars Banquet*, before taking the disc out of its inner sleeve. "Original packaging. Do you know how much this is worth?"

Lars plopped down on the sofa, poured wine for both of them. He nodded.

"I mean, it's not going to secure your pension," Christian continued. "But it should bring in a few thousand. If you sell it to the right people, that is. And it's in excellent condition." Christian let the LP spin around his two fingers, studied both sides. "The jacket too."

"I'm more interested in the music. Do you know the album?" Lars slid the glass toward him.

Christian tapped his cigarette, crossed his legs on the floor.

"Yeah, I find it a bit boring." He took a sip of wine. His lips twitched slightly, then he laughed and took another drink.

"It's just rhythm 'n' blues," Lars said. What did the kid want? Progressive rock? "And they still manage to mix in samba, country, and music hall. Not too bad, eh."

Christian shrugged. "I've always preferred this one." He picked up *Let it Bleed* from the stack. "Wow, first edition too?"

Lars nodded. He couldn't help laughing.

"One of the first," he said. "Check out the number on the label."

"And with a hole in the cover to view the inner sleeve. Blue for stereo." Christian stuck his finger through the hole. "Do you have the poster?"

Originally, the record came with a poster, but one of the many previous owners had lost it, given it away, pissed on it. How should he know?

"Unfortunately not."

Christian got up on his knees, sent Lars a questioning look before lifting the pickup from the Lou Reed album and putting on *Let it Bleed*. Lars waited for the falling Fender Rhodes–like guitar chords that opened "Gimme Shelter," but instead the room was filled with a raw guitar boogie.

"'Midnight Rambler'?"

Christian gave him a crooked smile.

Lars laughed. This was like being eighteen again. "You think *Beggars Banquet* is too monotonous? And then you play the most Banquet-like track on the entire album?"

Christian was sitting cross-legged again. The glow from his cigarette reflected in his eyes; his face disappeared in a cloud of smoke.

Lars got up. "You've got to hear this cool version of 'Midnight Rambler.' He stepped over the chairs and record covers on the floor, hunched down next to Christian and found *Get Yer Ya-Ya's Out*.

"This," he said, "this is fantastic. Brian Jones has just died. They are on their first tour with Mick Taylor. This is the Stones at their best, before Altamont. You've heard of Altamont, right?"

"Yeah, of course. We've got an old hippie for history. But

why do you listen to music from the sixties? You're not that old, are you?"

"Thanks a lot! When I was your age, it was all punk and new wave, but I gradually discovered that music from the late sixties and early seventies—the Stones and Zeppelin—had the same vibe. But I can still listen to Joy Division."

He took *Let it Bleed* off the turntable and put on *Get Yer Ya-Ya's Out*. Call and response, harmonica and audience, drums and guitar. Christian began to rock back and forth, moving his lips to Mick Jagger's vocals.

I'm talkin' 'bout the Midnight Rambler,
Ev'rybody got to go

Lars closed his eyes. "What's so cool about this version is the break in the middle section where the guitars battle and Jagger sounds like an old Indian chanting and doing a sun dance."

Christian raised his eyebrows but said nothing. They sat quietly, listened.

On the turntable, the band joined in with heavy beats at the end of each of Jagger's lines.

I'm called a hit-n-run raper, in anger…
Or just a knife-sharpened tippie-toe…
Or just a shoot-em-dead, brain-bell jangler
Everybody got to go

"You know this is about the Boston strangler, right?" Christian lit another Benson & Hedges. His eyes were shining.

Did he know. He had stumbled upon *Let it Bleed* when he entered the police academy, where they had studied case material on the Boston strangler. He'd gotten shivers down his spine when he discovered the connection.

"Do you think DeSalvo murdered all of them?" Christian asked.

Lars was lying on the floor, staring up at the worn, nicotine-yellow stucco on the ceiling. He didn't need to think back.

"Hmmm. Thirteen women murdered and sexually assaulted between 1962 and 1964. They varied in age, between nineteen and eighty-five, as far as I recall. Some were strangled with nylons, a couple were stabbed. One died of a heart attack when he grabbed her." Lars shrugged. "I don't know. There were details of the crime scenes that DeSalvo knew about, details that hadn't been released to the press. Still, there were massive differences in the way the murders were carried out. And there's the victims' ages. The young ones were very young, right? And at the other end of the scale, from their mid-fifties and up to eighty-five. It doesn't sound like the same killer. Anyway, a couple of months ago the Boston police linked DeSalvo's DNA to the last and youngest victim. So he did kill at least one of them."

"What about—what are they calling him? The Sandman?"

Lars didn't answer. He stared at the ceiling through the billowing cigarette smoke. "Midnight Rambler" lapsed into "Sympathy for the Devil." Talk about the devil.

"Why is a young guy like you interested in such morbi—"

Suddenly Maria was standing in the living room. Neither of them had heard the door open.

"What are you doing? I thought we were going to celebrate your graduation?" She stared dark-eyed at Christian.

Christian got to his feet, smoothed out his shirt. He sent her a wry smile.

"Didn't we agree to meet here?" He went to kiss her.

Maria twisted away from him. "I've been sitting in ZeZe with the same club soda for over an hour. You didn't take my calls?"

Lars held out a hand, wanting to help smooth things over.

Maria looked at him, and his hand fell. He too had crossed some kind of line—that much was clear. But which?

"Darling." In two long steps Christian was in the corner where Lars had placed the bouquet. "These are for you."

Maria tossed her head but leaned forward to smell the flowers. Her face softened. "Thanks." She gave him a little kiss. "Come on."

They disappeared into the kitchen. Lars was alone in the living room with his cigarettes, half a bottle of Ripasso, and his forty-year-old records.

Maybe it was just time for bed?

AUGUST 1944

THE KITCHEN WINDOW is open. The checkered curtains
hang motionless on the warm summer evening. Twilight
is descending, but a faint afterglow still clings to the sky. She's
sitting on the stool in the corner by the stove, her heart fluttering in her chest. He's making the crossing tonight. Father has
arranged for a boat to Sweden, agreed to the time and place
with one of the local fishermen. Jack will send word when she
can join him. Her head is light, she has a strange feeling in her
stomach, as though something inside her is going to break.

She gets up, runs a finger along the brass pipe that circles the
black cast-iron stove. She starts at a sudden vision of a deathly
pale face with blood running down the cheeks appearing in the
dim light in the corner behind the stove.

"Jack?" she whispers. Then she clenches her teeth. Jack is
hiding in the bottom of a fishing jolly in Øresund. In an hour,

he'll be safely in Sweden, and in a month or two she'll be in his arms again. En route to Stockholm or London, she'll be listening to the silly odes he sings to her eyes. She shakes her head. No one can find rhymes for grey-blue and green like Jack. He's the first person who has been able to name her imperfections without her getting upset.

She laughs to herself. A young girl's fantasy, dreamy as the last embers of the purple light that is fading in the evening sky.

She gets up, dances, hums. The curtains, the dish towel, the entire kitchen still smells of the basket of Danish meatballs she made for Father and Jack to take with them. From the living room, she hears the soothing clicks of Mother's knitting needles as they knock together with soporific regularity. Everything is calm; no evil can reach them. What does it matter that nations are crumbling all around them? As long as they have love, everything else is so profoundly trivial.

Outside, the garden gate opens and shuts. Could Father be returning already? The steps on the garden path are firm like Father's but more supple, rapid. A young man? Her heart leaps inside of her.

No, it can't be him. He would only come back if something went wrong. And not in full view of the entire neighbourhood. Her proud Jack would come crawling through the bushes at the back of the garden, in from the swamp where no one could see him.

At the front door the knocker strikes the brass fitting. In the living room, Mother gets up with some difficulty, puts down her knitting. Laura is on the kitchen floor, quiet as a mouse, wishing time would stand still.

Mother's voice whispers through the house. It's for her. Arno. Can she go out to the garden?

Like a sleepwalker she leaves the kitchen, dragging her feet in her worn clogs. Her gaze is lowered, her blood filled with ice.

She doesn't want to. And yet she must. She cannot. But she has to. Her mother has returned to her knitting and the soft chair in the corner.

He stands under the old copper beech, the one that is practically strangled by the climbing hydrangea. He calls her, standing there in his uniform with his hands folded in front of him. In his shiny boots, riding pants, and cap. Why is he here tonight? She doesn't want to be seen with a member of the HIPO Corps, not even if he is an old classmate.

He starts talking before she's even reached him. His voice is thick, his cheeks flushed. He talks about the two of them, about the future, about happiness and marriage, children. But she cannot — she will not — listen. Arno is pleading. He's down on his knees. But she doesn't notice Arno. And she knows he can sense it, that she's somewhere else.

And then, as he gets up, his eyes harden. The tears have left dark lines on his cheeks. The vision returns, the one she had inside the kitchen. Arno's face is ashen, the pale face of a corpse in the white night. And she does not want to but must look all the same. Arno's hands open to expose the horrible secret they hold.

Two eyes with sea-grey pupils, two eyes that — clear and alive and full of expectation and love — got drunk on the sight of her only a few hours earlier. She can still see herself, as Jack saw her, reflected in the dead iris and all the white that is now caked in blood with the severed nerve endings resting in Arno's trembling fingers.

Then the garden gate squeaks behind Arno. It's Father returning. He nods briefly at Arno, avoids her gaze. He walks up the garden path and disappears into the house.

Then she knows.

The scream comes from deep down inside, rises from her bosom. It tears upwards through flesh, sinew, and bones, passes the tiny life that grows beneath her navel. But when the blood-wind reaches the oral cavity, it has lost all strength.

Only a faint whimper passes her lips. The sound that comes from the mice in Father's trap behind the kitchen cupboard in the morning.

SUNDAY
JUNE 22

CHAPTER 41

LARS CLIMBED THE many stone steps in the rotunda to the second floor, down the narrow dark red corridor, and through the green door.

The department was empty. He hurried into his office and closed the door behind him with a silent click. It would soon be over. He would move on and the department could move on without him. Why Kim A had even bothered to file a complaint, he didn't understand. He threw his blazer over the back of the chair beside the door and sunk into his office chair.

One final case and it would all be over. He had been here for ten years. Now all he could think about was getting away.

He plunked his feet on the desk, considered lighting a cigarette despite the smoking ban. He still had a rapist to catch.

Lars forced himself to watch the DVDs from the surveillance cameras at Nørreport once more. Maybe there was a tiny detail, a microscopic clue in the way he moved, his clothes? Something which, seen with fresh eyes, could break the case? But there was no sudden flash of clarity. The lightning didn't strike.

The previous evening was still fresh in his mind. Cigarettes, wine, and records. The Stones. Maria's boyfriend smoking Benson & Hedges. Something about his hair and eyes, the way he acted. Lars got up and moved to the window.

The door to Maria's room had been closed when he got up. Christian's jacket hadn't been in the entrance. His shoes were gone too, but maybe he had taken them into Maria's room? He wasn't sure. Had he heard the front door open during the night? Not a sound came from her room. He hesitated outside her door, stood with his hand raised, trying to decide if he should knock. Then he had turned on his heels and gone into the shower.

At the department he could hear his colleagues walking back and forth down the corridor, collecting reports, chatting about suspects being brought in for questioning. But no one knocked on his door. The operation with Lene had not been his idea; in fact, he had been against it. But nothing stuck to someone like failure.

He glanced at the report from the operation on the table. Brown rings from countless cups of coffee covered the thin sheets in a psychedelic pattern. A photo of the bench in Hans Tavsens Park with white circles marking where Lene had leaned on the bench to get up. Had he seen Christian in a photo? In here? He quickly leafed through the sloping piles on the desk, moved on to the drawers, and pulled out a large pile of black and white photos. The sudden movement caused the photos to sail across the room in a perfect arc, landing with a dry rustling on the floor. A single sheet landed face-up, fluttering haphazardly before settling on the floor by his feet.

The photographs from Penthouse. Lene dancing with her arms above her head. And in the background, behind the very last person in the row at the bar. There wasn't much to see, but there was something about the hair, the way he stood. The eyes were pointed down; they weren't visible. But it certainly could be him.

He shook his head, threw the photograph on the table. What had he expected? Of course it wasn't Christian. But what if it was? He shuddered. Christian's interest in the Boston Strangler, the morbid Stones number. He glanced at the picture, then forced himself to look away. Was that really something you did these days? Talk about serial killers the first time you meet your girlfriend's dad?

Barely able to control his shaking fingers, he managed to slip a King's Blue out of the pack. To hell with the smoking ban. He opened the window, lit up, and took a drag. The nicotine unfurled in his lungs, raced through his bloodstream, hit his brain like a burst of projectiles. He removed a piece of tobacco from his lips, glanced at the picture again.

Then he picked it up, held it up with two fingers. The height and build were right. A figure dressed in black. Blond locks peeked out from underneath the hood.

He shot up suddenly, grabbed his jacket and flung open the door.

The open-plan office was filled with his colleagues now, several of whom he had worked with for longer than he cared to think about. None of them looked up. Frank and Lisa were sitting by Ulrik's secretary, speaking in low voices. Toke was nowhere to be seen.

He hurried toward the green door, and ran down the corridor. He practically barged into Sanne at the foot of the stairs.

Only a quick stop and an adroit sidestep on her part saved them from colliding.

"Hi Lars. I've been thinking about calling..." Her voice trailed off.

Lars fidgeted with the railing. "I'm the one...Thanks for dinner. The other night, I mean." He went quiet. *Pull yourself together.* "It was nice. Maria had a lovely evening." *Was it Martin, her boyfriend was called?* Images of doing the dishes, the silent cab ride home with Maria appeared in his mind's eye. He clenched his fist.

"Listen, I'm sorry about..." Sanne began. "The complaint and—"

"I'm leaving anyway." He shrugged. "Where are you going? You seem like you're in a hurry."

"Out to question a witness. And you?"

"I'm just swinging by Forensics and then I'm going out to Hellerup." Lars took a step down the stairs, hesitated. "It's just an idea I had."

"We could drive together? I'm going to Gentofte."

"Do you have a car?" A tingling feeling ran down his neck and into the pit of his stomach.

Sanne handed him a set of keys.

"Here. My Fiat 500 is in the parking garage. Do you want to head down and start it up?"

Sanne leapt up the stairs. Lars gazed after her. For a brief moment, his eyes followed her slender legs, her tight buttocks. Then he continued through the door to the rotunda, cut across to the exit, and rounded the corner to Hambrosgade.

The white Fiat 500 was well hidden behind a row of rundown and dirty patrol cars. It was surprisingly clean inside. Lars put the key in the ignition, eased down on the clutch, and put the car into gear. Then he pulled up by the stairwell, stopped, and opened the door to the passenger side just as Sanne came rushing down.

"Stress will kill you, you know." He pushed the gas pedal and the car jumped forward.

Sanne laughed, slammed the door shut, and fastened her seat belt. They drove out on Hambrosgade, then took a left down H. C. Andersens Boulevard. She pulled out a pile of papers from her purse, flipping them back and forth.

"I'll never learn to keep track of all the streets here," she said. Then: "There. Brogårdsvej."

"Is this about the black prostitute?" Lars drove past City Hall. "I read about it in the papers."

"Yeah, the guy who reported it has been interviewed, but I'd like to . . ." She broke off. "It's unbelievable. No one saw anything. But when their peace and quiet is disturbed because she's standing in the street, screaming in pain and horror, then they call to get her carted off."

Lars zigzagged through the traffic out of the city, continued along Gyldenløvsgade. "Hey, is it all right if we swing by my place first? There's just something I need to pick up." The sun glistened on the waves on the string of lakes marking the border of the inner city. Sanne nodded.

"Sorry, I interrupted," he said. "Was that your guy?"

"It looks like it. Frelsén is quite certain. Same incision, same MO. Enucleation, removal of the eyeball. Well, except that she got away. What do you need to do?"

"Oh, there's just a couple of things I need to check."

Lars turned right on Lundtoftegade. At Folmer Bendtsens Plads he pulled up opposite the elevated railway.

"I'll be back in two minutes."

Up in the apartment he went into the bathroom, squatted down, and pulled out an evidence bag from his inside pocket. He opened the garbage can with a pen and rummaged through the Kleenex, hairballs, and toothpaste tube. There it was, half hidden by a mascara box. Pale yellow and wrinkled, tied in a knot. He knew he had no right to do this. His eyes quickly flickered, then he poked the pen inside and lifted the used condom into the brown paper bag.

When he came down to the car, she was leaning against the window, staring at the dashboard. He climbed in.

"Is something the matter?" he said.

Sanne didn't answer; she was somewhere else. She jumped when he slammed the door.

"What?"

"You look like something's wrong."

"It's—" Sanne closed her eyes. "I made a fool of myself yesterday. Ulrik...Oh, never mind." She looked out the window. Lars gave her a quick glance. Then he turned the key and started the engine.

CHAPTER 42

FRELSÉN HAD HIS legs up on the table. His red-and-purple-striped socks led to a pair of worn, brown leather shoes. Some loose sheets of paper were strewn across the floor. His gold-framed glasses were resting on his forehead, and his eyes were closed.

Lars raised his hand to knock on the open door.

"It's called meditation." The forensic pathologist kept his eyes closed, his mouth hardly moved. "And you don't disturb someone who's meditating. Sit down in the corner chair; I'll be finished soon."

Lars looked around the narrow office. The window at the end had a view of the parking lot behind the main building of Rigshospitalet. The enormous desk rested against the wall on the right; bookshelves, groaning under the weight of thick volumes, lined the wall on the left. Here, in the corner by the door, Lars found a chair, moved the reports and what looked like a complete set of *The American Journal of Forensic Medicine and Pathology* onto the floor, and settled in.

A few minutes later Frelsén's deep, steady breathing quickened. His eyelashes flickered; one leg fell to the floor.

"Okay, I'm back." The forensic pathologist opened his eyes; the grey pupils were staring intently at him.

Lars took the evidence bag out of his inside pocket. "I'd like you to do a quick DNA test. Quick as in: I need the results today."

Frelsén looked at the bag, narrowed his eyes. "You know it has to go down to Forensic Genetics. They can do a rush analysis in twenty-four hours. That's going to cost you sixty thousand kroner. Is that in your budget?"

Lars held out the bag for Frelsén. "I was thinking that maybe you could do a little magic—just you."

Frelsén took the bag, looked inside. "And why, may I ask, is it not going through the usual channels?"

"Let's just say, it's a...feeling."

"Unofficially, then"—Frelsén smacked his lips—"I can look at it and have something ready by the afternoon. But it can't be used as evidence; a proper analysis is needed for that. All the same, I can point to a suspect—and I guess that's what you're looking for?" The forensic pathologist's inquiring look was sharp as a scalpel.

Gentofte. 24 Brogårdsvej. Small trees and large bushes made a whitewashed house with black glazed roof tiles nearly invisible from the road. Sanne was halfway up the driveway before Lars had gotten out of the car. She took the stairs up to the front door in two steps and knocked. A man in his sixties appeared. His hair was silvery-white, his teeth gleaming against his tanned face. His bare feet were in light brown loafers.

"Yes?"

"Police, Mr. Lund." Sanne showed him her badge. "Sanne Bissen. This is my colleague Lars Winkler." Lars came up the stairs behind her. "Would you mind if we asked you a few questions?"

At the word "police," the open, smiling face transformed to scowling mistrust.

"What's this concerning?" He closed the door a few milli-metres, probably without realizing it. Lars prepared to move his foot inside.

"Two nights ago, at 2:10 a.m., you called emergency servi-ces and said"— Sanne pulled out the sheet—"'There's a Negro whore screaming in the middle of the road right outside my house.' You were quite worked up."

"Oh, that." His shoulders dropped a little. The smile returned. "Yes, your colleagues have already been out. It's rare for something so dramatic to happen out here. And it was in the newspaper too, so—"

"Can you tell us exactly what happened, sir?" Lars inter-rupted. "How did you discover her?"

Lund took a step back. "Come inside."

They dried their shoes on the mat and stepped inside. A beechwood staircase wound up to the second floor on the left side. The steps were worn in the middle. A long carpet led them through the entrance toward the living room. Lund waved them in.

The living room was a good size and parallel to the road. There were several thick rugs on the floor and a built-in book-case covered one wall. A row of hunting trophies hung between the three-light windows on the opposite side of the room. Lund followed Lars's gaze.

"They're not mine," he said. "They're my father-in-law's. But they kind of suit the house, don't you think?"

Lars nodded. Sanne stood with her back to the window.

"Can you tell us exactly what happened when you spotted the girl, Mr. Lund?"

"Yes, well, she was difficult to ignore. I was sitting in that armchair there, reading, listening to music. Mahler, if I remember correctly. The girl had a voice that cut straight through both walls and the orchestra."

Lars looked out the window. "The road isn't visible from here?" Bushes and trees blocked the view.

"Not from that window, but here..." Lund went to the very back window. "A little bit of the road is visible through the branches."

Lars and Sanne moved behind him. Sure enough, a good stretch of Brogårdsvej was actually visible from there.

"Of course it was dark and you couldn't see who was standing in the shadows," Lund continued. "I wasn't going to run outside and get attacked. And your colleagues arrived quite quickly."

"There's a police station up the road," Lars explained to Sanne, pointing his thumb over his shoulder. "And Gentofte hospital is only several hundred metres away. The ambulance must have been here shortly after?"

Lund nodded. "Within five minutes. I checked my watch."

"You stay up late, Mr. Lund?"

"When you get to be my age, it can be difficult to fall asleep." Lund smiled. "So a cup of tea and a good book helps. And of course the music doesn't bother anyone out here."

Lars nodded, scanning the bookcase. Classics, book-club purchases from the 1970s.

"What are you reading, Mr Lund?" Just then, he spotted the low table by the armchair, where a thick novel lay half-covered by a newspaper. Lund followed his gaze.

"*Crime and Punishment*, Dostoyevsky. The old Russian classics ought to be reread once in a while. After that it's *Fathers and Sons*. You know Turgenev, of course?" Lars didn't, but he tried smiling anyway.

"So there's nothing else? Nothing happened that night, nothing unusual?"

Lund shook his head. "I went to bed, it must have been around 11:00 p.m. I woke up again a little past one. Then I came downstairs and made tea and read. It wasn't long before the young girl started shouting." He adjusted the book. "Before that, I neither saw nor heard anything. I was listening to music."

Sanne nodded. "Thank you, Mr. Lund. We may return later."

Lars followed them to the entrance hall. On the way out the door he turned around. "Do you have any children, Mr. Lund?"

Lund looked a little taken aback. "Two daughters. Why do you ask?"

"Fathers and Sons, Mr. Lund. Fathers and Sons."

Lund's eyes flickered briefly. "We've all had a father, Detective."

CHAPTER 43

SANNE ROLLED DOWN the window. The smell of internal combustion engines and lilacs filled the car. People were strolling the gardens on Ole Olsens Allé. The sky was high and deep into summer.

Lars parked by the curb. An old elder tree leaned over the fence. Parked in front of them was an old roadster, an aubergine-coloured MG Austin-Healey Sprite. Lars opened the door and climbed out. A great tit flew out from the low branches, circled over the car, and squawked.

"Somebody's grumpy." Lars watched the bird fly away. "Do you want to come?"

"Yeah, why not?" Sanne climbed out.

A large box-like red-brick house with enormous windows towered at the bottom of the open garden. The window surfaces reflected the bright sunlight.

"Functionalism," Sanne said. "Looks like Arne Jacobsen."

"Really?" Lars turned halfway around on the way down the garden path to face her. Then they were at the door and he rang the bell. Møller, the door read. Ditlev, Margit, and Christian.

Thirty seconds passed. Dawdling steps dragged through the house.

Christian opened the door.

"Lars," he said. "Thanks for the other night." He was drying his hair with a green towel. "What are you doing here?"

"Hi Christian. This is my colleague, Sanne Bissen. Do you mind if we come in for a moment? Are your parents home?"

"Come on in." Christian motioned with his hand, stepped aside so they could enter. "Dad's at the clinic. Mom ... I don't actually know. Maybe she's out shopping? I was in the cellar." He smiled, then looked down.

"But the car out there—" Lars pointed over his shoulder.

"Oh, that's mine." Christian closed the door behind them. "Would you like anything?"

Lars shook his head, looked around. A staircase led upstairs. Doors opened up to the rest of the house. A large modern painting filled the entire wall to their right. Black and brown brush strokes, circles dancing across a white canvas.

"No thanks, just a couple of questions. We'll be off shortly."

"Any way that I can help."

Lars pulled the photo out of his jacket pocket. He'd had to fold it up and was doing his best to smooth it out again. He hadn't had time to consider how to tackle this. He'd just have to take the plunge.

"This picture was taken at Penthouse on Friday night. Can you confirm that that's you standing at the end of the bar?" He pointed at the figure, half hidden behind someone's back. Sanne leaned against the door frame, followed their conversation with an uninterested expression. But her eyes flicked from one to the other in time with their exchange.

Christian didn't take long. "Well, it is a little difficult to see, but I was there that night. I had just aced my Danish exam and I was celebrating." He nodded. "That must be me. Is that the girl who got raped?" He pointed at Lene.

"That's Lene, an officer-in-training. She was assaulted later that same night." He looked Christian in the eye. The boy stared back, his gaze expressionless. "But no, she wasn't the one who got raped. Can you remember when you left?"

"It must have been..." Christian thought about it. "It was late and I'd had a lot to drink. Around 1:30 a.m., I think. Maybe a little later."

Lars folded the picture, put it back in his inside pocket.

"Were you there with someone? Is there anyone who can verify that you left at one thirty?"

"Unfortunately not." He gave them a wry smile. "I like going out on my own."

"And your parents? Were they up when you came home?"

Christian shook his head. "Is this where I need to call a lawyer?" His smile broadened. Lars's cell buzzed in his pocket. He held Christian's gaze and took the call.

"Frelsén here. I'll spare you the details. You'd like to know if the DNA profile matches Stine Bang and Louise Jørgensen's rapist?"

"Yes."

Frelsén paused. "Unfortunately not."

"And Caroline?"

"Negative again. I'll send it over to Forensics immediately. We need to analyze the semen properly, of course, but that won't change anything. He's not the one you're looking for."

Lars thanked Frelsén, ended the call, and stuffed the phone back into his pocket.

"Good news?" Christian asked.

"Actually, yes." He shook Christian's hand. "Well, that was everything. Thanks for your help. And sorry for disturbing you. We may ask you to come into the station to look at some more pictures."

"If I can help..."

Lars nodded at Sanne. They could leave.

"Oh, by the way," Christian said. "I've invited Maria out here for dinner tonight. I hope you didn't have other plans?"

"No, that's fine. Do you know where she is now?"

"I'm sorry. I haven't seen her since last night." He wiped the back of his neck with the towel. "It's awful about her friend."

"Yes." Lars could picture Caroline's face. Then he forced himself to move. "We have to get going. Come on, Sanne."

The long line of cars was winding its way down Lyngbyvejen, racing to get home from work. It was summer, a time of rolled-up sleeves, rolled-down windows, and radios blasting through the air. Lars was back behind the wheel, following the rhythm of rush hour. He had been so certain. Christian's behaviour had been so bizarre the previous night. The blond hair and the blue eyes. And he had been at Penthouse on at least one of the nights. Everything had added up. But maybe a little too well? He passed a bronze Grand Vitara and slipped into the right lane. He started to sweat.

"What do you think?" Sanne said, observing his profile.

"What do I think?" Had she said something, had he missed something? Then he understood. "Oh, about Lund? It's your case."

"Come on, you're the experienced officer here. You know the neighbourhood."

On the radio, Chris Isaak crooned his way through "Wicked Game."

"Well, I'm afraid it didn't yield very much. He hadn't seen or heard anything."

Sanne raised an eyebrow.

"Most people get nervous, when the police come knocking," he continued. "They wonder what they've done: did they forget about a parking ticket, or run a red light? Is the butt from the joint they smoked yesterday still lying in the ashtray?"

Sanne laughed. "I can't really imagine Lund smoking pot."

"You'd be surprised when you discover how widespread it is. But that was just an example." He pulled out the cigarette pack, squeezed it. Only one left. He'd better wait. "I just don't think he had anything to do with the abduction and that operation—what did you call it?"

"Enucleation."

"Yeah, that's the one. The guy you're looking for is a loner. He's probably clashed with the law before, maybe arson or rape..."

"So the same profile you're chasing?"

"Yes, more or less." They both fell silent as they drove under the S-train bridge by Ryparken Station. Sanne pulled her cell out of her purse, disappeared into the tiny screen. Lars glanced at the phone.

"What are you doing?"

"Facebook. I just have to..." She went quiet. The steady stream of music from the radio continued above the engine noise, the rumbling of the tires. She put down the phone and stared into space.

"What's wrong?" he said.

She put the phone back into her purse and looked away.

"It was a message from one of my old colleagues in Kolding. She's asking if I know you—if I know what's going on."

Lars's shoulders suddenly went heavy. "It's not hard to guess where that story came from."

They had reached Hans Knudsens Plads when Sanne's cell rung. Allan was excited, but his words were lost in all the noise from the car.

"What was it?" Lars asked after she'd hung up. Sanne bit her lip and looked out the window.

"Elvir Seferi, one of the guys who gave the Bukoshi brothers an alibi—it turned out to be false. Allan has checked up on him."

Lars put the car in gear and crossed the intersection of Jagtvej and Lyngbyvej at Vibenshus.

"In February there was a break-in at a dental clinic in Valby," Sanne continued. "There was a single suspect."

"Elvir Se—?"

"Seferi, yes. During the break-in, several litres of glutaraldehyde were stolen. Dentists apparently use it for cleaning their instruments."

"Was he charged?"

"No, Meriton Bukoshi gave him an alibi and there was no physical evidence. Also—" Sanne pushed her hair behind her ear. "Allan has also discovered what Elvir did for a living before he fled—Kosovo, I mean."

Lars didn't say anything, waiting for her to continue.

"He was a veterinary surgeon."

CHAPTER 44

MARIA STOOD WITH her hand on the garden gate. It was a warm evening, and the thin cardigan made the sweat trickle under her arms. Or was it the thought of meeting Christian's parents? The evening sun drew gold lines across the pale blue sky. There was an almost imperceptible smell of salt in the breeze that blew in from Øresund.

Christian had pestered her for days. It was almost getting embarrassing, the way she'd had to resist. But it was far too early. She didn't even know what she wanted herself. That was probably the reason she had gotten upset when she found him at home with Dad.

The air was heavy with lilacs. Maria leaned her head back, breathed in the sweet smell of flowers mixed with the fresh-cut grass. Her blood was racing, her body sang.

She straightened her hair, swallowed, then pushed down

the handle on the garden gate.

Christian's parents lived in an enormous red-brick house covered by layers of green ivy and with deep red flowers along one wall. The house was on Ole Olsens Allé, a stone's throw from Gentofte Hospital.

A ghostly figure moved behind one of the enormous windows, then withdrew at the exact moment she spotted it. Maria was sweating again. The small bouquet of flowers in her hand, a present for the hostess, Christian's mom, suddenly looked like she'd picked it up from the garbage back home at her father's.

Christian opened the door before she could ring the bell. He looked good as usual in his fitted jeans and loose white shirt. His hair was carelessly tousled. He winked at her, pulled her inside, and gave her a deep kiss.

"Mom, Dad. Maria's here."

She blushed. Her stomach refused to settle. She tugged at his shirt to get him to stop, but he just laughed, letting his lips brush her cheek. He placed an arm around the small of her back and led her into the house. She heard footsteps on the second floor.

"Welcome." His mom's voice was no more than a whisper, just as thin as the grey cardigan over her shoulders. The top button nearly reached her chin. She rubbed her hands together before extending her right arm.

Maria shook her hand: a pale, dry echo of a handshake.

"This is my mom, Margit." Hidden behind her back, Christian's hand moved down to squeeze her buttock. The contact sent electricity pulsing through her.

"Thanks for inviting me." She held out the flowers, bit her lip. A thin smile creased Margit's face, then it was gone.

Christian laughed. He held her arm firmly, spun her around. "And this is Ditlev."

Ditlev came down the stairs in a blue-and-white-striped

shirt and worn jeans. There was a hint of a dark red silk cravat around his neck. His prominent forehead was wrinkled and tanned from too much sun; his eyes hard and hungry.

"Well, what do you know?" He looked her up and down. "The boy has inherited his father's good taste." He clicked his tongue. "Welcome. Time for us to have a drink."

On the terrace a small table was set with glasses, bowls of nuts, and a bottle of rosé in a wine bucket. The ice cubes sparkled in the sun. Patches of sweat were spreading under Maria's arms. Now she couldn't take off her cardigan. Her heart was racing.

Ditlev asked Christian to open the wine and pour it.

"My son tells me your dad is in the police. Homicide?"

Maria nodded.

"Fascinating job. Should maybe be better paid?" Ditlev winked.

"Stop it, Dad." Christian placed a glass each in front of Maria and Ditlev, then went back to pour wine for himself and his mom. Panic set in every time Christian was more than a few steps away. She held her arms by her side, tried keeping her body still. She was trembling uncontrollably.

Margit said nothing, while Ditlev's sticky gaze practically devoured her.

Christian's dad laughed, drank wine, and ate nuts in a steady stream as he talked.

"The boy has alway been morbidly fascinated by police work. Well, you bloody have." He raised his voice when Christian tried to protest. Ditlev leaned over the table, placing his entire weight on his elbow. The teakwood tabletop creaked beneath him as he lowered his voice. "He couldn't have been more than eleven or twelve when he came home and announced that we had a killer in the neighbourhood. He had found a bone in someone's garden over by—Søbredden, isn't that right?"

Christian turned his back to them. Why was he making her sit alone with them?

"Did you ever manage to show the bone to the police?" Ditlev laughed. "Okay, he's angry now. Never mind him. I'm sure we can have a good time anyway." He smiled invitingly. "Now where were we? The bone, yes. We had to spend several days convincing him that it was from a dog. Crazy kid. Cheers." He took a drink, laughed.

Margit sipped from her glass, toyed with the hem of her skirt. "I think dinner's ready now."

They ate inside. It was easier to talk in there, undisturbed, as Ditlev put it. Margit drifted back and forth between the living room and the kitchen, carrying in carafes of water and various delicacies that Ditlev insisted Maria try. Neither Ditlev nor Christian seemed to take further notice of Christian's mom. A creature without body, a spirit floating around the table without quite being let into the circle. Christian didn't say much. It was Ditlev who kept the conversation going, offering Maria new dishes, more wine.

Before dessert he got up. "Now let's have a proper glass of wine. I'll just run down to the cellar."

Margit got up, began collecting the plates.

"Let me help." Maria grabbed a tray and the side plates. Margit opened her mouth. She mumbled something unintelligible. Maria figured it was an appeal for her to stay seated, but she insisted on helping her clear the table. Christian's eyes bore into her back. Was he angry that she was helping out? It didn't make any sense. Everything was so different here.

The kitchen was a lavish space with brightly glazed floor tiles, inch-thick beechwood tabletops, and glass cabinets on every wall. Ditlev had purchased the enormous porcelain sink in France, Christian had told her. Above the sink was a gigantic window with a view of the garden, vibrant and enchanting in the twilight. She placed the tray and plates on the counter, turned on the water, leaned over the sink, and started rinsing.

The splashing water drowned out all other sound: the low, classical music in the background, engine noise from the road, Margit and Christian exchanging monosyllables in the living room. She rinsed gravy and food scraps into the sink, where they accumulated into a brown mush around the drain.

Suddenly she sensed something right behind her, then felt someone's hot, heavy breath on her neck. She only managed a half turn before greedy hands grabbed her breasts.

"Christian?" she whispered.

"Christian? He doesn't have the balls for this!" The voice seethed with arousal. A hand moved over her stomach, buried itself into her skirt.

Nausea rose up in her throat. She stood petrified against the porcelain sink while Ditlev's greasy cauliflower nose chafed her neck. A section of the living room reflected in the dark window. She didn't dare say anything; she hardly took a breath. Where was everyone?

Just then, Christian stepped into the kitchen. Her eyes widened in a silent plea for help. He stopped in the doorway when he spotted them. His eyes were empty. A chill sent icy knives through her.

Margit appeared behind him with her arms full. She looked down at the floor, tripped through the kitchen, and put the plates down on the table next to her husband and Maria.

"Are we having coffee with dessert?" she asked, and then was on her way out again.

Ditlev let go of her. He stroked his greasy hair back with one hand, adjusted his fly with the other. A single drop of saliva bubbled in the corner of his mouth. He gave her a lecherous look, then turned his back to her and walked over to his son, patting him on the shoulder.

"I found us a bottle of Pomerol, 2001. Chateau l'Évangile."

Christian didn't look at her; he just followed his dad into the living room without a word.

CHAPTER 45

I'M JUST GOING to buy some cigarettes." Lars got out, handed her the keys. "It will only take a minute."

Sanne nodded, locked the car. Lars ran into the corner store at number 4. It was the young guy behind the counter again.

"Two twenty packs of King's Blue?" he asked. The pimples quivered on his chin.

Lars nodded. Then he thought about the empty cupboards upstairs. "Hey, do you sell wine?"

"Sure, but don't you think you should go to Føtex instead? If she's the one you're taking upstairs, I don't think our booze is good enough." He laughed.

Lars's gaze wandered. Sanne stood on the sidewalk, waved at him.

"That's not—oh, to hell with it. Give me the best bottle you've got."

"Sure. This one, I guess." The guy placed a bottle on the counter next to the two packs of cigarettes. Lars paid without looking at the label.

Sanne raised an eyebrow when he came out of the store. "Are we having wine?"

"If you feel like it. I can take your car in tomorrow." His cheeks warmed. "I didn't mean—"

She laughed. He liked it when she laughed.

"Just one glass," she said.

They walked up the stairs. Lars put the key in the lock, said a little prayer that Maria hadn't left the apartment in a state of disaster, and then turned around.

"I have literally just moved in," he apologized, but it didn't look like Maria had left behind a big mess. Both the bathroom and the kitchen looked presentable.

Sanne sat down on the sofa, while Lars fetched two glasses from the kitchen and opened the bottle of wine. Sanne looked around the living room.

"How's it going?" she asked. "With the divorce, I mean?"

"Well, we speak as little as possible. It's best like that."

"And Ulrik?"

"I avoid him." He poured them both a glass. He considered for a moment whether he should tell her about the problems selling the house. But there were only a few subjects more boring than property sales and equity. Instead, he raised his glass.

"Cheers."

"Cheers." Sanne grimaced as she took a sip. "Well, it's not exactly a Chateau L'Évangile."

"A what?"

"Chateau l'Évangile. A wine from Pomerol, Bordeaux. It's close to Pétrus. Do you know it?"

Lars shook his head. Sanne took another sip.

"It's not that bad," she said. Then she burst out laughing.

"Are you some kind of wine expert?"

"Martin would certainly like to be. He's always reading about it on the Internet. But I haven't tried that one. The name just stuck." She dried her eyes, put the glass down, and looked at him. "Just let me know if you don't want to talk about it. About the complaint."

Lars shrugged. "Ask away."

"Well, I don't understand...you and Ulrik..." She hesitated. "You're—adversaries. But what's the deal with this complaint? Kim A doesn't have anything to do with you and Ulrik, does he?"

Lars was biting his cheek, thinking. The alcohol burned in his mouth.

"It's a long story. It goes back nearly twenty years."

Sanne looked at him, waited. He sighed.

"In 1993, both Ulrik and I had graduated from the police academy and started probationer duty at Station One. On May 18, after the referendum on the Maastricht Treaty for the European Community, we were on our usual patrol downtown. This was early in the evening, mind you, before our colleagues fired into the demonstration. As the evening wore on we realized it was getting more and more violent on Nørrebro, but we were told to keep to this side of the lakes, by the intersection at Frederiksborggade and Nørre Farimagsgade. Just when the fighting was at its worst, a riot police officer, Kim A, comes running toward us with someone in handcuffs. He opens the door, practically throws the young guy into the back, and starts searching him and swearing at him, saying all sorts of nasty things. The other guy is pretty wound up too and starts shouting back. Ulrik tries to calm them down. Kim A starts pushing the guy and he pushes back. All of a sudden, Kim A punches him in the stomach. He doubles up right there in the back seat, gasping for air. I looked at Kim A in the rear-view mirror and told him that if he laid another hand on him, I'd drive us straight to the station and report him for assault. You should have seen his face. Then Ulrik asked what the guy was being arrested for. Kim A mumbled something, but kept staring at me in the rearview mirror."

"Then what happened?"

"He let the guy go. And then he just sat there. For two minutes, staring me down. After that he got out of the car and left, out toward Nørrebro." Lars shrugged. "For a few months, he tried to get the better of me. But Ulrik had seen everything, so he risked being reported for assault. There's been bad blood ever since. This is the first time Kim A's worked on an investigation that I'm leading. It was bound to go wrong. On the other hand, you would think that after nearly twenty years..."

Sanne was looking out the window. "In Kolding, some of the usual suspects occasionally get a once-over in a patrol car. Not everyone does it—I have never taken part. But I know it happens. And generally, they deserve it."

"Maybe I see it from a different perspective."

"What do you mean?"

Lars hesitated. Sooner or later she would find out. She might as well hear it from him. "Before I joined the force, when I was in high school, I was a punk. This was just at the beginning of the squatter's movement. I helped occupy a few houses."

The glass rattled as Sanne set it down on the table.

"Easy." He put his hands up, tried laughing. "I haven't thrown stones or dropped toilets out of windows or anything."

She looked him in the eyes, held his gaze for a long time. "Tell me."

It was in the 1980s. The nuclear threat, the economical ruptures following the oil crisis in the 1970s, youth unemployment.

There was nothing to do if you couldn't quite bring yourself to conform. Years earlier, the first punks had proven that it was possible to start a movement, create your own scene. It started out on Nørrebro, before Lars was old enough to participate. First an abandoned bread factory, then a derelict, empty factory that in happier days had produced bicycle tires — he'd read about the movement in the papers, heard it on the radio. His mom encouraged him to participate, to rebel. But he had no ideology, no political conscience, only a vague need for something to happen, though he did not know what. It was more out of defiance that he was attracted to the activity and vibe around the young punks and squatters. Something was happening here; people were trying to get an alternative scene going, something untainted by the adults' eternal ideological trench warfare. There was colour, life, parties. There was no violence back then either, nobody threw stones or Molotov cocktails. It was just a group of rootless kids who wanted something different. And then there was the music: wild and intense; hard, fast, and frenetic. Beautiful as a rock slide and filled with the poetry of destruction. It tore away the dust and the haze that numbed the senses, liberated the mind and exposed the bleeding flesh. He had heard the punk band Sods on the radio, and another that called themselves Bollocks. And then there was Ballet Mécanique. And Kliché.

At the end of October 1981, he read about a demonstration for a youth house. It was a dark day. Heavy grey clouds were suspended above the flatbed truck that was being used as a makeshift stage. It looked so small in front of the enormous City Hall. A trio with short hair and leather jackets was playing hardcore punk. The wind hurled the sounds back and forth across the large open square. A number 6 bus pulled into the square from Vesterbrogade, and the passengers were staring thunderstruck at the motley crowd shuddering in front of City

Hall. It had been announced that the demonstrators would walk to Nørrebro, but when the punk band finished their set, instructions were shouted into megaphones for people to follow those in the front. The crowd started moving, picking up speed, and suddenly everyone sprinted down Vesterbrogade. The police officers assigned to monitor the demonstration were caught completely off guard; they couldn't keep up. Several hundred people tore down one of the widest and busiest streets in Copenhagen.

Lars found himself more or less in the middle of the crowd, his legs pumping. He was filled with a total sense of freedom. Everything inside him was bursting with the knowledge that he was doing something, that he was a part of something. The leaders of the demonstration had secretly planned for the demonstration to occupy the old shelter for the homeless, Abel Cathrines Stiftelse, on Abel Cathrines Gade. They'd even arranged to have ladders there so people could climb in through the second-storey windows. That night was a party, an intoxicating collective of colours, music, and people. Lars blissfully jumped from group to group, had a few drinks here, took a drag on a joint there. Suddenly he found himself in the corner of a small room with a pretty redhead. The music and the voices faded into dull blasts from a distant world. They kissed hard and awkwardly, their hands wandering over each other's clothes. But the restless energy tore him away, kept him moving aimlessly around the building, then out into the neon-illuminated night. Whatever happened to the girl, he never found out; he never saw her again. But he frequently returned to the occupied house to see concerts by ADS and Under For.

Lars stubbed out his King's in the ashtray, followed the smoke that rose up toward the ceiling in lazy billows. Outside the twilight was about to lapse into night.

Sanne was silent, her face was hidden in the shadows.

"The point," he said, trying to catch her eyes, "is that during the entire occupation there was not a single confrontation with the police and everyone left the building voluntarily several months later. But to this day there's still bad blood between the police and the squatters."

Sanne blinked, drank a little of her wine. It was clear that she had difficulty understanding him, but she tried.

"Does Kim A know about all of this?"

"I don't know." Lars shook his head. "But it wouldn't surprise me if he had ploughed through all the records to find something on me."

Sanne nodded, rubbing her temples. "But if you didn't do anything then surely you're not in the police records?"

He smiled indulgently.

Sanne tried to laugh. "A police officer with a past as an anarchist? There's a first for everything."

"Anarchist? I was a punk and a bit on the fringes when it all began," he said. "At night, I went home to my mom and did my homework. That's not very rebellious, is it? But I'm glad you can laugh at it." He took his glass, emptied it, and grabbed the bottle.

"More Chateau l'Évangile?"

"You're out of your mind." She laughed, held out her glass. "How did you end up joining the police then?"

Lars poured more wine for both of them, took his glass, and swirled it around.

"Yes, why did I? After the occupation of the building called Allotria—you've heard about that, right?"

Sanne nodded. "I was born that year, but of course I've heard about it. Squatters digging a tunnel under the street and leaving the house under the very boots of our colleagues."

Lars shook his head, smiled. "Well, everything started getting more violent, then. You've heard about toilets being thrown

284

at the police from the windows of occupied buildings, Molotov cocktails...When that started, I pulled out. I'd started playing music and spent a lot of time on that." Lars took an almost imperceptible pause. He'd revealed enough already; better to slam the door shut now. "I moved to New York, lived with my dad for a year—went to eleventh grade in a high school over there. I came home, was called to the conscription board when I finished high school and hoped I'd get out of the army. But there was really no way of getting around it."

"You could have been a conscientious objector?"

"That's what my mom said too. She was furious. But I was tired of the alternative scene. I was way too stoned all the time. So the military became an easy way out, a clean break. And when I'd completed my service, a job with the police didn't seem like such a big leap."

Sanne nodded, pulled her feet up under her, and looked at him above her glass. "Have you got a spare cigarette?"

Lars lit her cigarette. The ember pulsated in the darkness between them, lit up her eyes. Her pupils were large, burning into his.

Outside, an S-train zipped into the station. Farther away, the cars roared down Nørrebrogade. The Ring Café was open now; they could hear shouting and bottles clattering. They sat close on the low sofa.

"What was that about work? In the car..."

Sanne shook her head, put a finger to her lip. "Shh. Not now."

He looked at her, almost as if in a trance. Her face drew closer. The cigarette smoke rose from her hand. The front door opened in the hallway below, and they heard steps shuffling on the staircase. Dark eyes with a little too much makeup burned into his; her tongue carefully slipped out and wet her lip. He was just about to say something, when her lips touched his. A flash of skin and light.

His head began dancing in triple time. He opened his mouth, kissed her back, and closed his eyes.

Then the door slammed in the hall, and a sobbing filled the apartment. Sanne shot back on the sofa, dropping the cigarette. They both dove to the floor, searching for it. Maria stepped into the living room, her face grimy from smudged makeup. She was shaking.

"Maria, what happened?" He was up, his arms around her before the sentence was finished. Sanne had found the cigarette and got back on the sofa, pushing her hair back. Maria snuggled up to him.

"What happened?" he asked again.

Maria shook her head. "Just hold me, Dad."

He held her shivering body close. He could still taste the kiss on his lips. Sweet. Light.

Sanne got up, picked up her purse from the floor, and checked its contents with her fidgeting fingers.

"Well, I've got to—" She nodded at them and slipped toward the entrance.

"See you tomorrow," he shouted after her. Then the door slammed, and he was left with his daughter in his arms.

A few minutes passed. Neither of them said anything. Then he craned his neck back, attempted to lift her face so he could see her eyes.

"Weren't you supposed to be at Christian's?"

Maria's shoulders twitched. Tears mixed with snot. He rocked her back and forth until she calmed down. Then he moved her over to the sofa and sat down beside her. He stroked her hair.

"There now, dry your eyes. What's the matter?"

Maria shook her head and wiped her nose. Lars got up to fetch some paper towels. When he came back, she was staring at the two half-empty glasses. She looked up at him.

"What have the two of you been up to?"

"Police stuff." He handed her the paper towels.

"And red wine? Honestly, Dad."

He shook his head. "It's not good for a teenage daughter to know everything."

CHAPTER 46

THE DUTY OFFICER called just as Sanne stepped out of the entrance to Lars's building. She switched off her cell and threw it in on the passenger seat. She climbed into the car without even thinking about the couple of glasses of wine she'd had. She put the siren on the roof and drove off.

Now she was crawling through shrubbery and down the bluff toward the crude tent at the edge of the small lake in the middle of Østre Anlæg Park. The white concrete walls of the National Gallery of Denmark rose up on her left. A group of police officers stood around the tent at the water's edge, congregated by a single yellow cone of light. One of the police generators sputtered in the darkness, drowning out the faint drone of traffic on Øster Voldgade and Sølvgade.

Ulrik turned as she arrived. He still hadn't said anything about the interview with Langhoff.

"Sanne, glad you could make it. I called your place and spoke to Martin, but he didn't know where you were."

Sanne mumbled something in reply, hoping Ulrik couldn't see her blushing.

"Is it him again?" she asked, forcing herself to focus.

Ulrik nodded, pulled her along down to the water's edge and into the tent. Frelsén waved. Bint shook her hand. A couple of officers she didn't know stood on the other side. The naked body of a blonde woman was lying in the middle of the circle, half-submerged in the dark lake. The light gave her skin a strong yellowish tone. Small waves lapped up against her almost hairless genitalia and the tattoos on the lowest part of her stomach, leaving trails of seagrass and waste on her abdomen and thighs. The body had the same small hole by the groin that Mira's body did and the same entrance wound from the fatal bullet above the left breast. Empty eye sockets stared up at the roof of the tent.

Sanne remembered the horror on Abeiuwa's face. It could just as easily have been her.

"Another prostitute?" she said.

"The tattoos would suggest that." Frelsén sounded tired. Apparently, they wouldn't have to listen to his usual spirited, slightly inappropriate commentary tonight. "They should also help us with her identification. The body and bone structure is Scandinavian. She's presumably Danish, around thirty-five years old. So somewhat older than the first girl and the African who escaped."

"Abeiuwa." Sanne turned to Ulrik. "Who found her?"

"They called from the museum." Ulrik nodded toward the white colossus. "The Danish Bankers Association was having its annual meeting tonight. One of the guests was out stretching his legs. You can see the remains of his buffet dinner over there." He pointed at a tree close to the water's edge.

"When did he find her?"

"Around ten o'clock, so just under an hour ago. The park closes at eight."

"Have you spoken to him?"

Ulrik shook his head. "I let him go home. He's one of the chief executives of Nordea. He was completely beside himself. You can speak to him tomorrow."

"Okay." She sighed. "I'll speak to him. And I'll be nice."

"The killer drove her up to the entrance of the museum," Ulrik continued, "dragged her over the fence, down the path, and down the bluff here. Bint found the tracks." He pointed. It was the same path she herself had taken.

One of the officers whispered to his colleagues, "She could have shaved properly down there."

"She did, as a matter of fact." Frelsén pointed at the body's genital area. "Observe the small tears. They're from pubic shaving a few hours prior to the time of death. But not all the body's cells cease functioning when you die. Some can continue for hours, days, and, in favourable instances, even weeks. So often it can appear as though the hair has continued growing, but it could also be caused by the skin shrinking, revealing the hairs growing on the inner layer—before they emerge from the skin, that is. Morticians often need to shave male corpses before interment."

The officer spat in disgust, looked away. A sudden weariness threatened to knock Sanne over.

"What's that on her hand?" she said. The body's hand was positioned at an unnatural angle. Sanne crouched down, tentatively held the wrist. It felt strange, like hard rubber. She lifted the hand. The skin was torn, as if someone had been filing around the wrist.

Sanne looked up at Frelsén.

"Yes." He placed his gold-framed glasses on the bridge of

his nose. Suddenly there was some life in his weary eyes. He hunched down beside Sanne, examined the wrist. "That's odd. For the time being, I would say she's been bound with a coarse rope, shortly after the time of death. The tissue is destroyed, but there's no trace of blood vessels."

"Who would tie up a dead body?"

Behind him the paramedics were on their way down the bluff with a stretcher.

"Yes," he said and blinked. "That is precisely the question. Who would do that?"

CHAPTER 47

WHEN THE BLOODWIND has raged, only the essence remains. Mahler. Cabbage soup. Urgrund. Mother is dead. She lay screaming in her old room until the end. Everything that must not be said comes raging out. She fades away, collapses as the words flow out of her. Father is Grandfather, Grandfather is Father. Now he finally knows the truth: Grandfather *and* Father. He understands where it comes from, the power that roars inside him. When he looks down between his feet, straddling the continental plates, he sees a point turning on its own axis: dark red, pulsating. Incredible, blazing heat. It radiates a frightening force; everything melts before the Urgrund. The flesh falls from the bones, the blood boils. The body secretions spit, rise in columns of white and yellow steam. The eyes drip, run sizzling out of their sockets. This is life's primordial force, so infinitely greater than anything he has ever before experienced. So vigorous and omnivorous that everything must bend to its iron will. That is the bloodwind. The fissure is open. It can no longer be closed. Nothing can contain that which wants out. He is the servant of the bloodwind. This house—these beams, stones, and trusses—is the seat for the all-consuming Will that will brand the world. To be its instrument makes his chest swell with pride. He who could not see the bloodwind's pure, unthinking workings. The naked instinct consuming everything in its path. Now he is bearer of the wonder. The rebellion, the girl's insubordination, all was part of a greater plan. They too have had their role to play. And this knowledge makes his burden easier to bear. For the Will should know it has not been easy to release the children, to hurt the ones you love. But when the purpose is clear, its pure workings shine, he can bear everything. He looks at Sonja and is filled with love. She is the only one left now. Hilda had to go, like Karen and the others before her. The cabbage soup steams on the table. He pushes the plate across to her. Eat, my girl. I miss them too. But we must all make our sacrifices. And the bloodwind has shown me that we will soon be complete again.

Sie sind uns nur vorausgegangen
und werden nicht wieder nach Haus verlangen!
Wir hohlen sie ein auf jenen Höh'n
im Sonnnenschein! Der Tag is schön
auf jenen Höh'n!

MONDAY
JUNE 23

CHAPTER 48

THE SOUNDS OF morning from the street: a drunk throwing up outside the Ring Café, the S-train whizzing into the station, birds singing in the courtyard. Maria was in the shower. Lars opened his eyes. He had not felt drunk yesterday, but now he felt a sharp pain shooting behind his eyes. No more drinking cheap red wine.

Last night came back to him. Images of him and Sanne on the sofa. The story about the occupation of Abel Cathrines Gade had more or less been the truth. But why had he not told her about the demonstrations afterwards? About the street fighting, the drunken feeling as the cobblestone flew out of his hand, sailed across the sky toward the police lines? About the adrenaline-pumping high he got from running from his future colleagues, a bandana covering his face? The romanticizing of street partisans? The drugs?

He coughed, tried to focus on the previous night. He and Sanne kissing, Maria coming home crying. He rubbed his eyes and pulled himself up on his elbows. He wondered how both of them were feeling today.

The shower stopped. Maria poked her head out the door, humming. Her hair was wrapped in a pink towel, her body covered by a larger blue one. Small drops of water trickled down from the wisps of hair on her cheek.

"Did you sleep all right, Dad?"

He grunted, then sat up. He was still amazed by how quickly his teenage daughter could move from one end of the emotional spectrum to the other.

"Are you okay?" he asked drowsily.

"For sure." Maria smiled. "Remember, I'm going to a party at my classmate Christina's tonight." She disappeared into her room.

He considered asking about the party, but his cell rang. He swung his legs out of bed, answered the phone.

"Lars." He felt like a smoke, even though he knew it wouldn't do his headache any good.

"Toke here." Toke paused on the other end, but Lars didn't answer. Toke sighed, then continued. "Yesterday Kim A and Frank tracked down someone from the group outside the 7-Eleven. You know, the kids who met Stine near Nørreport the night she was raped. His name is Jesper Lützen. He's twenty-three years old and works at"—Toke flipped through the pages—"Cosmo Film. It's probably one of those jobs where you don't really get paid. Kim A and Frank spoke to him last night. He was on a shoot."

"And?" Lars's tongue was thick and sticky. He could do with some water. Or juice.

"The guy on the video—the one we thought was following Stine—got into a cab straight after."

"So he didn't follow Stine?"

"Not according to Jesper."

"We've got the time-stamp from the video from Danske Bank…" Lars grabbed a T-shirt from the floor and tried putting it on without taking the phone away from his ear.

"Kim A and Frank are already working on the cab drivers."

"I'm on my way."

Lars hung up. Unbelievable. Kim A and Frank had been working on their own.

"Would you mind putting some coffee on?" he shouted to Maria. "I'm just jumping in the shower."

Half an hour later he went out into the street. The sun shone from a cloudless sky. Maria was going out to a classmate's to study, but she had plenty of time. She was probably upstairs in the apartment with her feet on the table. He patted his pockets. He must have forgotten his cigarettes up there. He turned around and took one step back when he saw the *Ekstra Bladet* placard outside the corner store.

THE SANDMAN STRIKES AGAIN
Another Body with No Eyes
Bank Director Discovers Body

His jaw dropped. He was staring at the placard's black, yellow, and red graphics. He went into the store and asked for a pack of King's Blue and a newspaper. He paid with a crumpled two hundred kroner note. An older, dark-skinned man with an impressive red beard and a bulky stomach took his money. The young Danish kid must be at school. Middle Eastern pop music was booming from a cheap stereo in the back room. He took his change and hurried to the 5A bus stop on Nørrebrogade with the paper under his arm.

The bus was packed, but he managed to find a window seat near the back. A tall, overweight man sat down next to him and he was forced to squeeze up against the hot window. Lars flipped to the articles about the dead woman on pages four, five, and six. He skimmed the spread on pages four and five. A blurry night photo, shot with a telephoto lens from the other side of the lake, showed a group of police officers by a set of generator-powered police lights standing at the water's edge. He thought he recognized Ulrik. And was that Sanne standing there, on the way into the tent shielding the body? They had probably called her just as she'd left his place.

He flipped over to page six. *Boom*. Another headline.

COPENHAGEN IN PANIC—WHERE ARE THE POLICE?
How much longer will the rapist be given free rein?

His eyes scanned the article, stopping at a quote that was emphasized in boldface: "Sources in the Homicide Department tell us that the head of the investigation has lost control. Important leads are not being investigated; resources are being used improperly." At the bottom of the article was a picture of Lars on the tailgate of a police car, soaking wet, trying to light a smoke. The caption read: "*Ekstra Bladet* can today reveal that Detective Lars Winkler, who ran the abortive operation in Hans Tavsens Park on Thursday night, refuses to follow normal investigative procedures. The question is, can the people of this city be confident in the police?"

He clenched his hands, nearly tore the newspaper in half.

"Hey, buddy, take it easy. That paper never did anything to you." The portly man sitting next to him laughed. Lars let go of the crumpled paper, folded it up, and handed it to him.

He sat with his forehead resting against the window and

looked out into nothing while his thoughts churned. The bus continued down Nørrebrogade and had gotten as far as Griffenfeldsgade when he jumped up and pressed the stop button. He waited impatiently for the bus to stop outside the Grob Theatre.

He needed peace; he needed to go home. It was time to start from the beginning, to go all the way back to square one.

CHAPTER 49

IT WAS PAST two in the morning before she'd arrived home. Martin had been ready for her, angry and drunk, ready to interrogate her. Where had she been? What had she been doing and who had she been with?

She hadn't gotten much sleep on the hard sofa either, and when she woke up, the argument continued. There was a throbbing behind her eyes as she climbed the stairs to the dark red corridor and walked to the green door at the end. *Don't think. Coffee, lots of coffee. And then straight to work.*

Balancing a brown envelope from her mail slot in one hand and a plastic cup in the other, she managed to open the door to her office. She hurried in, slammed the door behind her, and practically fell into the chair. Cold, sticky sweat drops ran down her forehead and got caught in her eyebrows.

She drank the lukewarm coffee. The burnt, bitter taste

made her throat constrict and her stomach implode, but it was strangely invigorating. Then she grabbed the end of the envelope between her teeth and tore it open with her free hand. She shook two DVDs out of the envelope. Yesterday's footage from the surveillance cameras at the entrance of the office buildings of the Danish State Railway on Øster Voldgade, just across from the National Gallery of Denmark. Someone had been working fast.

She turned on her computer and popped in the first DVD.

The recordings started at 5:00 p.m., just as the thick rush of office workers was streaming past. The warm summer afternoon had drawn the jackets off the sweaty bodies. Employees marched past in shirt sleeves and T-shirts. She fast-forwarded to 7:30 p.m., let the video play at double speed. She stared at the screen for more than an hour until the timer showed 10:03 p.m.: the time when a guest at the Danish Bankers Association event had found the body.

Nothing.

Sanne swore and started from the beginning. She had just printed the pictures of the passersby when Allan knocked. "Are you ready?"

She looked up. "What?"

"Seferi is waiting in my office."

Elvir Seferi. Of course.

"Sorry, I'm a little . . ." Sanne got up and followed Allan into the office he shared with Toke. She closed the door behind her and sat down next to Allan. Bent double on the other side of the table was a small man with a bushy moustache and stubble up to his eyes. He had close-cropped white hair, and the top of his head was tanned. A greasy ivy cap lay on the table next to his restless fingers.

Allan turned on the recording device and introduced himself. Then he leaned over the table. "You know why you're here?"

"No." His fingers were fiddling with the cap.

"Break-in at a dental clinic in Valby in February, does that ring a bell?" Sanne crossed her arms, observing the man from the other side of the table. He was sweating.

"But that wasn't me. You know that?"

"Do you know the Bukoshi brothers?" Allan said.

"Buk...?"

"They both claim that you can give them an alibi for the evening of May 4. You were playing cards with them in Shqiptarë?"

The light brown eyes came to life.

"Yes." He nodded. "That's right."

Sanne and Allan looked at each other.

"But that evening you were in lock-up in Middelfart." Allan pushed the report from their Funen Island colleagues across the table.

"Um, yeah," Seferi mumbled.

"You came here from Kosovo in 1999?" Sanne smiled. "You're a trained veterinarian?"

Seferi nodded. Then he shook his head. "Doctor. Difficult to get work at a hospital, better as veterinarian."

Sanne's heart jumped an extra beat. She tried to stay calm, but the adrenaline was pumping. "What was your specialization? Gastroenterology, cardiology...ophthalmology?"

"No specialization, just doctor." Seferi straightened in the chair.

Sanne took out the box with the reconstructed glass eye from her purse and placed it on the table. "What is glutaraldehyde used for?" she said.

"Glutaraldehyde?" Seferi gave them an inquiring look. "For cleaning instruments after surgery. Why?" Neither of them answered. "Ah, the stuff stolen from that dentist? But I told you, that wasn't me."

Sanne opened the box, placed a napkin on the middle of the table, and laid the glass eye on it. The pupil stared up at Elvir Seferi.

"Did you do any eye surgery in Kosovo?" she said.

Seferi shifted in his seat. "No."

"You know we can get the hospital records from Pristina and Skopje, right?"

Seferi blinked, folded his hands. He watched Sanne as she placed the glass eye back in the box. Allan gathered up the break-in report from February, closed it.

"I think we'll take a break here," Allan said. "Elvir, you're going to detention in the meantime."

Sanne walked through the canteen door. Lars was nowhere to be seen. She went up to the counter and asked about the daily special.

It was lunchtime, the canteen was packed, yet she was still able to find a place on her own. She forced herself to eat. Strangely enough it helped. She felt better. Her headache faded.

Back in her office, she sat down by the desk, lingering over the pile of printed pictures. The anonymous mass of faces fluttered up at her. She had to close her eyes and press her thumbs against her eyelids until it hurt before the flickering disappeared.

The door opened and Lisa poked her head in. No "Hi," no attempt at any kind of greeting, just the bare essentials of the message.

"Ulrik wants to see you. Now."

The door closed behind Lisa with a dry click that made Sanne's heart skip a beat. This was it; Langhoff had filed a complaint. Ulrik couldn't use her anymore. She was going back to Kolding. She was freezing on the inside, her skin blazing hot.

"Sanne, thanks for coming." Ulrik looked up from his place by the desk in front of the window. The smell of linoleum, dust, and stale sweat was even more pronounced today.

Kim A stood next to Ulrik in front of the window. The *Ekstra Bladet* tabloid was open on Ulrik's desk.

"Lisa didn't mention what this was about." Without thinking, Sanne stood with her legs slightly spread, her hands behind her back, in the middle of the room. Her fingernails started clicking before she was even aware of it. It was a habit she had not been able to shake.

Ulrik cleared his throat, exchanged looks with Kim A. Then he turned the paper so Sanne could read along.

COPENHAGEN IN PANIC—WHERE ARE THE POLICE?
How much longer will the rapist be given free rein?

"Where is Lars?" Ulrik asked.

She closed her eyes for a moment. "I don't know."

"That—" Ulrik pointed at the newspaper article. "There's no place for this." He took a deep breath. "I'm not accusing any of you of the leak, but..."

Sanne focused on Tivoli Gardens' Star Flyer ride behind her two colleagues. What was Kim A doing here?

Ulrik folded the newspaper and threw it into the wastepaper basket.

"There—that's where it belongs." He coughed. "The attorney general called the police commissioner, and he has spoken with the head of Homicide. We're all under pressure. I have," he looked at his watch, "about an hour before I have to issue a statement. It's not something I'm happy about, but I have no choice. This affects the entire squad."

Sanne didn't answer. She looked at Kim A through half-closed eyes.

An irritated grimace crossed Ulrik's face. His thin fingers were tapping the table.

"Lars is off the case until further notice. Kim A is taking over. I've asked you to come in to . . . Right now you're the only one Lars speaks to."

Sanne blinked, a sharp retort on the tip of her tongue. But what could she do? She nodded, accepted the Judas mission. Went along with it, as usual. She tried forming the words in her head, the way she would say them to Lars when she got hold of him. But the sentences kept unravelling.

Ulrik placed a hand on Kim A's shoulder. "Come on. Let's go brief the others."

Sanne slumped into her office chair. What had just happened? And where did she and Lars stand after yesterday?

She grabbed the phone and dialled Lars's number. "Come on," she mumbled while the ringing echoed in her head. When Lars's voice mail came on, she hung up and slammed the receiver down.

Just then, the door flew open and Allan ran in. His face was split in two by a broad grin.

"This just came through the wiretap—Meriton and Ukë's shipment, it's down at Strandhuse, in the southern part of Zealand. Just as you had predicted."

MAY 4, 1945

"**A**T THIS MOMENT, Montgomery has just announced that German troops in Holland, northwest Germany, and Denmark have surrendered. This is London. We repeat: Montgomery has at this moment announced that German troops..."

The contractions hit her. Her back arches over the bed of ammunition sackcloth. The voice drones from another world. It is only after a long time, between two contractions and interrupted by the cheering and shooting outside, that she understands: the war is over; the Germans have surrendered.

But for her, everything ended months earlier. Her Jack is dead. And last winter, Mother quietly faded away. In the end, there was no one left. Father has kept her down here ever since her bump could no longer be concealed. Hidden away, wrapped in the smell of dust and gun oil. If she concentrates, she can still capture Jack's scent, the last thing she has left of him. That and his eyes in the jar on the shelf above her. Two whitish lumps floating in the yellowish liquid, blind and silent, suspended in an eerie dance.

The gunshots outside are getting closer now. Then they disappear. She feels another contraction press on her lower back and pubic bone. She is one single throbbing vein.

When she comes around again, she is drenched in sweat. Someone has switched off the radio. The kerosene lamp flickers on the table in the corner, its light caressing the machine gun on the tablecloth.

Father observes her with feverish eyes. It'll be over soon he says. It's a big day. Then the contractions return and she disappears in the pain.

Over the next few hours, she slips in and out of consciousness. She hears herself panting; she is a foaling mare. When she comes to, Father is back, bringing news from the outside world. The HIPOs and collaborators are everywhere. There's shooting by the town hall. He has been in a firefight with a group on Brogårdsvej. Arno won't bother them anymore, he tells her, as if it's an afterthought. She knows not to ask.

Something is on its way, sliding through her, moving out between her legs. The pain slips away; everything disappears. Then with a disgusting sound it bursts its way out of her. When she looks up, Father is standing by her feet. Something wet and living is moving over her stomach. Blood and fetal fluids soak through her already drenched shirt. Tiny clutching hands open and close around nothing. A small greedy mouth seeks, sucks blindly in the empty air. Father's rough hands tear open her shirt, find her breasts, and then he gives the creature a nudge. She gasps as the child latches on, clings to her, and sucks greedily.

"Look at him, look. My son." Father tries to turn her head, but she refuses to look.

Father is between her legs again, pulling more out of her. A pair of scissors glistens under the light. He cuts, then throws something in a garbage can while the child feeds.

"Look or don't look. It's all the same to me." Father sits down by the machine gun and lights his pipe. "Don't count on getting out of here until my son's finished breast-feeding. And then, if anyone asks, the child is your cousin's. It's our duty to support and protect the family. We can't have the neighbours gossiping." On her breast the child lets out small whimpering sounds.

Father leans forward and turns the knobs on the Bakelite radio. "We shall give him my na—"

"I'll call him Jack," she whispers and turns her head away.

In that moment she swears never to speak to that which she has brought into the world. From that moment on, she will never speak again.

The radio crackles, the tubes come to life, glowing behind the rough felt. Then comes the voice.

"We repeat: Montgomery has reported that the German troops..."

CHAPTER 50

SANNE WAS SITTING with her legs up on the back seat. The car tore through the bright evening. Allan drove; Ulrik was in the passenger seat. No one spoke. Bint was in the Crime Scene Unit's vehicle behind them. They had three quarters of an hour before they were meeting Gregers Vestberg from the local police near the village of Sjolte.

Allan looked at her in the rearview mirror.

"I had a colleague in Pristina ask around a little. It doesn't look like Elvir Seferi was involved in any kind of eye surgery there."

Ulrik followed the conversation but said nothing.

Green fields and woods streaked past. What a way to spend Midsummer's Eve.

"Well, he could still be involved," she said.

"Well, yes."

Ulrik turned in his seat. "Did you get hold of Lars?"

Sanne shook her head.

"Me neither." Ulrik closed his eyes and leaned back against the headrest.

No one said anything. The asphalt kept rolling away beneath the car.

The first bars of "Upside Down" filled the car. Sanne bent down and dug her phone out of her purse. A German number?

"Yes?"

"Frau Bissen? *Hier* Dr. Henkel *aus* Mülheim. I just thought I would get back to you. I spoke today with an older colleague . . . and well, between us, we recalled another colleague—unfortunately he died in a traffic accident a few years ago. We both seem to remember him having had a Danish student in the 1960s."

"A Dane?" Sanne sat up, shushed Ulrik and Allan. Neither of them had said anything.

"Yes, a young man. Our colleague fired him rather quickly. The young man was incompetent. Comical, really. I think his grandfather was a doctor."

Sanne held her breath, counted to five. "And can you remember the name of the young man?"

"Unfortunately not."

When she had hung up, Sanne got Professor Lau's number from the duty officer. Moments later she threw the phone down on the seat.

"Isn't his voice mail picking up?" Allan accelerated, passed a red Opel.

She shook her head and forced her breathing down.

CHAPTER 51

HIS CELL PHONE hummed in his jacket pocket. Lars pulled the steering wheel, swerved around a slow-moving Peugeot on Bernstorffsvej, only to immediately pull over to the side. He had picked up the car at the depot on Hambrosgade earlier in the day, but avoided going into the precinct. The Peugeot passed him, leaned on the horn. The sun burned the sky golden beneath the last leaden clouds. The wind blew the remains of a heavy shower across Øresund. In the villas along Bernstorffsvej, windows lit up; people were sitting around the tables. A few dads were out in their gardens, pulling the tarpaulins off the waiting bonfires for Midsummer's Eve. Some had already placed the symbolic witch, a scarecrow figure clad in black rags, on top of their bonfires.

Lars was running out of time. He was fidgeting in his seat and his nose was burning. He pulled out his cell.

"Yes?"

"Lars?" It was Sanne. A lump dissolved, trickled through his body, bubbled, and combined with the chemical substances that kept him going. "Where have you been?"

He laughed. "Sanne? Thanks for last night." Short pause. "I've been home, thinking. But, you—"

She interrupted him. "Have you seen *Ekstra Bladet* today?" Suddenly he realized that she was worried. She continued before he had a chance to respond. "You're off the case. Kim A is now in charge of the investigation."

She stopped, waited. But Lars had long since passed the point of anger. He sniffed, ran a finger under his nose.

"It doesn't matter. I'm doing this on my own from here on in. I have a clue. Maria . . ."

"Lars—"

"I'm glad you called. But I'm busy. I promise I'll call later. Bye."

"Lars, just a mo—"

He turned off his cell before she could finish the sentence, then put the car in gear and roared out on Bernstorffsvej.

He was on his way to a party.

The house, an enormous whitewashed box with a black-glazed mansard roof, was secluded from Egebjerg Allé. The noise from the traffic on the nearby Bernstorffsvej was by and large gone. On the right of the house, a towering gable faced the road. It had a bay window with sashes and a balcony on the second floor. The garden was simple and well looked after. Light and laughter streamed through the open terrace doors. Glasses clinked. A mediocre stereo played Maroon 5, "Payphone." Lars had stumbled across the video on YouTube. He did not watch it all the way to the end.

The driveway was flanked by two white pillars, which anchored the black wrought iron gate. A towering private security guard stood out front.

Lars parked the Ford on the other side of the road and climbed out. It was getting dark now. The air smelled of lilacs and freshly mown grass. Torches lit the driveway and spotlights sent cones of light up from the pillars by the gate.

The guard stepped forward. "Can I help you, sir?"

"I need to talk to my daughter. She's in there." He nodded toward the house.

"It's by invitation only. I'm sorry."

Lars sighed, pulled out his police badge, and walked past him without waiting for an answer.

"Stop," the guard shouted at him. "You can't just..."

Lars didn't react; he just continued up the driveway. A well-maintained vintage Jaguar gleamed in the light of the torches by the house. He whistled quietly and allowed himself to indulge in the car's slender curves for a few seconds before he entered the garden and approached the terrace. He was greeted by a crowd of young people in suits and short dresses; the graduates were outside in their caps, smoking. Maria was not among them.

He stepped onto the terrace, moved in and out past the couples. He didn't fit in. He was too old, too poorly dressed.

The volume on the stereo was turned up in the living room and a group of girls spread out on the dance floor. The hard pumping beats faded out and were replaced by an old song that played in his head.

Then the youth go off to dance
On your bidding good Saint Hans...

"Hey, I think you're lost, Grandpa." The voice was just

behind his right ear and pulled him back into the present. He tried turning around.

"Now, let me help you." Firm hands grasped his arm. It wasn't exactly hostile but someone found it amusing. A joke at his expense. Lars tried to break free, mumbling something about Maria.

"Let him go." The voice sounded both familiar and unfamiliar at the same time. "Lars?" A young man forced his way through the crowd and stood in front of him.

"Simon?" Lars took a step to the side. He had to support himself on a chair. Maria's ex? Here?

"Is he drunk?" someone asked.

"Maria?" He had lowered his voice, his gaze fixed on Simon. "Is she here?" Just then he spotted her. She walked down the staircase inside the house, her hand resting lightly on the sweeping railing. Her white, sleeveless dress glowed against her dark hair, and she had a shawl draped over her shoulders. She spotted him, smiled, and the voices merged around him.

"You can't be here. This is a private party."

"Why didn't the guard stop him? What does he think we pay him for?"

He reached into his pocket and pulled out his badge. "Police. I need to talk to my daughter."

The hands released him immediately. The group moved a couple of steps back.

Maria's face froze. She quickly jumped down the last few steps and ran across the dance floor. She pulled him out of the circle of light, away from Simon and into the garden.

"Dad, what are you doing?" she whispered with a pleading look on her face. "Don't say anything to Simon about Christian!"

The momentum had made him lose his balance. He fought to stay on his feet on the soft grass.

"What are you doing here? I thought..." Her eyes were shining. "You can't just come in here waving your badge around. I'm making friends here. Finally."

Simon was holding a glass, keeping an eye on them.

Lars still could not get it to add up. Maria dragged him further away into the shadows along the wall.

"I wanted..." Lars looked up at the terrace again. Something prickled inside his head, but he couldn't hold onto it. It slipped away, disappeared.

"Yes?" Maria was impatient now. "Pull yourself together, Dad. Have you been drinking?"

"I've been working on this rape case all day and..." He tried again. "At the hospital, Caroline..." His voice disappeared. The prickling feeling returned; everything stood on end. Simon on the terrace under the bright evening sky. Maria at a party with the Øregård clique.

Then the words spilled out of him, tumbling over one another. "The other night, in your room. That wasn't you and Christian?"

For a moment she stared at him in confusion, then her look darkened.

"So you did come home?" She pulled the shawl around her shoulders, looked down. She couldn't possibly be cold on such a warm summer evening. "That's disgusting, Dad. How could you think I'd want to be with Christian?"

The pieces fell into place. The condom, the DNA profile they had thought cleared Christian. It was Simon's DNA, not Christian's. He looked up at the terrace. His eyes searched among the guests.

"I need to find Christian. Now. Where is he?"

"What's with you? You're acting so weird."

"Sorry." He went to reach for her but then let his arms drop. "It's important."

317

Maria looked away, covered her mouth with her hand. "He was here half an hour ago. Just before Simon got here. Some of the boys got rid of him." She looked away. "I don't want anything more to do with him."

What had happened at Christian's house the night before? He was about to ask when a drunk guy walked over to them. His tie was hanging loose over his unbuttoned shirt, his eyes were swimming.

"Have you seen Christina? We're trying to find the key to the liquor cabinet."

Maria shook her head. "Anders, you saw Christian out. Did he say where he was going?"

Anders smiled; his eyes were swimming. "He was completely out of it. Kept going on about blood and bones. And about the Sandman, that he knew who he was." He stumbled to one side. "Crazy shit." Then he disappeared.

Lars remembered only too well his conversation with Christian at the apartment: "Midnight Rambler" and the Boston strangler.

Maria had gone completely white. "Christian's dad said Christian thought there was a murderer living in the area, back when he was a kid. On... by Søbredden? Does that name mean something?"

Lars didn't answer; he just stared off into the shadows. In a flash, he saw the roundabout by Brogårdsvej in the sunlight the day before, Sanne in the passenger seat. Out of the corner of his eye, the road sign on the right. Søbredden.

He grabbed her, had to make an effort not to squeeze her. "What did he say?"

"I don't know. Let go, Dad."

The kids on the terrace were watching them. He let go.

"Sorry, I didn't mean to frighten you." He stroked her cheek. "Is Mom home?"

"Yes, she—"

"Go home to her. Now. Lock all the doors, close all the windows, and wait for me to call."

She nodded and pressed her cheek against his chest.

CHAPTER 52

THE LAST BLACK clouds scurried out over the sea. Sanne closed her cell, held her nose in the air, and breathed in. It was lovely to get away from the city air. Pine needles, grass, sea salt, and the faint smell of manure; it was almost like home. She leaned against the car, concealed behind dark trunks, and crossed her arms. Lars had sounded... different. Something metallic in his voice.

The ruin of the three-winged yard was about one hundred metres away, a dirty grey speck in the deepening twilight. The forest behind it was a dark and threatening wall. Six of Gregers Vestberg's vehicles from the South Zealand and Lolland-Falster police force were parked deeper in the woods; two were positioned discreetly along the roads leading to the property from the highway. Now it was only a matter of time.

There was a rustling from inside the car. Ulrik tapped on

the window. Sanne opened the rear door and climbed inside.

"We've gotten word from the unit in Sjolte." Allan turned toward her. "They've just driven past. They'll be here in a few minutes."

Sanne blinked and stared into the woods, trying to get her eyes accustomed to the dark.

"Ukë and Meriton?" But she already knew the answer.

"They're still driving around Copenhagen." Ulrik slammed his fist on the dashboard. "Why aren't they coming?"

"They've been tipped." Sanne leaned back in the seat. She was completely calm. The time for waiting was over.

"None of my people..." Ulrik started.

Sanne just looked at him. He didn't finish the sentence; his hand was resting on the megaphone on his lap. Nobody said anything for a few minutes.

"Have you got your vest on?" Ulrik asked for the umpteenth time. She nodded and took the service weapon out of the shoulder holster. The thick, viscous smell of gun oil. Sanne put the pistol back in the holster. Twilight slipped into night.

A set of headlights from a minivan turned from Sjoltevej down toward the woods. Sanne caught herself holding her breath and forced herself to take deep and steady breaths.

"This is it," Allan whispered.

They opened the doors almost simultaneously, slid outside and toward the house, moving from tree to tree, three shadows among the hundreds of others in the woods. The minivan rumbled down the dirt road, around the corner where the small stretch of woods began, and into the yard by the three-winged ruin. For a brief moment the headlights revealed the collapsed wall of the house. Then the engine went silent and the darkness closed in around the ruin once again.

Allan whispered into the walkie-talkie as he ran forward, hunched over. She could glimpse her colleagues moving along both sides of the wooded road. The moon was making its way above the treetops; an errant beam glinted briefly on a weapon barrel. Her heart pounded against her ribs. They had to be able to hear her from a long way off down there. But nothing happened. She ran bent double across the road behind Ulrik, drew her service weapon, and slipped in behind the trees to the left of the derelict property. The uniformed officers fanned out counter-clockwise and in behind the barn.

Inside the barn, behind the battered door, there was movement, light. White cones shone out in the night through the collapsed wall and the holes in the roof. Faint music. Voices.

"*Wann kommen sie?*"

"*Bald, Alexandru, bald. Hab doch ne bischen Geduld, he?*"

Allan and Ulrik got into position on either side of her. A couple of female voices burst into giggles. Music from a radio.

A crackling came from Allan's radio. He nodded at Ulrik, who stepped into the yard, raised the megaphone, and shouted, "This is the Danish police. You are surrounded. Come out with your hands in the air."

Immediately the radio was switched off and the light disappeared. A cuckoo sounded in the distance. Otherwise everything was completely still. Sanne counted eight cuckoo clucks before the barn door began opening centimetre by centimetre on creaking hinges. Seven young women tottered out, one after the other, and huddled together in the middle of the yard.

Ulrik raised the megaphone again. "We know there are two more inside. Come out with your hands in the air."

Whispering was heard, scraping. A hoarse voice shouted. "*Ein moment.*"

Ulrik motioned to Allan who passed the message on. Their colleagues moved in closer. The net was closing.

Allan waved the girls away from the yard. The door creaked again and a figure appeared. At least four flashlights were directed at him and the automatic weapon in his hand. The barrel was pointed at the ground.

"Put the gun down. Now!" Ulrik barked into the megaphone. The girls, now standing behind them, jumped. Two policemen escorted them to the other side of the road.

The man in the doorway waved his weapon back and forth. *"Nicht schiessen, nicht schiessen."*

Why didn't he drop his machine gun? And where was the other one?

Sanne's eyes swept the barn. It was pitch black. From her position, she could see partway around the corner. Her colleagues had reached the rear of the building now.

Behind them, a shadow rose up.

"There. Behind you!" she shouted, then broke into a run across the yard. The man in the doorway took a step back into the barn, raised his weapon, and fired off a short salvo, then another. The dry, crackling sound echoed in the night; bullets tore up small fountains of gravel and dirt by her feet. A rapid series of hard cracks followed and the automatic weapon went quiet. An unearthly rattle came from inside the barn, then she reached the corner and darted past two uniformed officers.

She launched herself into the darkness, following the sounds of snapping branches and twigs. Something flicked through the night, tearing her hands and face. Another salvo from an automatic weapon shot past, close, and tore the bark and wet wood off a pine tree behind her. She drew closer; she could hear him panting. Behind her the dogs started barking.

"You cannot escape. Stop," she shouted. Her blood pumped adrenaline, fear, and rage through her body. The fugitive accelerated; then, the sound of his feet was gone. Her colleagues were close behind with flashlights. Streaks of light danced between the trunks. She stumbled into a deep trench, then regained her balance on the way up the bank. A shape jumped into view and took off. Her colleagues' flashlights caught him in the crossfire of light beams, and he stopped. He had mousy hair and was wearing dirty jeans and a medium-length grey jacket. He stood with his back turned, shoulders bowed, arms by his side.

"Get down! On your knees, hands behind your head," she shouted. The pistol was raised, ready to shoot. Where was his weapon? There was no doubt he had heard her, but he didn't react. He remained standing with his shoulders and head drooping. She couldn't see his hands. Slowly she circled around in front of him, just as her colleagues arrived.

"He's unarmed," she shouted, when she could see his empty hands. Where had he dropped his gun? Two officers had him now. They locked his hands behind his back with plastic straps. Two more officers arrived, one of them gave Sanne a flashlight. She started searching the ground between the trees. Dry branches, dead underbrush, animal excrement, pine cones. She followed their tracks back through the forest, over a fallen tree trunk, in and out between the bushes. Something flashed in the darkness some ways off the trail. She stopped and aimed the light at it. A Heckler & Koch MP5K PDW was half hidden behind a pile of withered leaves.

"Sanne?" It was Allan.

"Over here." She waited for Allan to reach her. He gasped for breath.

"Are you hit?"

She shook her head, showed him the weapon.

"The other guy had one just like it. What were they planning to do, start a small war?"

In a flash, Sanne saw the guy jump up in front of her, into the cones of light. Why this burst of energy? She was about to lose his trail. It had happened exactly when she passed the ditch.

"Follow me." She handed Allan the weapon, then found the place where she had stumbled in the ditch. She took note of the direction. A little further out, where she thought she had seen him jump up, the ditch continued zigzagging. Sanne swept the edge with the flashlight, back and forth. The stench of rot and topsoil rose from the oily water and the pulp of half decomposed leaves that covered the bottom.

A tree root edged into the ditch. Sanne traced its winding movement with her flashlight. Something glistened beneath it.

Allan stood at the top of the ditch, looking down at her.

"He could have stayed down there and picked us off one by one as we came barging in."

Sanne dug between the wet leaves and damp earth. She pulled out the elongated pack from the small opening, where it had been wedged between dirt and root.

"He'd heard the dogs. He knew we'd catch him eventually. Here," she said. The flat package, sealed in thick, transparent plastic and brown tape, landed by his feet.

"What is it?"

"This is what he ran off to hide." Sanne climbed up from the ditch. "Let's go back and take a look."

A couple of officers had placed the wounded man on the ground, turned him so he was lying on one side, and opened his mouth to prevent him from choking on his own vomit. The man was bleeding heavily from his neck and thigh. Someone had lightly dressed the wounds. His legs were kicking in short, abrupt spasms, and his eyes had rolled back so only the whites were visible.

Ulrik wandered off with his hands in his pockets, kicking the gravel. He looked up when Sanne approached. "You okay?"

Sanne nodded. Two officers were placing the other man in

the back of a patrol car. Allan went over to help the other officers with the trafficked girls. Gregers Vestberg came out of the barn.

"Quite the operation, Ulrik." He pulled out a pipe from his pocket, began to pack it. He looked briefly at the wounded guy in the yard. "He'll be dead before the ambulance arrives." He lit his pipe with two matches. "What happened to the two brothers? Weren't they the ones you were supposed to catch?"

Ulrik ground his teeth. The sweetish smell of pipe tobacco billowed across the yard. The scent took her back to her childhood in the 1980s, her father's evening pipe in front of the TV. Clips of riots with punks and squatters in Copenhagen on the evening news. Had Lars been among them?

"I've just spoken to the officers staking out the Bukoshi brothers." Ulrik looked away. "They're sitting in the club on Abel Cathrines Gade. Playing cards. What happened?" Sanne was just about to say something when he continued. "No, you don't have to answer." He ran his hand across his forehead and down his cheek. He looked tired. "Sorry. Nice work."

Sanne handed him the package. "Maybe this will cheer you up. Girls aren't the only thing Meriton and Ukë are smuggling across the border."

Ulrik took the package, weighed it in his hand. The white powder gleamed in the light behind the thick plastic. "There must be at least two kilos."

"That's why he started shooting." She nodded at the wounded guy, still twitching on the ground. An officer attempted to hold the dressing in place on his neck. "His buddy needed time to hide it."

Gregers lit up, puffed on the bouncing pipe. "Excellent. We'd best get the girls and the package to Næstved."

Ulrik shook his head. "The preliminary wiretaps were carried out by us, hence the crime scene falls under Copenhagen

Police jurisdiction. Everything's going to Politigården."

Behind them a couple of Gregers's people were questioning the seven women. Sanne shivered. Two of the girls resembled Mira. Allan left the group of girls and the officers who were questioning them and positioned himself next to Sanne.

"They've got some nerve," he said. "You'd think they were already in Vesterbro. If my wife heard the propositions they were making... To top it all off, two of them are from the Middle East. Surely this behaviour isn't normal for Muslim women?"

"What did you expect?" Sanne looked over at the group. "A handful of terrified and banged-up girls, half-dead from starvation and thirst?"

Gregers drew on his pipe. "Your colleague is right. Denmark was not their first stop. They were broken long ago. Beaten and raped. They're making the most of the few opportunities they have."

CHAPTER 53

H **E PARKED THE** aubergine MG Austin-Healey Sprite roadster by the curb and turned off the engine. His hands were shaking and his heart was beating rapidly. Maria had been distant at the party, cold and dismissive. They all ended up being like that. He knew he had to take a different route now. He had to go through the same wild garden that he visited on another Midsummer's Eve, six years earlier. Behind the elder thicket and the decaying picket fence, there was someone just like him. He was going home.

He slid out of the seat, put the key in his pocket, and closed the door behind him with a quiet click. He leaned against the trunk, lit a Benson & Hedges while observing the driveway. He took a drag on the cigarette, let the nicotine penetrate his lung tissue and permeate his body. He enjoyed the slight dizziness and the warm evening air while he blew the smoke out through his nose. Most of the houses were empty; the residents had gone down to the bonfires along the lake. He knew the ritual.

Christian stubbed the cigarette out with the heel of his shoe and disappeared into the shadows.

The moon was rising above the lake as he moved along the elderberry thicket by the rotten stump. He saw the old picket fence through a tangled and twisted bush; the red paint had almost peeled off. And in there, behind the branches, was the small mound where he had buried the neighbour's cat.

The enchanted garden with the house on the small built-up hill rose before him, bathed in the moon's pale silver gleam. Far back, in another world, he heard the crackling of the bonfires. Stanzas of "The Midsummer Night's Song" drifted across the lake.

His eyes searched for the house: the empty façade with the dark eyes, the windows' black, lifeless rectangles and squares. He took a deep breath and slipped away from the shrubbery, but stopped just as he stepped inside the looming shadow of the house.

The front door was ajar.

Moving carefully, he stepped closer, tiptoed up the three steps to the front door. He looked around. The garden was empty; he was trembling with anticipation. Christian filled his lungs with air, took a final step, and pressed lightly on the door handle with one finger.

The door slid open.

Black, impenetrable darkness. The air inside was drier, more pure than the air outside, which was moist with dew and fumes from the lake. He shut the door behind him, stood still, and listened. Nothing moved. There was no indication that he'd been heard, only the usual sounds of an old house: branches against a window, beams creaking, a tap dripping. Somewhere inside a clock struck. One, two, three—eleven strokes, he counted. He started walking to the right. The planks groaned under his feet. He moved past the foyer and the old staircase. An indeterminable, alluring smell wafted out from an opening on the left, at once both chemical and organic. Rot and solvent? He forced himself to continue, taking the small flashlight out of his jacket pocket. He hazarded a little light. Old fabric wallpaper in paisley print on the walls. A doorway led to a small, old-fashioned kitchen. In a corner, an old cast-iron stove. Firewood piled up in the log basket.

Across from the kitchen a doorway led to an empty room. The moonlight shone through the dusty windows, creating expanses of light on the worn wooden floor. A rocking chair was silhouetted amongst all that silvery white.

In front of him, between the kitchen and living room, a closed door blocked the way. He hesitated, switched off the flashlight, and listened.

The entire house was holding its breath, waiting. From far off came the roar from Lyngbyvej. The slightly off-key voices rang out across Gentofte Lake.

He knew he had to go through that one door to get where he needed to be. He took a step forward, grabbed the handle, and opened the door. He stood on the threshold and waited. Nothing happened. In the darkness he could make out a heavy desk in front of the window, a lamp, and something large and solid stretching along the walls. He waited with bated breath. Thirty seconds, a minute. Still, nothing happened.

Christian took two steps forward, switched on the flashlight, and stifled a scream. It was staring at him, looking right through him. Caught in the pale circle of light, in glass jars, meticulously stacked on racks of varnished wood, everywhere he looked, eyes were staring at him. Fifteen to twenty glass jars were lined up, the pale white spheres floating idly in the clear, yellow liquid. Their round shapes had begun to blur, dragging fibrous trails behind them. And in the racks were pile after pile of grey-blue and green, hard and solid. *Glass eyes?* He blinked.

He had to support himself on the desk. The light from the flashlight strayed onto a jar. Two eyes with a tail of frayed fibres, remains of muscle tissue, white with age, rocked silently in a yellowish liquid.

A rustling came from behind him, the sound of fabric on fabric.

"Welcome." The voice was flat and toneless, hard and cold. The sound coming from the depths of a boulder. Before Christian could turn around, the coppery voice continued. "I've been expecting you."

Christian leaned against the table, his heart pounding in his chest. The walls, all of the eyes, spinning. He swallowed, pointing the flashlight at the voice.

A powerful figure was seated in an armchair in the corner. The upper half of his face was in shadow, the lower half illuminated by the flashlight. The soft lips moved. A pink tongue moistened yellow teeth. There was something about that voice. Rage and excitement surged through Christian: the memory of the last time he had been in the garden, bathed in the moonlight.

The figure stood up, towered over him.

Christian attempted to point the flashlight at his face but a heavy arm struck out. The flashlight flew out of his hand, landed on the floor, and flickered before going out. Christian stepped back into the corner between the bookcase and the desk.

"The police are on their way," he began.

"There's a better way. I know what you are. I can show you."

Christian dared not take his eyes off him. His mind was racing. "My parents, they…" It was pathetic, he knew it.

The man in the shadows laughed. Then he tilted his head to one side. "Would you like to meet my family?"

His muscles tensed, he bent his knees and jumped on the table. But a heavy arm struck out from the darkness, sweeping his legs out from under him. He fell, hit his back on the lamp, and tumbled over the edge of the table, pulling the jar with the two eyeballs down with him. The jar shattered on the table, shards of glass cutting his forearm. He hit the bookcase, the floor rose up to meet him, and the last thing he saw before he disappeared, was hundreds of eyes descending on him.

Darkness. A nothingness darker than anything he has ever known. Somber music and dim string instruments form a swaying monotone backdrop for a single-tone horn. A female voice singing, more beautiful than he thought possible.

Das Unglück geschah nur mir allein.
Die Sonne, sie scheinet allgemein.

Pain, greater, sharper. Unbearable. His head is being torn open. Something has forever changed.

There's a mumbling. He is lying on his stomach, naked. He tries turning around but he's strapped down. He can't move a muscle, only his head. He tries to blink but something is missing. There's nothing for his eyelid to cover and a silent dripping, running inside his head.

He's crying blood.

The scream moves up and out as powerful fingers spread his buttocks and a pillar of fire penetrates his sphincter with explosive force, bursting upwards and in. For a brief moment the pain causes him to lose consciousness; then the same pain brings him back to life.

Above him, the monotone mumbling turns into comprehensible words accentuated by each thrust.

"Welcome my son." Again and again, the pillar of fire tears his insides apart and his own protracted wailing rips his throat as the blood flows down his cheeks.

Then, just above, there is the sound of scraping. Someone is walking around upstairs.

CHAPTER 54

THE LINE OF traffic headed north toward Copenhagen. The silence inside the car was oppressive. Allan drove, while Ulrik sat in the backseat. Sanne stared out into the dark. The hood devoured the white lines.

They passed the exit for Køge when Sanne's phone rang.

"Lau here. Someone called me from this number?"

"Professor?" Sanne straightened up. "This is Sanne Bissen, Copenhagen Police."

Professor Lau laughed. "Oh, it was you? How can I help?"

Sanne recounted the conversation with Dr. Henkel.

"Does that ring a bell? A young Danish student?" she concluded. "Listen, is it all right if I put you on speakerphone? I'm sitting in a car with two colleagues."

"Of course. One moment." Professor Lau was silent at the other end. "Yes, now that you mention it," he began, "Koes, the former chief surgeon at Gentofte Hospital—I believe his grand-child trained as an ocularist in the former West Germany for half a year. It must have been back in the early sixties, just after the chief surgeon died. But it didn't work out and he was sent home again. Seeing as it was Koes's grandchild, we found him a job as a hospital porter when he returned. Yes, that was as far as his talents could take him."

"Koes's grandchild?" Sanne almost couldn't breathe. "What's his name? Is he still employed at the hospital?"

Allan had slowed down the car. Ulrik leaned forward.

The receiver crackled. They could hear Lau's breathing.

"It was...Jack? I'm not sure. Rumours spread at the hospital that he was born in Koes's cellar during the final days of the war. Some even said it was on the day of Denmark's liberation. Koes insinuated that the father was a wounded English pilot who had been hidden in his cellar. But, of course, these are just rumours."

"Was Koes a resistance fighter?" That would explain the Husqvarna gun.

"Ha, he was a regular war hero. On the eve of liberation, he was in a gunfight with a group of HIPOs. He even killed one of them. He loved to tell that story. He got medals after the war and all."

"And where can we find Koes's grandchild today?"

"Well, as far as I remember, he stopped at the hospital in the mid-nineties. His mom got sick. After..." Lau let the sentence hang in the air.

They hung up. Ulrik had already found the number for Gentofte Hospital.

Two minutes later he switched off his phone, looked from Sanne to Allan.

"Jack Koes. 14 Søbredden—Gentofte Lake."

CHAPTER 55

IT TOOK LESS than ten minutes to drive from Egebjerg Allé to Søbredden. There was a constant rumbling from the highway, a strong stench of gasoline, and a web of fine particles hung in the warm summer evening.

Lars parked behind Christian's aubergine-coloured MG, opened the glove compartment, grabbed a Maglite, and got out of the car. The weight of the Heckler & Koch in his shoulder holster was awkward; he was unaccustomed to carrying his service weapon.

It had to be here. Christian's MG was parked at the end of the long driveway that led to an L-shaped property.

The light from the houses along Søbredden spilled out onto the gardens. Laughter and song. Midsummer celebrations. There were probably a lot of bonfires by the lake tonight. He made himself light, tried not to think.

He kept to the decaying, half-rotten fence along the drive-way, worked his way quietly toward the garden.

The house grew out of the darkness. It seemed to oscillate in the bright night.

The telephone rang in his jacket pocket, and Lars took a step back into the shadows of a wild hazel thicket.

"Sanne," he whispered, "Listen—"

"Not now, Lars." There was engine noise in the background. She was out driving. Someone said something. Was it Ulrik? Sanne cut him off. "Be quiet and let me talk to him."

"Sanne—" Lars looked up at the house. It stood on its small rise at the back of the garden, dark and brooding. "I'm standing on Søbredden in Gentofte. Christian, Maria's—"

"Did you say Søbredden? Number 14?"

Lars looked back. The number on the fence out by the road was unclear, flickering in the dark.

"Yes, I think—"

"Listen: The old chief surgeon at Gentofte Hospital, it's his grandson who lives there now. Jack Koes. He was training as an ocularist in Germany in the 1960s."

A fleeting glimpse of a naked yellowish-white body moving by the water's edge, sea grass up to one leg.

"But—"

"It's a long story. The emergency response—"

"There's no time." Lars swore, looked up at the house. "Christian is in there."

"Don't go in there alone. You'll have backup in ten minutes."

Lars narrowed his eyes. Was there something flashing inside behind the windows?

"Just get them out here. Now."

He switched off his cell and crawled slowly along the edge of the garden, merging into the shadows. Near the corner of the house he ran, hunched, across the grass. A bat swept close by his face in a gentle curve, a faint gust of wind graced his skin as it passed. He flattened himself against the wall of the house. His heart pounded. Drops of sweat broke out on his forehead, his back, his armpits. Lars listened. There was a rustling in the grass to his right; a thin shadow slipped through the fence from the neighbour's side, stopped, and looked at him with luminous eyes before it disappeared in the dark. A cat on the prowl.

He tried to control his breathing. The roar from the motorway was fainter now, the night sounds from the thicket behind the house and the swamp down toward Gentofte Lake more clear. Bush and thicket groaned in the breeze. A bird shrieked. A sudden change in the wind carried a stanza from an old song coming from the lake.

> . . .but against the spirit of strife
> over field under beach
> on our forefather's burial mound we will give the bonfire life
> every city has it witch,
> and every parish its trolls . . .

There was a burnt smell in the air.

Lars edged his way forward to the corner of the house, ducking below the large living room window. Still no sound from inside. He looked around the corner with his hand on his weapon. The moon's pale reflection lit up something just outside the wall. Lars took another quick look.

The back door was open. He crept forward carefully, avoiding the rusty garden furniture leaning against the wall, drew his pistol without releasing the safety, then slipped quietly inside. It smelled stale and musty at the same time. Mildewy. He tried to orient himself, stepping over the hoe and gardening shovel. His foot struck something hard—steps leading further up. Then wooden planks. He stopped, listened. Adjusted his eyes to the darkness inside. The old house groaned in its joints.

Contours loomed up from the darkness: the wall's lighter surfaces, dark doorways, shapeless furniture. He stopped in a corridor or entrance hallway of some kind. He listened one final time before stepping on the floor, cautiously feeling his way forward before planting his feet. He hadn't gone more than two steps when the floor gave a loud creak. His heart pounded in his chest. Then came a noise from the staircase. A branch against a window? He waited, did not dare to breathe.

He moved on to the kitchen. Plates with old leftovers were stacked in the sink. It smelled stale and rotten. No sign of either Christian or Jack Koes. His gaze fell on a small piece of cloth hanging from a hook on the side of the kitchen table. He lifted it carefully with a pen, held it up to his face. He turned it in the sparse light coming through the window. A G-string, black, nylon.

Something fell over with a crash below him. The noise echoed through the house. The floor shook. Lars dropped the underwear, which fluttered to the floor. Where were the stairs to the cellar? He looked around the kitchen. There was only one doorway to the entrance hall. Not even a door to the garden.

He returned to the entrance hall. The door between the one leading to the kitchen and the one to the living room was ajar. Lars opened it quietly. A mess of smashed furniture almost spilled out into the entrance hall. Cupboards and bookcases had been tipped over. The air was acrid and smelled of chemicals. When he stepped inside, his foot squelched on something wet. He slipped, and something soft and tough snapped beneath him. Inside, in the middle of the floor, under flotsam and jetsam, a flickering flashlight. Its beam cut through strips of wood, papers, and water, and several balls that floated around on the floor. A moment passed before he realized what he was looking at. He bent down and picked up one of the balls. A glass eye, grey-green iris, asymmetric curvature. Surprisingly light.

Lars carefully put the eye down and returned to the entrance. A speckled, irregular trail led to a closed door between the staircase and the bureau. Blood. With his ear to the door, he listened for a long time before opening it. A deep and impenetrable darkness assailed him.

He crossed his arms in front of him. One hand held the Maglite, and the other the service pistol. He released the safety on the pistol, turned on the flashlight. He found the first step, then shifted his weight forward, lifted the other leg, and found the next. Mildewy, damp air drifted up from the cellar, and with it the sweetish stench of rot and a strong chemical smell. The light from the Maglite danced in front of him, revealing worn steps on a wooden staircase that once had been painted red. He passed piles of old clothes, dusty furniture, half-decomposed cardboard boxes, and several garden tools. And there, on the floor at the foot of the stairs, the flashlight captured a pair of unmistakable red stains.

He had only two steps to go when the stairs creaked treacherously under him. Lars swore, jumped over the last step, and took a quick step to the side when he landed on the floor. The silence seemed to suck away all sound. More blood stains, this time on the floor, led to a large hole in the wall.

He ducked down, felt with his hand until he found a switch.

At that exact moment the music begins. From somewhere deep down two clarinets meander in slow spirals. A female voice begins to sing, and the orchestra kicks in.

"Police," he shouts and switches on the light.

CHAPTER 56

SØBREDDEN WAS AS far from the idyllic picture of a Danish suburban road as you could get. The blue, oscillating lights of the police cars flashed psychedelically against the backdrop of the green hedges, two-storey houses, and curious faces. Uniformed and plainclothes officers kept getting in each other's way in the growing crowd of neighbours and reporters.

The driveway to number 14 was blocked. The row of emergency response vehicles stretched all the way into the garden. As far as Sanne could see, no one knew what was going on.

They parked in front of an MG roadster. Ulrik climbed out and grabbed hold of a uniformed officer who was standing at the edge of the curb.

"Where's the emergency response leader?"

Sanne and Allan climbed out of the car, taking in the chaos. A steady stream of drunken Midsummer's Eve guests were emerging from their backyards and houses. The bonfire circles by the lake would be empty now. Everyone wanted to have a piece of the action.

"Um, I don't know..." the officer began.

"I can see that," Ulrik snapped, then walked across the sidewalk toward the driveway. Sanne and Allan followed.

Ulrik had called the duty officer, but someone somewhere along the communication lines had messed up. There were far too many officers from far too many precincts. With police officers from both Copenhagen and Gentofte, it was impossible to get an overview of the situation.

"It's the Sandman," Allan said. He trotted, huffing on Sanne's heels. "Every colleague would give their right arm to be a part of this."

Sanne nodded. You could see the glint in the officers' eyes, the way they looked at the house.

A dark blue Ford was parked on the opposite side of the road, across from the driveway. The doors opened at the exact moment Ulrik turned down the driveway.

"Ulrik." Kim A flicked a lit cigarette butt onto the road and crossed the street without looking. Frank and Lisa were behind him.

"Kim." Ulrik stopped, waited. "Frank. Lisa." Sanne and Allan kept back.

"What the hell is going on here?" Kim A hissed.

Ulrik held his hands out in front of him. "Take it easy. There's no reason to get all worked up."

Sanne was watching Lisa and Frank, who stood right behind Kim A. She caught an almost imperceptible shudder in Lisa's gaze.

Kim A ignored Ulrik's comment, raised his voice. "He's breaking all the rules, shitting on the chain of command. I'm the one who..."

The onlookers started to turn.

"Come with me," Ulrik said. He pulled Kim A up the driveway. The two officers on the sidewalk had enough presence of mind to stop the onlookers who tried to follow. Sanne and Allan slipped in behind them, Lisa and Frank followed.

Ulrik stopped Kim A with a hand on his shoulder. "We have a colleague in there with the Sandman. By all accounts, he's taken my stepdaughter's boyfriend hostage too. We need to get Lars and Christian out. Then—"

Kim A closed his eyes. When he opened them again, he focused on a point behind Ulrik's shoulder. The jaw muscles pumped. In, out, in, out.

"You'll have my resignation on your desk in an hour." He turned to Frank and Lisa. "Come on," he said, as he started walking back to the car.

"Kim, god…" Ulrik took a step toward him. Frank and Lisa looked at each other. Frank followed him.

"Come on." Sanne pulled Allan's arm. "Let Ulrik take care of this. We need to find Lars."

When they stepped into the garden, four officers from the emergency response team came out the front door.

"Gustafsson," Allan shouted. "What's going on?"

"I thought you knew?"

Allan nodded at the house. "Where's Lars?"

"There's no one in there." Gustafsson removed his helmet, scratched the back of his neck.

Sanne took a step forward. "Are you sure?"

Gustafsson opened his collar, wiped a drop of sweat from his Adam's apple with a dusty hand. He nodded.

"It's completely empty. It looks like there's been a fight in there. Bookcases and furniture are all over the floor. Everything's swimming in some kind of alcohol and broken glass. And eyes, both glass and real."

Sanne and Allan exchanged looks.

"Over here," a voice shouted on the other side of the house. Allan and Sanne started running, followed by Ulrik and the emergency response team officers.

A uniformed officer pointed a flashlight at an open door by the garden.

"Someone has broken in here."

CHAPTER 57

THE GLARING WHITE light forces Lars to close his eyes. Blue and yellow dots dance in a sea of red. He opens them again, slowly, allowing them to adjust to the sharp light.

A steep staircase in front of him leads three, four, five metres down. Another cellar, deeper than the first. Piles of dusty wooden boxes line the walls. Clunky rifles with wooden butts stand in a rack in a corner. Sackcloth is strewn along the far wall, and along the wall on the right, there is a kind of field kitchen with a gas burner and flasks. A large pot simmers on the burner. The air is tight and humid, thick with the smell of boiled cabbage mixed with a chemical stench.

On a box next to the burner stands a portable phonograph; an LP is spinning under the pickup. A warm female voice is singing in German, sombre tones drifting in the stagnant air.

Next to the field kitchen is a table and four chairs. A naked woman sits upright with her hands on the table and her face turned away from him. She is completely lifeless. Her blonde hair, strangely dry and lifeless, falls across her shoulders. Between her hands is a steaming bowl filled with a greyish-white substance. A spoon sticks up from her clenched right hand. Across from her a young man is sitting, he too has a bowl in front of him. Motionless, slumped, his whole stance so utterly different from the erect woman sitting opposite him. But he is naked like her, his blonde hair combed back. Dark lines are running down Christian's cheeks.

The chemical smell becomes sharper and more potent. Arms appear from behind, hold him in an iron grip. He struggles. Then everything turns black.

When the world returns, there is nothing but nausea. His head is pounding, his hips hurt. His heart is galloping away. He lies on his back with bile and stomach acid in his mouth. He doesn't want to die. He must not choke on his own vomit. His leg twitches, and from somewhere far away comes the sound of someone softly humming to the music.

Strong hands lift his legs. Something tightens around them.

Lars opens one eye, slowly. A narrow slit, allowing him just a glimpse of his surroundings. A towering figure, Koes is wearing only a white shirt; he's naked from the waist down. He hovers over him, turned to one side, securing Lars's legs with focused movements. Lars is lying on a table or a box of some sort that is raised above the floor. Koes is standing between him and the table where Christian and the naked girl are sitting. Lars turns his head; he knows what is coming. In a moment, Koes will be finished with his legs and will turn his attention to his arms. He must strike before then.

Koes tightens the strap, clicks the buckle in place. Lars closes his eye and drifts off. Just then there's a clattering. Koes curses and Lars can hear him bend down. Lars looks around desperately. One of the antique rifles is leaning up against an ammunition box close to his head. He reaches out to grab it. The cold metal is smooth and oily in his hand. As Koes turns back to him, he thrusts the weapon, butt first, until he hears a gruesome crunching, then a curse. Koes staggers back, collapses in the chair next to Christian. The table behind him rocks back and forth. Some of the grey-white liquid in the bowl between the naked girl's arms sloshes out onto the table. Neither she nor Christian is moving. Lars forces himself up, tearing at the tightened leather straps holding his legs in place. Koes's eyes are rolling around in his head. He resumes his humming, his chin resting against his chest. The blood streams down his mouth and chin; his nose bent at an odd angle on his busted face.

"Oh Augen!" The words gurgle from his crushed lips.

Lars grabs the barrel of the rifle, turns the bayonet blade toward his feet, and begins filing away at the leather straps. Piece by piece, he manages to cut through the old, well-cared-for leather straps. Koes is now standing on wobbly legs, the blood dripping from his nose and broken mouth.

Lars turns the rifle, hits Koes in the face again. Blood and snot spurt out in a fan, to the right and over Koes's shoulder. The large figure staggers, takes one step back. Lars quickly cuts through the last strap, screams as the bayonet cuts the skin and flesh in his calf. He lets go of the rifle, which falls to the ground, and throws his legs over the side. Standing up, he tries to find his balance. The pain keeps the world at a breaking point.

He looks around, spots a worn steel tray, a handle on each side, displaying surgical instruments from another time, spread out, ready for operation: scalpel, suction cup, cloths, liquids, hypodermic needle. He vomits thin, bitter bile. Remains from his last meal, from he doesn't know when, splash on the concrete floor. Then Koes is on him. A fist planted in his kidneys makes his legs double up. He gasps for air, crawling in his own vomit. The blows are raining down on him. Everything is nausea, pain, tremors, and loud, piercing laughter. He tries to ward off the blows with one hand while the other feels around on the floor. Where's his service pistol, the Maglite? His hand closes around something cold and greasy. The barrel of the rifle. He raises the weapon and thrusts it with all his might, until he hears a rib crack, then break. The rifle strikes something soft and hard. He jumps to his feet and plunges forward. The weapon slips through—a startled grunt and a hard crack. Then everything goes quiet.

The cascade of blows has stopped. He crawls back, gasping for air, squeezing his eyes shut.

Time ticks away. Second follows second. Throbbing pain tears through his body, sending waves of shock through his trembling flesh.

"Bloodwind," Koes whispers. Lars opens one eye. Something is glistening. He blinks, opens both eyes. And sees Koes's broken face, the nose pointing sideways and up to the right. His lips are swollen sea cucumbers, the skin torn off the cheeks in large, bloody wounds. Broken teeth stick out of the bloody pulp of his mouth.

Lars pushes further back to survey the damage. The rifle sticks out from Koes's shoulder at a grotesque angle. His last desperate lunge with the bayonet has impaled Koes and pinned him to the wall of ammunition boxes.

Small, vigilant eyes follow Lars while the blood seeps from the shoulder wound, drenching the shirt's soft cotton material. Koes's right hand is twitching. Soon he will be able to pull the bayonet out.

Bracing himself against the ammunition box, Lars rises to his feet. He takes his handcuffs from his belt, places one bracelet around Koes's free hand and attaches the other to the rope handle at the end of the ammunition box. When Koes, who is too weak to resist, is secured, Lars sits down on an empty box. His legs are trembling. His fingers dig around for the cigarettes in his pocket. The package is crumpled; almost all the cigarettes are broken. He manages to light one, takes a greedy drag, lets the nicotine fill the lung tissue and stream into the blood.

He pats his other pocket and pulls out his cell phone.

"No service," Koes snickers.

Lars ignores him, but Koes is right: he can't get a signal.

"Dad hid weapons and ammunition down here during the war. The Germans never found it. You'll never get out."

Koes's laughter ends in a sputter. Blood is spilling out over his shirt and onto the rough floor.

"And him," Koes nods at Christian. "He'll be awake soon."

Lars twitches. "He isn't dead?"

Koes starts humming again, then turns his head.

Lars reaches over and feels Christian's neck. The carotid artery pulsates reassuringly beneath the skin. He slumps down on the empty chair next to the boy. Thank God. Then he looks down: two jello-like lumps lie in the bottom of the boy's bowl staring up at Christian in a pool of blood.

The empty eye sockets, hollows of nothingness on his ruined face. Christian's body twitches. The boy raises his head, then shakes it from side to side, as if there's something he can't understand. Then he screams.

Just then, a groan passes through the house. The foundations shake. Koes's eyes gloss over and his bloody lips part in a grotesque grin.

Lars gets up. *Out*. He must get help. He takes a step toward the staircase, staggers. Another step and his knees buckle. Everything is spinning.

CHAPTER 58

A **MAP OF** the area was spread out on the hood of a police car that was parked halfway into the garden. Allan was investigating potential escape routes out in the swamp. The night air smelled of lilacs and midsummer bonfires.

Sanne clicked her thumb and ring fingernail together. Where was Lars?

The emergency response team had returned to the house. A crackling came from the radio Gustafsson had given to Ulrik.

"We've just heard screaming! It came from beneath us."

The windows in the dark building shook. A small spark appeared behind the black windows and, before she realized what was happening, grew to a huge ball of fire and exploded up through the roof into the still night. People were screaming. The crashing roof echoed across the lake. Sparks and roof tiles rained down everywhere. The sudden heat made her skin prickle, contract. The house was being torn apart from the inside out.

"Goddammit," Ulrik shouted, grabbing the radio. "Get out of there. Now!"

"But Lars is still in there." Sanne stared, hypnotized by the flames, which blazed through the roof with terrifying speed.

Ulrik shouted, "What's keeping the fire department? Dammit, has nobody called them?"

No one answered. Everyone stared at the flames, frozen.

Then, a movement. A uniformed officer appeared, dragging a bystander with him.

"This guy claims to know something." He had to shout to make himself heard above the roaring flames. The onlooker, a man in his mid-forties, nodded.

"My dad often talked about the eye doctor who lived there. During the war, he was the leader of the local resistance group. He dug out an extra cellar under the house. Folks in the neighbourhood used to say he used it as a weapons store."

"You're saying there's another cellar—beneath the cellar?" Ulrik had turned away from the house. His hands were suspended in mid-air by the bystander's chest, ready to grab him by the collar.

The man nodded. "The Germans never found it."

Now the sirens wailed.

Sanne left the car, walking toward the house in a trance.

"Stop," Ulrik shouted. "Where are you going?"

"We have to help Lars," she whispered.

Gustafsson grabbed her just as he came out of the front door. "It's too dangerous in there. The whole thing could collapse at any moment."

Police officers were jumping into the emergency vehicles in the driveway, attempting to pull to the side so the fire trucks could get through.

"Over here," a female voice shouted, barely audible above the roar of the fire. Sanne ran over to the other side of the house. By the end wall, opposite the garden door, Lisa was tearing at the thick vegetation along the house. Hidden under the overgrown thicket was an old cellar entrance, plank shutters locked with a heavy padlock.

Gustafsson disappeared, returning immediately with a pair of bolt cutters. Seconds later, the padlock was cut and with a joint effort, Lisa and Sanne managed to open the cellar door. Gustafsson shone his flashlight into the darkness below. Dead leaves, dirty rags, all sorts of garbage and debris covered the dark staircase. Sanne looked up at the roofline. The glow from the fire spread across the sky. The house groaned and a shower of embers poured down from the roof, landing in the dewy grass. She shrugged and went down the stairs. Lisa, Gustafsson, and the rest of the emergency response team followed.

Narrow bands of smoke seeped through the cracks of the beams. The old house rumbled.

The flashlights scanned the whitewashed surfaces in the low cellar, revealing damp patches and spots of mould. Piles of old clothes and junk, cardboard boxes, books, and shoes filled most of the area.

"Where can a person hide in here?" Lisa asked.

"There must be a set of stairs leading to the second cellar, somewhere under all this junk." Sanne narrowed her eyes. The smoke stung her eyes and throat.

The others began moving the piles around haphazardly. They scraped at the floor with their boots to locate a possible trapdoor. Sanne moved to the bottom of the staircase that led up to the house. She stood at the end of a long blood trail that led from the consulting room to the cellar. She looked down. The floor was somewhat clear here. No cracks, no chinks in the wood, no trapdoor leading to a second cellar.

The stench of smoke got stronger. Above her the roar increased. It was a matter of minutes before they would be forced to give up.

"Forget that," she shouted. "It's over here somewhere." She could hear water raining down on the house. The fire department had gotten the hoses attached. Lisa left the corner where she'd been searching and approached Sanne.

"Where could you conceal a trapdoor in here?" Sanne mumbled to herself, wiping a dirty lock of hair off her forehead. Her chest rose and fell. It was difficult to breathe.

Her gaze followed the cone of light, from the boxes of old kitchenware, across piles of brown-green knitting and old newspapers, and the low bookcase with the heavy, leather-bound medical books, to the vitrine on the opposite wall. Where could it be? If the Germans couldn't find the secret cellar, how were they going to be able to in the few minutes they had left before the house collapsed? The panic stuck in her throat. She looked around at the kitchenware, knitting, bookcases, vitrine, newspapers. Kitchenware, knitting, bookcases, vitrine, newspapers. It had to be somewhere.

Bookcase.

Sanne straightened up with a sudden movement, almost smashing her head against a ceiling beam. She reached the bookcase in a single jump and started pulling at it.

"Help," she hissed. Her eyes stung now, and she wheezed when she breathed. She sensed more than saw Lisa next to her, then came the shadows of Gustafsson and his team. Between them they managed to push and wriggle the heavy bookcase aside. Nothing. Sanne cursed. It had to be here. Gustafsson was down on his knees, pushing on the wall where the bookcase had been. Nothing happened.

He shook his head, got up, and took a step back.

Sanne cast her gaze from the wall to the vitrine, which hung a good metre above the floor. The glass doors were smashed, and the shelves contained old, chipped porcelain and a blue-fluted dinner service. Everything was covered in a thick layer of dust. She stuck an arm inside, swept aside the contents of the first shelf. Nothing. The next shelf gave the same result. Something fell through the stairwell above her, striking the railing on its way down. The noise was ear-splitting. The vitrine shook.

Sanne slid her hands across the empty shelf. Air pockets under the greasy shelf liner bulged under her hand. The little finger on her right hand slipped across a nail head, at the back right corner. Instinctively, she pushed down on the nail with her index finger. Then she pulled it back and felt the rough head slip. A creaking came from behind the vitrine as it began to swing out. Smoke and light leaked out of the hole, illuminating the hidden cellar. A voice shouted from inside.

"In here. Lars Winkler, police. I need help."

Gustafsson and his team pushed past Sanne and Lisa and crawled in through the opening. Lisa ran outside to report that they'd gotten through and needed help.

Sanne took a deep breath, then crawled through the gap.

Lars lay at the bottom of the stairs. His hands and face were covered with blood and cuts. His head rested on the bottom step, one arm hanging over the other. He had tried to pull himself up. One of the emergency response team officers was bent over him, holding two fingers against his neck.

Time stands still. The man bending over the figure at the foot of the stairs doesn't move; the scene is frozen, a tableau. By a table in the right corner sits a naked boy. His mouth is open in a muted scream, blood is pouring down his face from empty holes that will never stare again. Seconds, minutes pass, before she accepts the vision as the young man Lars had questioned the previous day. Sitting at the table with Christian is a naked woman, two dead eyes glistening on her dim face. Her skin has the same yellowish-white colour as Mira and the other nameless woman they found in Østre Anlæg the night before.

Leaning against the ammunition box, his face broken, blood and snot all over his head, shirt, and naked lower body is Jack Koes. One arm is shackled to the farthest handle of the box, the other hangs loosely at his side, the shoulder fixed to the ammuniton box by the bayonet of an antique rifle.

"Is he alive?" Gustafsson whispers.

The officer, still bent over Lars with his fingers against his throat, nods at Gustafsson and with that one signal, time marches on again. The man pulls Lars's arm over his shoulder, and helps him up the stairs. He is alive. Sanne half stumbles, half runs, grabbing Lars's other arm, trying to help. Between them, she and the other officer manage to drag him up the stairs even though his feet keep giving out beneath him. Out of the corner of her eye, Sanne sees Gustafsson cutting off the handcuffs that hold Koes to the ammunition box. One of his men pulls the bayonet out. The other officers help Christian to his feet.

The groaning and creaking of the house gets worse with every second.

Gustafsson and the other officer get Koes to his feet. His body goes into spasms as he glances at the dead woman by the table with a look of longing and doom. Then he is on his way up the stairs, with Gustafsson and the other officer on either side supporting him.

Suddenly Koes turns and hits the other officer with a savage blow with his elbow, sending him tumbling down the stairs. In the same movement he clamps his jaws around Gustafsson's nose. Gustafsson screams, his fingers attempting to find Koes's eyes, but Koes jerks his head back and forth while his jaw muscles are working. The lower jaw is making sawing movements. Then Gustafsson falls backwards, releasing a wailing howl and a plume of blood. The officer Koes has knocked down the stairs has his service weapon out and fires two shots. The first goes directly through Koes's wounded shoulder, sending a red mist of blood and chunks of flesh across the staircase. The other shot hits the railing near Sanne's head.

Koes looks up at the ceiling and spits out something red and wet. Then he catches Sanne's gaze and raises his healthy arm, holding Gustafsson's service weapon. From above, the crashing becomes more violent with every second. The officer on the floor searches for a line of sight, but dares not shoot for fear of hitting his colleagues.

Koes laughs, but all Sanne sees is the film of tears covering his eyes.

Then he positions the barrel under his chin and pulls the trigger.

TUESDAY
JUNE 24

CHAPTER 59

THE ROOF COLLAPSED with an ear-splitting crash; sparks and steam leapt up into the night sky. The blue light from the emergency response vehicles gave the entire scene a disjointed and surreal glow. Firefighters and police got in each other's way. The lawn was covered with firehoses, the water pouring over the burning house. Gustafsson and Christian had already been taken to the hospital. Koes's body was left on a stretcher on the grass. People kept back. A blanket covered the mangled head.

"What happened?" Lars was on a stretcher inside the open ambulance, half lying, half sitting. He nodded at the flame-engulfed house. Sanne sat next to him.

"It looked like a gas explosion. But everything happened so quickly. It appears that Koes rigged some kind of bomb to the house."

Lars attempted to sit up but the pain in his side was too much.

Sanne gave him a pillow for his back.

"One of the officers brought these up from the cellar." She placed a stack of Polaroids on the blanket. Lars picked them up, flipping through them with a mix of surprise and revulsion.

Photo after photo of family gatherings, holiday celebrations. Christmas Eve: Jack Koes in a Santa Claus outfit, smiling happily in front of a tree swelling with presents, surrounded by three female Christmas elves with rice pudding, red wine, and gifts. Coffee service: Koes in shirt and cardigan, laying out the seagull dinner service, with the women in evening dress, heavily made-up, the dead glass eyes staring blankly ahead. Bedtime: Koes in pyjamas in bed, apparently deep in sleep with a woman's corpse on either side.

Lars's heart was pounding. He felt a throbbing behind his eyes, passed the pictures back. He didn't want to see anymore.

"Why?"

"Most likely, we'll never know," Sanne said. "There are many lonely people out there who miss having someone to be something for. Some of them find — other ways to deal with it."

"Most people would probably just say he wasn't right in the head."

"That's probably an understatement." Sanne placed the pictures in an evidence bag. "Koes worked as a porter at Gentofte Hospital; you saw his upper body. The job gave him free access to chloroform and glutaraldehyde."

Something moved, stepped out of the chaos.

"Well, that's some bonfire you've managed to put together for Midsummer's Eve!" Frelsén poked his head into the ambulance. His gold-rimmed glasses reflected the gleam from the burning house. Bint stood behind him, watching the roaring flames and shaking his head.

"You'll have to sift through all of that." Lars motioned at the garden with his head, then clutched his side. "There are more victims than the three we already know of." He pointed at the evidence bag with the photos in Sanne's hand.

"Damn." Bint stared at Koes's body. The blanket covering his head was soaked in blood.

"Sanne. Lars." Lisa nodded at Frelsén and Bint. "I'm glad you made it out."

Lars grimaced. "Where's Kim A?"

"Lisa got us into the cellar when the fire started," Sanne said. "You have her to thank for us getting you out."

Lisa smiled. "Never leave an officer behind. Kim A has quit, by the way. He wants to transfer to the Secret Service." She shrugged.

"Secret Service, huh? Thanks," Lars mumbled. His eyelids were closing. His head sagged against his chest.

"Well, time for him to go," was the last thing he heard.

Someone was stepping down from the ambulance; a door slammed. Then he was gone.

Lars opened his eyes. A glaring white light. Was he dead? He heard voices, then a scream. As soon as he realized it was Maria who was screaming outside, he tried dragging his body out of bed. Then the door opened and Elena poked her head in.

"Lars? Are you awake?"

He nodded, fell back in bed. His entire body was hurting.

Elena pushed Maria, who was pale as a sheet, into the room in front of her. She put an arm around her, pulled her closer to the bed.

"Dad?" Maria took his hand, laced her fingers with his.

He tried smiling at her. "Was that you screaming?"

Maria nodded, bit her lip.

"The parents of the boy—Maria's—" Elena coughed. "Apparently he's in the same ward. His dad tried talking to Maria. Ulrik managed to stop him."

What had happened at Christian's house, with Christian's parents?

"Ulrik...can he?" Elena made a gesture at the door.

He closed his eyes, shook his head. God, he really needed a smoke.

"They say you just need a few days of bedrest. A few broken ribs is the worst of it." Elena held out her hand, hesitated. Then she patted the comforter above his leg.

"Where am I?" he asked. She looked lovely but the flutter of longing was gone.

"Rigshospitalet." Elena took her purse off the end of the bed. "I'm going out to Ulrik." She looked at Maria, stroked her cheek with her finger. Then she turned around and walked out of the room.

Maria held his hand in hers, gazing out the window behind him. He closed his eyes, imagining what she saw: the treetops in Fælledparken, the diagonal lines of the paths. Was the sun about to rise?

"They say it was Christian..." she began. "That he was the one who attacked Caroline and the others?"

He kept his eyes shut, nodded. Maria squeezed his hand so hard that it hurt. Neither of them said anything.

"What did you want at the party yesterday?" she asked.

Lars swallowed, looked at her. "Caroline said that the rapist was humming...during. I didn't recognize the melody, but..."

"I'm sorry, Dad." She shook her head. "I don't remember."

Lars turned his head, looked out the window. Jagger, the old Indian, chanting from somewhere in his brain.

Talkin' 'bout the Midnight Rambler,
Did you see me jump the bedroom door?
I'm called a hit-n-run raper, in anger
Or just a knife-sharpened tippie-toe . . .

The sunbeams crawled across the floor. Her other hand moved across the comforter, grabbed his.

Sanne poked her head in the door. "Am I intruding?"

"Maybe," Lars began. But Maria looked up, waved Sanne in.

"It's okay, Dad. I wanted to go see Caro. But there was one thing you didn't tell us: was it the murderer who Christian . . . ?"

Lars and Sanne looked at each other.

"Yes, Christian was right." Sanne came over, stood beside the bed. "But he should have stayed away. This was a matter for the police to handle."

"I heard what he did to Christian." Maria moved her hand in front of her mouth. Then she let it fall and stood up.

Lars reached out for her, but she was already on her way out.

"She's going to be fine." Sanne looked after her retreating form. Then she turned to him. "Toke and Lisa raided Christian's home last night. They found a black tracksuit. I've just spoken to Frelsén. The black fibres found at the crime scenes are a match." She sat down on the edge of the bed in the same place Maria had sat a moment ago. "What do you think he wanted with Koes?"

Lars grimaced. "Maybe he felt a kinship? I know it sounds sick, but Stine Bang was raped the night after Mira's body was found."

Lars closed his eyes; neither of them said anything. The seconds ticked by before Sanne broke the silence. "Hopefully we'll find out more during questioning,"

Lars turned his head and looked out the broad window,

across Fælledparken and Østerbro. A flock of swans shot across the sky in a pointed V toward the artificial lake near Edel Sauntes Allé. The swooshing, melancholy sound of their flapping wings bounced against Rigshospitalet's raw concrete surfaces. A new day was skipping across the fountain. His body began to feel light, practically floating from exhaustion. Then he started to laugh.

Sanne stared at him. "Do you really think there's anything to laugh at?"

He shook his head, stopped. "Yes, it's over. I'm free. Kim A, Ulrik." He made a sweeping gesture with his arm, reaching out for the sky.

"And now you're going to North Zealand's police?" She fiddled with the chart hanging at the foot of his bed.

He was still bubbling inside. Exhaustion and lightness, the final stages of the amphetamine high. He would collapse soon.

"It won't be Elsinore. I think I'll go see my dad."

"In New York? What about Maria?"

"She'll come with me."

Sanne's cheeks went red. She looked down. "And—you and me?"

Christine Fogh stepped in with her hands in her pockets. Her sharp eyes were peering at them from behind her red glasses.

"The patient needs rest now."

Sanne stood with her back to Christine and rolled her eyes.

"I'll come by again tomorrow." She walked backwards to the door, held his gaze.

Christine closed the door behind her. "Look at you!"

"You work in this department too?" He let his hand collapse on the comforter.

"No, I heard you were admitted."

"And?" He pointed at the door.

Christine shook her head, walked over to the end of the bed, and placed her hand on the metal frame. She looked out the window, closed her eyes for a moment. The sun spilled in, making her face glow.

"So you found him."

"Yes. Too late."

"But you found him, and if you hadn't shown up, that boy would have been killed."

"Maybe he deserved that?"

Christine looked out the window. "I think we should be happy it's not up to us to decide what others deserve. It must be a terrible responsibility." Then she lifted the chart at the end of the bed, let her eyes slide down the page.

"Remains of chloroform and . . . amphetamine in the blood?" She looked up, her eyebrows raised, and let the chart drop. It clattered against the metal frame. The sound echoed in the silent room. So it was chloroform Koes had sedated him with? Not surprising that his heart had protested; mixed with the speed he had taken, that was some cocktail.

Christine moved to the headboard. For a moment, the space between them was crowded with what was left unspoken. Then she shrugged.

"Oh well. It's none of my business." She leaned over him. For a moment, her right breast rested on his shoulder, heavy and warm behind the white coat. Her lips brushed his forehead.

She stood up, adjusted her coat. "You could call me sometime?"

Then she was gone.

CREDITS

Kindertotenlieder is from a cycle of poems by Friedech Rückert, written in 1833–34. Music by Gustav Mahler 1901–04. Quoted from *Wienerphilharmoniker Lorin Maazel: Mahler. Symphony no. 3 Kindertotenlieder.* Mezzo-soprano, Agnes Baltsa. Produced 1985.

"De berusedes vej" by Søren Ulrik Thomsen, Digte om natten.

Midnight Rambler by Mick Jagger/Keith Richards, *Get Yer Ya-Ya's Out,* 1971.

Midsommervisen, text by Holger Drachmann, melody by P. E. Lange-Müller, 1885.

Author photograph: Robin Skjoldborg

JAKOB MELANDER was born in 1965. He entered the eighties punk scene as a bass player and guitar player in various
bands. He lives in Copenhagen.